A. L. BIRD

lives in London, where she divides her time between writing and working as a lawyer. She has an MA in Creative Writing from Birkbeck, University of London, and is also an alumna of the Faber Academy "Writing a Novel" course, which she studied under Richard Skinner. Amy is a member of the Crime Writers' Association. For updates on her writing follow her on Twitter, @ALBirdWriter.

the
GOOD
MOTHER

A.L. BIRD

W✺RLDWIDE.

TORONTO • NEW YORK • LONDON
AMSTERDAM • PARIS • SYDNEY • HAMBURG
STOCKHOLM • ATHENS • TOKYO • MILAN
MADRID • WARSAW • BUDAPEST • AUCKLAND

Recycling programs
for this product may
not exist in your area.

ISBN-13: 978-1-335-92664-7

The Good Mother

Copyright © 2016 by Amy Bird

A Worldwide Library Suspense/January 2018

First published by Carina, an imprint of HarperCollins Publishers

This edition published by arrangement with Harlequin Books S.A.

® and TM are trademarks of the publisher. Trademarks indicated with ® are registered in the United States Patent and Trademark Office, the Canadian Intellectual Property Office and in other countries.

www.Harlequin.com

Printed in U.S.A.

the
GOOD
MOTHER

To my little one—welcome.
May I be the best mother to you, always.

PROLOGUE

THE GIRL GETS into the car that's waiting for her. She looks over her shoulder first, like he's told her to, to check Mummy isn't watching. Would Mummy really mind? She can't be sure. But he seems to think so. And he knows best, right? So she does the covert glance then slings her school bag into the back seat, like all the other times. He holds his cheek towards her for a kiss, which she dutifully bestows. Then he starts the engine with a vroom. Familiar buildings pass by. Buses on their way to places she recognises: Muswell Hill Broadway; Barnet (The Spires); North Finchley. There are a couple of kids from school. She raises her hand to wave but the man, seeing her, says, 'Best not.' So she lowers her hand and plays with the hem of her skirt, gazing absently out of the window.

Gradually, the territory becomes less familiar. The other man, the man they are going to meet, always insists on meeting outside of her home area. Says it's safer that way. She hopes he'll buy her a hot chocolate again. That was nice. Lots of whipped cream. Mummy always says whipped cream is bad: 'You'll end up big-boned. No one wants to be big-boned.' The girl commented that the women at Mummy's cupcake studio don't seem big-boned. And they have lots of cream. 'That's because they spend a lot of time in the bathroom after each session,' Mummy explained. That didn't make much sense. But still, after the last visit, she hung round in the bathroom for a good ten minutes, so that the cream didn't invade her bones and make them puff up.

And if there is hot chocolate, the girl thinks, it will be something to keep me busy. Because there's not a lot of talking on these trips, so far. The other man doesn't seem to know what to say. He looks at her a lot. Taking her in, from top to toe. She can feel his gaze travel down then up, up then down. Sometimes he gives a little smile. Other times a frown. She wants to please him, of course. She wants to please everyone. But when she tells him about the usual stuff—school, Mummy, music, boys even—he doesn't say much back. And the two men glare at each other whenever they're not looking at her. She can't figure out why they keep hanging around together. Or what they want her to do on these occasions. So perhaps better just to concentrate on pushing the little wooden stirrer stick up and down in the hot chocolate to make holes, revealing the hot chocolate below. You have to get it to just the right meltiness to drink it. Then it's delicious. She licks her lips in anticipation. Last time, the other man, the man they're going to visit, looked like he was anticipating hot chocolate the whole time. Kept licking his lips. If he wanted some of her drink, he should just have said.

This might be the last time at this place, though. Because the previous time the other man, the man they're going to see, had suggested they meet at his home. More relaxing. They could learn more about each other. He'd even given directions.

'I just want us to be close, Cara,' he'd said. 'You'll be quite safe. You'll have your chaperone there throughout.' He said 'chaperone' in a funny way. Like he was making a joke. Perhaps he only used that word because he didn't know what to call the man who brought her. She didn't, either, not really. Not once they'd had the little chat that evening in the car, his hand on her knee. Everything changed after that. She couldn't be herself around him, couldn't think of anything to say to him at all, never mind his name. She'd settled into the pattern after a while. But it was still odd. Of course it was odd. She would have asked Mummy. If Mummy were allowed to know.

Anyway, whatever he was called, the chaperone didn't seem to like the idea of going to the other man's home. So here they were, driving fast to the usual café. A bit faster than usual, maybe? Were they late? She looks at her watch, then realises she doesn't know what time they're meant to be there. And she doesn't really know where 'there' is.

So there is nothing to do but sink into the seat. It's out of her hands. But she's perfectly safe. Of course she is. It would be like all the other times. See the men. Then go home to Mummy. She looks across at the chaperone to smile, to show him she still trusts him after everything. But he doesn't smile back. He looks ahead and he frowns.

ONE

MY EYES FLASH OPEN.

There's a bed, a room and a blankness.

I leap off the bed, a strange bed, a single bed, and collapse straight onto the floor.

Where am I? What's going on? Why am I so weak?

I put my hands over my eyes. Remove my hands again. But nothing becomes right. I've still no idea where I am. Why am I in this alien room? In pyjamas? Is it day, is it night, how long have I been here?

And, oh God.

Where's Cara? Where's my daughter?

Look round the room again. It looms and distorts weirdly before me. I don't trust my eyes.

I try to pull myself to my feet but black spots and nausea get in the way.

OK, Susan. Stop trembling. Try to remember.

A hallway. At home. The doorbell ringing. Delivery expected. Chain not on.

Going to answer the door.

Yes, that's it. A door. I see a door now, in this room. Maybe Cara is on the other side?

Crawl over the floor. One hand in front of the other. Grunt with the effort. Feel like I'm Cara when she was learning. Past a tray of partially eaten food. White fish. The smell makes me want to vomit.

Approach the door, in this room. Lean my hands against it, inch them higher and higher, climbing with my hands. Finally at the handle. Pull and pull. Handle up, handle down. Please! Open!

Nothing. It stays firmly shut.

In my mind, in my memories, the front door of my house opens. I've answered the door. Then blackness, blankness. Nothing but: Cara, my Cara, I must see Cara!

I'm shouting it now, out loud. Screaming it. Black dots back again before my eyes.

Come on. Comprehend. Don't panic.

Slide down from the door. Look around the room. It's clean, too clean, apart from the half-eaten fish. White walls. A pine chest of drawers. Potpourri on a dresser. Beige carpets. All normal. My hands ball in and out of fists. It is not normal to me.

And you are not here.

But why, Susan, why would she be here? Was she even at home when that doorbell rang? She's fifteen, why would she be there, at home, with Mum? She might be safe, somewhere else, happy, even now.

I shake my head. Wrong. It feels wrong. I need to know where you are. Something is telling me, the deep-rooted maternal instinct, that you're not safe. I need to see you.

Footsteps! From the other side of the door.

A key in the lock. I watch the handle turn. Slowly, the door pushes open.

Him.

How could I have forgotten about him?

We face each other, him standing, me on the floor. Bile rises in my throat.

So.

This is the now-known stranger who has locked me in here. Wherever 'here' is. It's been what—two…three days? He must have drugged the fish. That's why it took me a while, for any recollection to return.

He's holding a beaker of water.

'Thought you might like something to drink, Susan.'

He knows my name. A researched, not random, snatching then. Watching, from afar? For how long?

I stare at him.

'Where is she?' I manage. Not my usual voice. My throat is dry. The words are cracked, splitting each syllable in two.

'You mustn't hate me, Susan,' he says.

I wait for more. Some explanation. Nothing.

Could I jump him? Could I run past him, out of the door? I must try, mustn't I? Even if there is no 'past him'. He fills the whole doorway.

Stop thinking. Act! Forget the shaking legs. Go, go, go! Storm him, surprise him!

But he is too quick. He slips out. The door closes. The lock turns.

'They'll come looking!' I shout, slamming my hands against the door.

Because they will, won't they? Paul, even now, must be working with the police, following up trails, looking at traffic cameras, talking to witnesses. Find my wife, he'll be shouting to anyone who'll listen. Neighbours, dog-walkers, Mrs Smith from number thirty-nine with that blessed curtain twitching. My afternoon clients, they must have raised the alarm, when I wasn't there. Right? I must be a missing person by now. Please, whoever has lost me, come and find me.

And, please, let Cara be with you. Let my daughter be safe.

Images of Cara frightened, hunched, bound, dying. No!

Just focus. Look at the room. How to get out of the room.

Look, a window! High up, narrow, darkness beyond it, but possible maybe?

There's a kind of ledge. I can pull myself up. Hands over the edge, like that, then come on—jump up, then hang on. Manage to stay there for a moment, before my weak arms fail me. Long enough to judge the window isn't glass. It's PCV. Unsmashable. And, of course, there is a window lock. And no key. Locked, I bet, but if I just stretch a hand—but no. I fall.

OK, so I need to put something under the window. That chair. Heavy. I push and pull it to under the window. Placing my hands on the back of the chair, I climb up onto the seat. With my new height, I stretch my arm to the window, then to the window latch.

Locked.

Still. A window is a window. People can see in, as well as out. When it's day again, I can wave, mouth a distress signal.

So do I sit and wait in the dark until morning? Until I can see the light again?

Or does this man, this man out there, have night-time plans for me? Because you don't just kidnap a woman and leave her in a room. You want to look at her, presumably, your toy, your little caged bird. Maybe he's looking at me even now. A camera, somewhere? I draw my legs up close to me and hug them. I stare at the ceiling, every corner. No. No. No. No. I can't see one.

Which means he must have another agenda.

I shudder.

Think of Cara. Be strong. What's your best memory of Cara? Proudest mummy moment?

Apart from every morning when I see that beautiful face. I will have that moment again. I will. Just as I've had that moment every day since I first held you.

Little baby girl wrapped in a blanket. So precious. Be safe, be warm, always.

But apart from that.

The concert!

Yes, the concert.

All the mums and dads and siblings and assorted hangers-on filing into the school hall. The stage set up ready, music stands, empty chairs. Hustle, bustle, glasses of wine. Me chatting to Alice's mum—Paul working late—about nothing and everything. Then, the gradual hush of anticipation spreads round the room. The lights dim. On comes the orchestra! And there's Cara. Her beautiful blonde hair hanging loose, masking her face. She'll tuck it behind her ear in a minute, I think. And she does. Then the whole audience can see that lovely rose tint to her cheeks, the lips so perfectly cherub-bowed to play the flute that she holds. I want to stand up and say, 'that's my daughter!' Instead I just nudge Alice's mum and we have a grin. Then there's the customary fuss and flap as the kids take their seats. All trying to look professional, but someone drops their music, and someone else plucks a stray string of a violin. Not Cara, though. She is sitting straight, flicking stray glances out to the crowd, holding the flute tight on her lap. Come on, Cara, I say to her in my head. Just do it like you've practised. All those nights at home, performing to me sometimes so that you have an 'audience'. You'll be fine.

And she is fine. When the orchestra starts to play, it's like she has a solo. You can see the musicianship. All nervousness gone. Head bobbing and darting, fingers flying, like a true flautist. No pretention. Just perfection. Then her actual solo. The flute shining out, beautiful, clear. Wonderful phrasing, beautiful passion. Then she's frowning slightly—was that a wrong note? Just keep on, keep on, no one will notice. And she does, she keeps going, right to the end.

But what makes me proudest, happiest, is, when her solo is over, she has this magnificent pinky-red flush over the whole of her face, and she gives this quick smile of sheer joy at her accomplishment, a brief look into the audience, before she bows her head and gets back to playing with the rest of the orchestra. Oh, my beautiful bold-shy Cara. How I adore you!

And then.

The memory is spent.

I'm just here again.

In silence.

Waiting.

Alone.

Hoping, praying, that my daughter is safe.

TWO

THE HEADMISTRESS OF Cara's school is occupied with a small handful of girls she has brought together in her study. They're sitting on chairs in a semicircle surrounding her desk, sipping the tea that she's given them. Patterned china cups usually reserved for the governors are balanced precariously on saucers. The girls are too busy to worry if they are spilling their tea. Their attention is focused on the man next to the headmistress. He's a rarity in a school that only has two male teachers. And neither of them have beards. Or wear leather jackets and open-necked shirts. It's clean-shaven and smart suits or the door for Mrs Cavendish's staff.

'Who do you think he is?' whispers one girl, skinny, ginger, to her companion, slightly rounder, brunette.

Her companion shrugs. 'New teacher? A friend for Mr Adams and Mr Wilson?'

The skinny ginger girl shakes her head. 'I don't think so. I think it's about Cara.'

'Everything's about Cara,' whispers back the brunette, rolling her eyes.

And it is true. The police cordons. The letters home to parents. The visit from a special psychiatrist. The thoughts, the prayers they have been asked to give her and her family in her conspicuous absence. The anxiety they have shared.

The headmistress clears her throat.

'Girls, thank you for coming,' she says, as though there is a choice to disobey the headmistress's edict. 'As you will have guessed, this is about Cara.'

The brunette shoots a 'see what I mean?' glance at her ginger friend.

'I've asked you bunch here in particular because of your friendship with Cara. I know you must be very upset right now. You're doing really well. I'm proud of you.'

There's a sniff from a blonde girl at the outer reaches of the semicircle. The headmistress advances to her and puts a hand on her shoulder.

'I don't want to upset you by going through the details again. We've all heard what the police had to say, and of course it's been all over the news. But we've been asked to help a little more.'

The headmistress resumes her seat at the head of the semicircle.

'I'd like to introduce you to Mr Belvoir, a private investigator,' she tells the girls. 'He wants—well, Mr Belvoir, why don't you explain?'

'Thank you,' the man says. He stands up. Then, perhaps realising he towers over the girls, he sits down again.

'Sometimes, when the police are looking at these things, their approach can be…limited. Now, I'm not doing them down, it's a bit delicate, but…well, I explained to your headmistress that I've got a private instruction to look at what's happened. Cara's family, you know. Got to ask my own questions. Make discreet enquiries, with close friends. I hope that's OK with you?'

Five heads bob in the room. The ginger head doesn't bob.

'Alice?' prompts the headmistress.

After a moment, Alice, the ginger girl, nods her head.

But she excuses herself almost immediately. He must ask his questions later, she says. She has English homework to do, she says. But, as she runs from the room, ignoring the headmistress's calls that the homework can wait, it's not thoughts of poetry composition that are spurring her on. It's the thought—or maybe the question—about secrets. Namely this: if your friend—your best friend, who's been your best friend since day one of reception—tells you something and makes you swear in confidence never ever to tell anyone, do you tell a man who is investigating something bad that's happened to that friend? When that man, after all, isn't even the police? And if it isn't even directly relevant? Or is it? Cara told her a secret and then—Oh Cara.

So Alice doesn't know what she should do. Cara would know what to do. She would just decide and have done with it. Impulsive and bold, that's Cara. Perhaps that's the problem. But Cara isn't here. Another problem. So, for once, Alice has to make up her own mind. The school hasn't prepared her for this sort of dilemma. Why don't they teach anything useful once in a while? Everyone knows it's friendships that count. Not books and sums and facts.

But she's stuck with those. And she'll just have to use them. And so she runs to the library, where she hides behind her textbooks. And until she has decided, she will avoid this Mr Belvoir. Even though she knows what she knows.

THREE

BITING MY NAILS. Putting my head in my hands. Walking about. Sitting down.

I can't do this.

I jump to my feet.

I shout. 'Let me out! Let me out! Let me out!'

Why am I here? Why aren't you at least in the room with me? He can't be scared of a woman and a girl uniting, can he? Not with all that muscle.

Do I just have sex with him and hope for the best? That he'll let me out without killing me, and we can all be a happy family again?

Or am I meant to just stay in here and finish that piece of fish? Is he fattening me up? Does he have a fat fetish? Did he think that the proprietor of a cupcake store and studio would be all doughy? That she wouldn't be a salad-eating Pilates junky who would have to close the store if she put on a pound? Because the yummy mummies of leafy North London don't want to associate cupcakes with saturated fats and weight gain, do they? That's not the lifestyle. No. Perhaps they're bulimic. I don't care. That's not my lookout. It's important to watch what you eat. Of course. But not for their reasons. So, when I see them running round Alexandra Park, I nod and smile and remind them of the 'how to do deluxe frosting' session but I don't follow them when they go to the bathroom.

Which is a good point. Bathroom.

I bang the door of my room from the inside. I have a question. Or at least, a ruse to bring that bastard in here.

I keep banging until I hear footsteps along the corridor.

'Yes?' says the Captor from outside.

'What if I need to pee?' I ask.

There's a silence.

'Do you?' he says.

I don't, but I want to know what happens if I do. If it gives me a way out. Some hope of escape. Or at least seeing if Cara is out there.

'Really badly,' I say.

There's a pause, then a key in the lock. I expect to be handed a bucket when the door opens.

But no. He is empty-handed.

'Turn round,' he says.

I do as he asks.

Once I've turned, he takes hold of both of my arms from behind, clamps them together with one of his paw-like hands. I feel like my wrists will snap if I struggle.

He twists me round and pulls me out of the room.

We're in a short corridor. Look about, quickly. Nothing I recognise. It's as blank and beige as the room. Like it's been deliberately stripped. Or like he has no life at all, apart from ruining other people's. We pass one closed door next to mine. My stomach jumps closer to my heart. Cara? Is Cara in there?

Baby in one room, mummy in the other. Let me see her, I need to see her!

'Hello? Cara?'

He pulls me faster along the corridor. We stop in front of an open door. I see a toilet and bath and a shower enclosure in the corner. White tiling. Clean. Probably forensically bleached before and after each visit.

He pushes me into the room.

And follows me.

What have I done?

'There we go, then,' he says, nodding at the toilet. He releases me from the arm hold and nudges me towards the toilet. He stands at the door, arms folded, facing into the room. Like he has no intention of leaving.

'Are you going to give me some privacy?' I ask.

He shakes his head. Apologetically?

'The door doesn't have a lock,' he says.

'You're going to stand here watching me?'

He doesn't respond.

'You could at least turn your back,' I tell him. Then I could at least try to jump you, I think, even if it is with my trousers round my ankles.

He still doesn't say anything. Just keeps looking at me.

So. I'll have to carry on. But I'm not going to let him degrade me. I'm not going to let him see how vulnerable I feel as I pull down my pyjama shorts. I'm not going to let him know how my flesh creeps, how my insides clench and my legs tremble. I keep eye contact as I lower myself to the seat. I expect his gaze to drift downwards, to drink me in while I urinate. But he keeps his gaze level with my eyes. I make a show of squatting up fully to wipe myself. Still his gaze stays at my eyes. At first. And then he allows himself a quick flick down, towards my exposed parts. I pull up my shorts in a hurry.

I move to the sink to wash my hands. I struggle with the taps; my hands are shaking. The Captor helps me out.

'Careful,' he says. 'The water is very hot.'

As he leans in, I catch sight of the two of us in the mirror over the sink. I almost gasp. I'm not who I remember myself to be. My eyes have purple patches under them—tiredness beyond black circles. Or maybe he has punched me? My skin is so pale it is almost translucent. My lips are dry and cracked. My hair, unbrushed, but in a ponytail, sticks up wildly. And if I thought he was twice the size of me, I was wrong. He looks at least four times the size of me. And about four times as human—pink skin (neatly stubbled), hair combed, lips moist.

Steam covers the mirror and the comparison is lost.

I notice my hands are burning and I pull them out from under the tap.

Then I present my wrists meekly to the Captor. He takes hold of them and escorts me back to my room.

When he leaves I'm sick on the floor.

I try not to think what will happen when I need to shower.

When Cara needs to shower. If she's here.

All I want to do is hide in the bed in a foetal position. But I must be strong, for Cara. I must show him that it's not enough to leave me locked in here. Like I've had my bit of outside and now I'm stuck.

So I take a big breath and unleash the banshee. I cry and I scream and I shout. Maybe we are in the middle of a housing estate. Maybe I'll alert the neighbours.

The door opens before I even hear the key in the lock.

'What's wrong now?' he asks.

What's wrong? I want to shout back. *What's wrong? You've kidnapped me, that's what's wrong. And done something, maybe, I don't know, to my daughter.* But I carry on with the wordless screaming. He moves towards me, closer and closer and closer, until—ow!

Stinging, on my cheek.

He's slapped me.

So I scream again. Louder.

He slaps me again, harder.

It brings tears to my eyes.

And there's a wet glittering in his.

'I didn't bring you here for this,' he says. There's a crack in his voice.

'Then why did you bring me here?' I hear my voice, high, wavering.

He shakes his head and moves back towards the door. I start screaming again.

He turns to me. This time his hand is in a fist. I flinch. He lowers his hand. But the warning is clear. No screaming. I lie down on the bed and face the wall. I can sense him standing there, watching me.

Eventually, I hear the door close. He's gone.

I fling myself over on the bed so that I'm facing the door that he's just exited.

Who is this man? I swear I hadn't seen him before I was abducted. What does he want? Can't he just tell me everything, like some kind of super villain confessing his evil plans? At least tell me he's got his cock out every night at the thought of me but he's just biding his time; tell me we had a chance encounter in a newsagent/restaurant/supermarket; tell me he has my daughter strapped inside a wheelie bin somewhere ready to be landfill unless I have sex with him. Just don't leave me here, not knowing.

I need to know what's happening. Why is no one telling me what's happening to my baby?

I need Cara. I need Paul. I need a hug, some tea, some air, some knowledge, some hope. I just need. Give me something. Please.

FOUR

The other side of the door

I COULD JUST have let her scream. Of course I could. I'm
prepared. Tough love, isn't it called? I've experience of
that. I've hardened myself for more. Had to. Grit your
teeth, get on with it, think of the greater purpose. The
purpose she'll realise in due course. Once that natural
obsession with her daughter has abated. Of course, she
wants to know. And maybe I should tell her. But not
now. Not yet. Little by little we'll get there. Together.
That's the important bit. We'll always be together. I've
succeeded in that much. However difficult it might be,
treating a woman like that when all you want to do is
hug her and kiss her and…all the rest. The groundwork
is done. We're together. Now I just need to carry on.
Day in, day out, as long as it takes.

Oh, she's resisting. Of course she is. Wants to be in
and out of that room like a jack-in-the-box. And it bothers me. Of course it bothers me. In an ideal world, she'd
take one look at me, one morning, and she'd love me
like I know she can. She'd thank me for the delicious
fish supper. Thank me for the warm bedding. Thank
me for taking care of her. But it's not an ideal world.
Don't we know it. All of us, under this roof.

So until that happens, she's got to stay there. Locked in that room. And sometimes I may need to use force. Judge me, you up there, if you want to. But just like you have your plans and work in mysterious ways, so do I. I didn't like slapping her. Of course I didn't. Yes, there was an element of me that liked the touch of her skin. So soft. English rose. Just like Cara. You want to caress skin like that, not hurt it. Needs must though. Even if she was more stunned than hurt. She'll forgive me in the end. She has to.

Slapping her, stopping her screaming, was the right thing to do. Selfish, partly. We need to communicate. We need to have a dialogue, even if for now it's full of hate from her. And I want to be able to hear her voice. Not just gaze at her from afar. If she's hoarse, we can't do that, can we? I've thought so much about her speaking to me nicely, silkily, calling me by name, that I don't want to ruin my chances by making her croak.

And there's the noise, of course. Screaming. I think we're safe. But I'm not big on attracting attention. Not now.

Of course, if she won't communicate as she should, however long she's in there, I'll need to come up with another plan. Perhaps I'll need to force her to understand. Something with more impact. Pierce that little bubble she thinks she can hide in, away from me, for ever. But for now I have to continue with what I've started. A new phase of life for us all.

FIVE

'Mum? Mum!'

It's just a whisper but it stirs me. My brain fumbles out of the half-doze it has been in.

Cara!

But where?

'Cara?' I call.

'Shh! He'll hear you,' comes the whispered response. That's my daughter: ever practical, ever critical.

That's my daughter. I was right. She is here. The maternal instinct hasn't let me down.

I flick on the light switch, hoping that the glow won't reach the Captor, or if it does that it won't alarm him.

'Cara,' I whisper. 'Where are you?'

There's a banging sound from the wall opposite the bed. She must be in the next room. I rush over; caress the plaster.

'Are you really through there?' I ask. 'But how can I hear you, through a wall?'

'Lean down,' she says. 'There's a grate.'

I do as she says, and she is, of course, right. My wonderful, wonderful daughter. You're alive! You're here! And you have found a vent between our walls! I lie right down on the floor to see if I can see her. Think perhaps we can join little fingers—our 'mother and daughter for ever' hook.

Her hand is so fragile, so tender. If I squeeze it, will she squeeze back?

But no. Hearing will have to be enough.

'How did you know I was here?' I ask her.

'You weren't exactly quiet,' she says.

No. I wasn't, was I?

'You're all right?' I ask her. 'He hasn't touched you, or hurt you, or…anything, has he?'

Silence.

'Cara?' I start to panic. 'He hasn't, he didn't—'

'I guess you can't hear when I shake my head,' comes her response.

I close my eyes with relief. 'Thank God,' I murmur.

There's a pause. Then we both start talking together.

'Do you know where we are?' I ask, as she says 'Do you think Dad will find us?'

Then, from her, 'I don't know,' as I say, 'I'm sure he will, sweetheart.' And at the same time I think, I hope so. Please, let him find us.

'I'm so glad you're here, Mum,' she says. 'I mean, it's awful that he got you, when I understood what was happening I…' She sounds like she's holding back tears. Or maybe letting them flow. My poor darling Cara. 'But I'm just glad, glad I'm not alone.'

I nod. 'I know,' I say. I hope she can hear that I'm hugging her voice with mine. Because I know what she means. I'm overjoyed she's here. She's here and she's safe and she's with me. I'd much rather she were at home, safer, with Paul, but at least I have this comfort.

She would be my desert island luxury, as I've often told her. I'll never let her go.

Such a beautiful baby. An item to treasure. Can't I keep her with me?

'What do you think he wants to do to us?' she asks. 'Just, like, keep us here? Or do you think he's got, you know, plans?'

Can I use the maternal cloak of little white lies to conceal the world from her? In theory, for one more year, until she is sixteen. But she is savvy. That's what growing up in London does to you. And she watches TV. We both know what she means.

'Let's hope he would have done that by now, if he was going to,' I say.

As if on cue, there is the sound of footsteps, and a door opening along the corridor.

'He's heard us!' I whisper. 'Quick, back into your bed! Don't tell him you know I'm here. He'll move us!'

'Mum!'

I hear the pain of separation in her voice. It rips through my heart. Worse, almost, than when they took her way from me, bundled up, in hospital, all that time ago.

'I'll think of something. Don't worry,' I say. Then I add, 'There's a window.'

But I have to scramble back to my bed because there's a key in the lock.

The Captor's face appears in the door frame.

'Did you call me?' he asks.

I shake my head.

He looks at the floor. 'Shame,' he says. Then I see

his gaze has shifted to my bed. Where I haven't quite pulled the cover over my exposed leg. I adjust the duvet quickly.

'I must have been having a nightmare,' I say. 'Thank you for that.'

He just continues to look at me. I feel tremors start in my hands. He must have plans, looking at me like that. Is it how he looks at Cara too? My Cara, just next door. Who I must protect, keep safe, now that she is here. That is my role, my calling, my mothering duty at its starkest. I grasp my hands, holding them both together to stop the shaking. I must not show him I am afraid. That makes me vulnerable.

I raise my chin and meet the Captor's stare. He looks away.

'Would you like some hot chocolate?' he asks.

'What, so you can drug it?' I ask.

He blinks at me. I knew it. He didn't realise he had such a clever captive.

'I don't want your drugged hot chocolate,' I say, more loudly than normal, so Cara can hear. Keep her safe, don't let her succumb. We don't want another generation started here in nine months' time.

'I'll go back to bed then,' he says. 'Unless…'

He stares again into my bed. I think he is going to ask if he can get into mine.

Instead, he says, 'Just tell me tomorrow if you want anything.'

'What do you want?' I hurl at him as he closes the door.

There's a pause in the door shutting.

'You,' he says.

Then the door shuts. And no one can see the tremors that have restarted. Because I know what that 'You' must mean. What it is building up to.

I'm pleased that Cara and I aren't face to face. That she can't see my fear. And I have her face in my mind anyway. Of course I do—any mother does. All her faces. From when she was born, that crinkly tiny tiny face, the shock of dark hair.

She's so small. So, so small. Could be crushed in just the palm of a hand.

Yes, that face, all her faces, right up to her now-face. That lovely blonde hair, about a thousand different shades, from gold to oaten, shorter now that she's older. Cool Cara. Beautifully smooth. Not for my Cara the acne and pockmarks of the mid-teens. Flawless.

'Cara?' I whisper. That same reverent tone as when I called her by name that first time, in the hospital.

'Shh, it's not safe,' she hisses, quietly. 'We need to find another way to communicate. And then we need to get out of here.'

She is right, of course. If he hears us talking, he will punish us. Separate us. Bring forward his plans. Whatever they are. But, for now, I need something.

'Cara,' I whisper again. She doesn't reply. Frightened, I suppose, of being overheard. Just this one thing then I'll heed her. 'When I tap, like this, on the wall—' I tap, twice, very lightly '—it means I love you, OK? And you tap back to tell me you're safe. OK?'

Nothing.

I know she's safe, as safe as anyone can be when they

are kidnapped, I've just spoken to her. But still my heart pounds at her silence.

Then, there it is. Tap tap.

I feel my soul relax, my shoulders unhunch, at her sound.

But it's only a temporary release. I must get her out of here. I must get her properly safe.

I look at the window again. If I could just escape, I could come back for Cara. Or maybe, now that we're both here, there's double the chance that someone will have seen something, reported something? One of Cara's school friends maybe? They're always to-gether and, when they're not, they're calling or mes-saging or Instagramming or whatever it is that they do on those devices of theirs. I don't know. She just helped me spruce up my website. 'It needs more jazz, Mum!' she said. 'And a picture of you! You're selling yourself, just as much as you're selling the cupcakes!' So per-ceptive, Cara. Such a good business head. Maybe she won't go to university. Maybe she can help expand the studio into a cupcake empire. And how lovely to have a daughter who's so proud of you that she insists on her favourite photo of you on your website. And that the photo is one of the two of you together—both with hair down, heads resting together, eyeliner on, black leggings showing off slim legs, big cheery smiles say-ing life is great, eat cupcakes.

Should I have been more careful, putting up photos of my daughter? Maybe. Maybe not. But she's probably all over social media of her own accord. She's fifteen. It's what they do.

Oh, to be back in that studio with you now, Cara!

I bend my head against the wall to Cara's room, as if I'm leaning against her head like on that website photo. Oh my darling. Please let that window help us escape. Please let one of your school friends have seen something. Please.

SIX

SHE WON'T TELL. She won't tell. Alice repeats the mantra of silence. Cara had entrusted her with a secret. What good would it do to tell anyone about it? 'La, la, la, I'm not listening', she says to the little voice inside her head that insists telling might do some good. I'm doing my English homework, she tells the voice sternly. And I am not telling that man what I know. That's a secret.

Alice's eyes wander to the passport-sized picture of her and Cara on her wall. They're wearing crazy red wigs, silver star-shaped sunglasses and moustaches. Both of them grinning madly. You can almost see the giggles. It was a party at school, and the teachers had laid on some 'fun' dress-up photo booths. And they were fun. What the teachers didn't know was that Cara had held on to the sunglasses and customised them— just in case they weren't tacky enough—with some glitter-glue cardboard rainbows. 'You're such a rebel!' Alice had told her. And they'd giggled some more. It seems hard to believe in now, the laughter.

'Alice! Come down here, please,' calls a voice. A parental voice.

'I'm doing my homework,' she shouts back.

'Now, please,' the voice calls.

Fine. Alice closes her exercise book in a huff. On

the front is a picture of Mr Wilson that Cara drew for her. It accentuates his big ears and has a funny caption coming out of his mouth. Well, it's only funny if you know Mr Wilson. He has a silly high-pitched voice like a parrot. So him saying, 'Good morning, class', while a parrot flaps round in the background, is a very funny picture indeed. All the funnier for being drawn in class by her best friend. Alice turns the exercise book over. I'm not telling, she says again.

Downstairs, her mum is sitting on the sofa holding a piece of paper.

'What's all this about you helping a detective?' Alice's mum asks her.

Alice stands next to her mother and peers at the piece of paper.

Oh. Stupid school. Of course they've sent a letter about Mr Belvoir. They send letters about everything. And if they don't send them, they hand them out, and Alice is supposed to give them to her mum. All such boring letters. And so much to remember. Cara always said she never told her mum about the boring stuff. But then, Cara never told her mum about the interesting stuff either. That, she kept for Alice. That was the blessing and curse of having a best friend.

Alice stands back from the piece of paper again. 'Oh, that.' She feigns nonchalance. She puts her hands on the arm of the sofa and does little stretches of her legs to either side. 'Just some man trying to find stuff out about Cara. No big deal.' Alice hopes her mum can't hear her heart beating. Or even see it beating. Great big red bangs out of her chest—boom, boom, boom.

Her mum puts the letter down and regards Alice.

'How can you say that, Alice? Don't be so fickle. If it's about Cara, it's important. You must tell him anything you know. Quite what he thinks he's going to add, I'm not sure. But you must help, do you hear me?'

Alice stares at the floor and nods.

'Otherwise I don't know how you can call yourself Cara's best friend.'

Alice keeps nodding. A single tear falls down her cheek. Her mum rises from the sofa.

'Oh, come here, love. I'm sorry. I didn't mean to make you cry.' Alice finds herself enveloped in a big perfumey hug. 'I know it's difficult for you. You're being so brave.'

Alice sniffs. 'I just keep thinking about how much I want to see her. Why did it have to be Cara? It's so unfair.'

'I know, love. I know.'

'And I just keep thinking about the last time I saw her, when—'

She stops herself. She's said too much. The secret risks slipping out without her choosing it to.

'When what, love?'

Alice shakes her head. 'When I try to go to sleep. I just keep thinking about that last time, when I go to sleep.'

Alice feels her hair being ruffled by her mum. Usually, she'd say she's too old for that, but today it feels nice.

'It's natural to feel like that, love. But if you talk to this man, who knows—you might make it all a lot better. You know I can't tell you that you'll see Cara again but, well, you never know, it might help.'

Alice nods. She knows all this. She is practically a grown-up—her birthday is coming up soon and then she'll be even older.

'Can I go and do my homework now, Mum?'

Another head ruffle.

'Of course you can, love.'

Alice leaves the room and strides up the stairs, almost managing two at a time. That was a close-run thing. It was bad having to lie to Mum. Because it wasn't so much thinking about the last time she saw Cara that was bothering her. It was the fact that she knew where Cara was going.

SEVEN

MAYBE THERE'S A RANSOM. Maybe that's what this is about. Maybe the Captor wants money for our lives. Or our body parts. Maybe I'll lose lock by lock of my hair, or finger by finger of my hand. He can take every limb from my body before he touches one strand of Cara's hair.

Will Paul pay? We've had the debate while watching late-night hostage thrillers. Me and Paul curled up on the sofa, Cara sitting on the floor between us (if we've quietly 'forgotten' it's a school night for the pleasure of her company). Is it ever right to pay a ransom? To give money to criminals? We've agreed that whether it's right depends on the circumstances. Do they have a wife and family? Because it's always the men, in these films, that go adventuring. All I did was stay safe at home. I even based the studio there. I hardly ever went out, not really, apart from to ferry Cara around— orchestra practice, concerts, parties, design classes, fashion shows… We deserve the safety we thought that gave us. I want to shout to him: 'Paul, it's always right to pay the ransom, if it's you and me and Cara. How- ever much money you have to raise'.

How much money could he raise, and how soon? Sell the house. The loft must have added a bit. Mine and

Paul's domain. Had there been a sibling it could have been her room. But no. So anyway, with the loft, with our Crouch End postcode—no Tube but lots of North London leafiness—we could be looking at £800,000? But the Captor might think it's more. This might be a rented place I'm held in. He might not be a Londoner. He might believe the press, think we all live in garages worth two million pounds. And he might think that Paul being an 'IT consultant' means something, something lucrative. A desk in a corner office in a City building, rather than a desk in the corner of our living room and, whenever his mobile rings, a jump in the car to some industrial estate company that's too broke to have a permanent IT team. The Captor might also think that because cupcakes are so popular, my company has been raking it in. That I'm doing corporate events or something. That millionaires come to my training sessions, not clever mums bored out of their wits by their decision to stay at home. He won't realise it's part inheritance, part being remortgaged up to the hilt that keeps us there.

So, all in all, I bet the Captor is asking for a million.

A lot of money.

It's nice he thinks we're worth it, Cara and me.

But why take both of us? Cara is the more valuable one and with both me and Paul outside we could raise much more money.

A thought strikes me.

Would Paul be willing to pay for Cara? Considering?

But yes. He must be. He can't negotiate over her. He can't say 'Nah, one million pounds? You don't know who you're talking to, mate. I'll just take the one. Five

hundred thousand plus another twenty for your trouble.'
Because he must know that if he gets me back, but not
her, he won't have me at all.

Why isn't it light yet? Where is the sun when you
need it?

The police might tell him not to pay of course.
Friends and remaining family might benevolently but
wrongly advise that I would not want all our hard-won
money given up without a fight. But what's money? I
would live in a caravan, overlooking the ocean. All I
need is family and freedom.

So pay it, Paul. Release what equity we have. Scrabble round beneath proverbial sofas to find the funds.
Call in old favours. Phone your sister. Crowd-fund. Or
find us, and shoot the place out (not us) with the police.

Find us.

I get out of bed, clasping the duvet to me, and go over
to the wall. Cara's wall. I nestle down there, close to her.
The separation of the wall is not enough to break the
bond. I tap-tap my goodnight kiss onto the wall. The
tap-tap comes back. I can breathe again.

My baby so close I can almost hear her breathe. Almost. Not quite.

I AWAKE TO beams of sunlight coming through the window.

Morning.

The window.

I jump up.

There's the chair, waiting for me. I clamber onto it,
peering over the ledge. It looks so beautiful outside, so

crisp. Unlike the air in here, already turning stale. Fully oxygenated out there—look at all those trees!

And not many people to clutter the atmosphere up with exhaled carbon dioxide, unfortunately.

I can see just one person. A girl. About eight. Scrawny, her brown hair in uneven bunches. Takes me back to when Cara was little. Except Cara's hair was always blonde. And her bunches were never uneven. The girl is skipping. Quite well. She must be concentrating hard, no risk of tripping on the rope. No risk of her seeing me, the Captor must think. I wave. I wave again. I try banging on the glass. Nothing. Just one-two-three-jump-two-three and the bunches bobbing up and down.

See me! I will her. See me, understand me, and run back to your parents' house—whether that's the other side of those trees or just round the corner, slightly outside my view—and bring them, so they can rescue Cara and me.

But she moves on to a more complicated skip, turning herself and the rope round in a circle while she jumps. I never taught Cara that one. Would never want Cara to have her back to her mother. Like the girl now has her back to me.

I come down from the window and slump in the chair. The window is not a solution yet. But I can make it one. If I just had a pen and paper, I could write up a big sign. 'Mother and daughter kidnapped—rescue us!' Or just 'Trapped—help!' Although whoever saw that would probably just think it was the wry joke of an angsty teenager, smile slightly and walk on by. If anyone were to see it. If the girl is observant when the rope is down. If anyone comes through the trees.

And if I had a pen and paper, I could do something else too—I could write to Cara! I go back over to the grate and examine it. Yes, a letter would go through there, easily! I want to call through my plan, but I daren't, after last night. He will separate us, I know he will, or punish us. Punish her. Which I can't allow. And, anyway, I can call out to him, tell him I want paper. Cara will hear, and she'll know I have some kind of plan. She'll be on the lookout for something new, something different, and she'll see it through the grate.

He told me, didn't he, that I was to call if I wanted anything? Well, I'll tell him I want to write a diary. That he'll be torturing me if he doesn't let me. That I'll scream again (although I won't).

So I bang on the door of my new prison.

'Hey!' I shout.

Silence.

'You!' I shout. 'Come here!'

Still silence. What's this? Is he sleeping? Has he topped himself? Will Cara and I starve? Has he left us alone?

Is he out collecting the ransom?

Is he just torturing me with denial?

Why doesn't he understand I must have my paper!

I search the room. I need the paper and pen now, now I have thought of it, this plan. I need to communicate with my Cara. I need to put up a sign to the outside world. I need the pen and paper.

I open the drawers. Nothing. No drawer-liner that

I could write on with potpourri. What kind of unci-
vilised place is this? I open the wardrobe, hoping for
those tissue paper covers the dry cleaner puts on coat
hangers. No. None. No clothes either. Just a lavender
clothes freshener. What does this guy have against natural smells? Am I in some kind of abattoir? Is this the
killing room, recently cleansed?

And the walls, of course, are paint, not wallpaper.
So I can't rip them down, write on them with the scent
of flowers. No.

Somewhere outside the room there is a sound of
slamming.

'Hello!' I shout again. 'Are you there?'

Footsteps now. He is coming. The key in the lock.

He is wearing a coat. So. I was right. He has been
out. If I had a watch, some way of telling the time, I
could record whether it's a habitual outing. Whether it
gives me time to speak to Cara. Whether we can use it
to break the doors down. Or if it's just a one-off, to collect ransom money. But perhaps he would have come
back in something nicer than an anorak if he'd just got
one million pounds.

I want to say a bitchy 'Nice day out?' but I don't.
Better to pretend I haven't noticed the coat. In case I
need to exploit it later.

Instead, I say, 'You told me to ask you if I wanted
something.'

His eyes become more alive. 'Well?'

'I'd like a pen and some paper, please. To write a
diary.'

'A diary?' His tone is curious.

'Of my captivity. Not,' I add, 'that I expect it to go on for long.'

He nods his head. He seems to approve of my request. I don't want your approval, I want to scream, I want you to let me and my daughter out.

But, short of that, give me a pen and paper.

'Anything else?' he asks. There seems to be hope in his voice, encouragement. Like I'm suddenly going to ask for him, himself.

Something to keep in mind for an escape.

But I'm not ready to go down that route yet.

For now, I just want to communicate with Cara, and the girl outside.

I shake my head. 'Just the pen and paper.'

The door closes, the lock turns. A few minutes later, he comes back with a notebook and a couple of pencils. The pencils are blunt, I notice. Maybe he thinks I would stab him with a sharp one. Maybe I would. But these will at least do for my first letter to Cara. I wait until he is out of the door again and the lock seals me in. Then I begin to write.

EIGHT

The other side of the door

WELL, YOU HAVE to give them what they want, don't you? Builds up trust, for when you need it. Means they no longer want to escape. Bit of tit for tat—I give you a pencil, you give me… Well. What I want. But slowly does it. I'm playing the long game here. Not that I won't take drastic measures if I need to. Haven't I already been drastic enough?

But can anyone blame me? I look at the photos again, lining the walls. So beautiful. That golden hair. Like mother, like daughter. Suze and Cara. Inseparable. What it would be like to touch it, for real. I sit back in my chair and let my fantasies run wild. I'm at the threshold of Suze's room. She stands there, hips jutting at a provocative angle, twirling one strand of hair in her finger. Slowly, she starts undoing her blouse (or, OK, that pyjama top I've got her in—the best fantasies are based on reality). Then just when the buttons have got tantalisingly low, she stops, leans forward, and grabs my belt. She pulls me towards her. Then she kisses me. It's a kiss that means I'm yours, I surrender, you can stop trying. It's a kiss that ends up with me on top of her, on the bed. Loving her, hard. As hard as she'll let me. Maybe harder.

I take a couple of deep breaths. Come on, cool it down. I know some men in my position would just go now and burst through the door, take what they want, and sod the emotional side. But that's not enough for me. I want her to want me. I will use what tools I have available. Perhaps Cara will be one of them, when it's appropriate. The diary is a good sign. It's like an acceptance that she's staying here. That's what I need. Acceptance is what I'm after. A step closer to recognition, forgiveness, to moving on to what should be our lives together.

Oh, that life together. It's like I can see it in a mirror but someone has steamed it over. Little by little, that steam will evaporate and there we'll be, clear as day. I've just got to keep everything fixed in front of the mirror until that moment. Help that steam on its way. And no, everything will not end up back to front, inverted in its mirrored image. It will be perfect. Well, one imperfection. But I can't do anything about that. Not now.

I've still got some little tokens of that life. Suze's phone. She had it on her when I locked her in. I confiscated it when she was sleeping. Switched off, of course. Good luck contacting her, anyone. And I have Cara's cherished instrument. She had it with her when she got in the car. Must just recently have had her lips against this very hole that I now lay my mouth on. Must have fingered its length to make her own melodious sound. Like I saw her do before. Oh yes. I've been there, to the school concert hall. I've stood at the back, in the dark, watching her. They stop monitoring the doors once all the parents have sat down and the lights have dimmed. Anyone could walk in.

I should take this to Cara's room. How I'd love to see her play, my own private performance. But I can hardly make her do that. I'm not deluded. Cara's not going to do anything to my bidding, any more than Suze is (yet). And it's Suze I've got to work on. Suze that holds the key to our happiness.

I get up and close the curtains. There's no room in the mirror picture for intruders. I can't risk answering the door and, if I'm clearly visible, there's no excuse not to. I've been out; that's enough. No reason to let them indoors wander free. I'll choose what from this house goes into the world. And what comes in.

NINE

Dearest Cara,
It's me! I'm writing to you! I got him to bring
paper and pencils (you might have heard). So we
can communicate without risk of being overheard.
But you must make sure he doesn't find this letter, or future letters, or the pencil or paper that
I'm enclosing. Look for a hiding place. And then
write back.

If I can't write again, for any reason, then remember this: *I love you.* And Dad loves you. And
between us, somehow, *we will keep you safe.*
Mum
xxxx

I RIP THE letter from the notebook and tear out some
other pages. I fold up the missive and wrap the other
pages around it. Then I change my mind and put the
letter on the outside, facing outwards, in case she otherwise doesn't see my writing. I place the pencil in the
centre. Then I advance to the grate and begin shoving it
through. The grate is small—each vent only the length
of a finger, and narrow too. I have to reduce the amount
of paper I send through and refold the package. The pencil itself, the essential tool of reply, I wriggle through.

I put my head to the wall and listen for rustling.
Nothing. I stay pressed like that. Maybe she is asleep.
Or worse. Not there. Maybe when the Captor left the
house earlier, he took Cara with him. Maybe he is ran-
soming us or disposing of us or…whatever-elsing us
one by one.

Shall I tap-tap on the wall? Or is that too much? Do
I need to limit myself, not show by my desperation for
her safety, how vulnerable we are? I raise my hand,
lower it again. Don't alarm her. Don't keep knocking.
Don't put the Captor on to us.

But please be there, Cara. If you are there and reply
to my letter, I know you at least are still with me. Only
in peril in the same way as me. Not in some dangerous outside place. Although there's a wall between us,
a daughter is safest nearer her mother, isn't she? Please
be there. Please let him not have taken you someplace
else. I can't bear for you not to be there.

*You'll always be this little one's mummy. No one can
take that way from you.*

Tears well. I let them fall. I rock back on my heels
and wait. And wait. What is taking you so long, Cara?
Why don't you reply? Should I risk a knock on the wall?
A whisper? But no. That might endanger everything. I
must have a little patience. Must breathe. Yes. Important
to remember. And fill my time wisely. The window!

Yes, of course, the window. My sign. It will be poxy
in small notebook paper and a pencil but I will do the
best I can.

What to write?

Keep it simple. Something like:

'Please help. Mother and daughter, Susan and Cara Bright, held hostage in here. Call 999.'

We must be all over the news—Paul will have done his bit insisting the media and police will be on the case. Right? Paul won't just think I've taken Cara on a trip? No. We were due to be at home, to eat together. The Captor snatched me from home and must have snatched Cara from school.

And Paul will find us. Then everything will go back to normal. I'll resurrect the cupcake business. Cara will go back to school—once I've spoken to the Head about security—and we'll all dine out on this trauma for the rest of our lives.

I sketch out the words for the sign lightly first. They cover six sheets of paper. Then I start pressing hard. Deep grey shading, to make it visible outside. But not too dark so as to destroy the pencil. It's all I have.

I'm so absorbed in my task that it's not until I hear the key in the lock that I know the Captor is coming.

Quick! Hide the sign! Why didn't I take my own advice to Cara and look for a hiding place? The door is opening, where can I put the sign?

I shove it under duvet, just in time. By the time the Captor's face appears, I am posing with the notebook, pencil in hand.

He bends down to place a tray down on the floor. Granola, yoghurt, orange juice, a cup of tea. An inch at the back of his neck is exposed. If the pencil were sharper, I could bring it down, now, spear it through the skin, force him to the floor. Or could I? He's a big guy. I'm not so huge. Maybe I need more than a pencil.

He stands up again. Moment or non-moment of potential escape gone.

He looks at me. 'Writing in your diary then?' he asks.

I shrug. 'I can't think of anything to write. Not much
happens in here.'

'Let me help with that,' he says. And he sits down
on the bed. Right on top of the part of the duvet that
hides the sign.

If he pushes the duvet back, I am finished. He is too
close to me. I can smell him. He smells of mould. Not in
a way that makes me retch. More that fragrant mould,
released in forests after the rain. Fine for forests. Not
so nice on a man.

He takes the diary and pencil from me. I want to
resist, want to claw them back, but we know who has
the power here.

He writes in the diary. Seeing as he is so close to me,
I try to lean in, see what he is writing, but he hides it
from me. He is concentrating. I couldn't, could I, stand
up and make a run for the door? He sees my head move
and follows my eye line. He puts one leg firmly across
mine. He is wearing big, heavy boots. I stay where I am.

Then I notice that when he moved, the duvet moved
with him. The edge of the sign I drew is now visible.

Shit.

I hold my breath, waiting for him to pull back all the
duvet, find out what is underneath. Punish me.

He is still focusing the notebook. For now.

I resist the urge to look at the sign again. He is observant. He will follow my eyes. Instead, I force myself to
stare at him, while he looks at the notebook. I scrutinise

the hair in his ear, the little lines around the edge of his eyes. This is a villain who has smiled more than he has frowned then. Not a good sign. Potentially sociopathic.

'There,' he says. 'Done.' He hands me back the diary.

I look at what he has written.

'Today is the day that I shared my bed. Sitting this time. But it's a sign of closeness. A sign of more to come. I will give that man what he wants—what I want, really—in time.'

I shiver. I look up at him. He smiles.

So. That is the plan then. He does, as he says, want me. But, apparently, I have to give myself to him.

He stands up. I want to break eye contact, let him know his plans revolt me. But I daren't, lest his eyes search out the paper sign instead. Holding his gaze, I shift along the bed, putting one hand behind me. I can feel the rough edge of the paper under my hand. I hope it is covered. I hope he doesn't think the gesture is an invitation.

He stays in the room, staring at me. A smile—or is it a smirk—crosses over his lips. He adds to the creases round his eyes. Then he turns his back and opens the door, and goes out. And locks me in again.

TEN

THERE IT IS—under the grate! A letter from Cara!

I was so busy trying to fend off, distract, comprehend the Captor that I must have missed it coming through. At least, I hope it's a letter. Not just a bundle of papers. I rush to pick up the pages. They shake in my hands like leaves.

And yes! Thank goodness. Here is Cara's wonderful handwriting. That beautiful, self-conscious, teenage script, with the dots of 'i's done in circles, the 'z's struck through, and all letters bulbous and round. That relief as real as when I used to look at you in your little bed, holding my own breath until your chest rose again. I clutch the paper to myself before I begin to read, inhaling it. Cara. Then I pull it away and study it.

Dear Mum,
Amazing. SO well done getting the paper and pencil. Totally get what you say about a hiding place. The room has a…actually, no, better not write where the hiding place is in case your place isn't as good as mine :).
So. What's the plan? How are we getting out of here? We will get out of here, won't we? Dad

must be coming, right? I reckon give him another few hours and he'll be here. Definitely.

How did you end up in here? I remember being by the school gates, then in a car, but not much else. Then…here.

I just wish we could get a message out. Let people know where we are. That we're alive. And so far, safe.

That first night, I think it was night, that was the worst. I just sat up in this horrible bed in the dark holding the duvet and shaking. I couldn't believe it was happening. I thought I'd never see you or Dad again. I would have given anything to know you were here. And now you are.

I love you Mum. I know you'll get us out of this.

You will, right?

Cara xxx.

I read the letter again and again. And again. I trace the loops with my eyes and then with my fingers. Cara. At once so strong and so vulnerable. So independent and yet still my little girl. I'd give anything to hug her. Kiss that beautiful face. To take her home, reunite her with the pink biro that I know this letter would be written in, had she the choice. She'd maybe cover it with some pink hearts, for extra measure, like the hearts she draws on the magazine articles and clippings that adorn her bedroom walls. Perfume ads, fashion pictures, cute animals—she's a real girl's girl. Then she recreates that physical space online, Pinterest and everything. I know.

She showed me a picture of one of my cupcake ads she'd 'pinned' on her virtual board. I felt so proud that she should be proud of me.

Much as I would love to write back immediately with outpourings of love, I can't write back until there is a plan. You can tell from the letter that she needs me to think of one, to keep her happy. What energetic and traumatised fifteen-year-old wants simply to hang round waiting for Dad to do something? I'm surprised I can't hear her ricocheting off the walls with pent-up frustration.

No. I must provide an alternative.

The window sign.

I tuck her note into my pillowcase and pull the sign from the bed. Quickly, I finish emboldening the letters that I had loosely pencilled in. There. That sign should be readable by the little girl outside, if she is still there.

I clamber up my chair ladder to the window and look out. No little girl today. But she must come back. Or somebody else must. And see the sign. I lean the pieces of paper against the window, facing out. They take up almost all of the window, leaving me just a small chink to look out of. The paper seems flimsy, like it could fall down at any moment. And however visible it is from the outside, it feels painfully visible from the inside. The Captor may see it. And, with it, my knowledge of Cara. Then he'll take down perhaps my only means of escape, and deny me my lifeline with my daughter.

So what I need is a prop. Something to keep the sign in position and also conceal it. But not arouse suspicion. From my chair, I look round the room. What would work?

The only contender seems to be a pillow. I have two. One should squidge up nicely to fit in the gap. I clamber down from the chair, seize the pillow and spring back up to the chair. Success. The pillow fits. It takes away most of the light and my room takes on a dungeon feel. But it's for a greater good. Our greater good. Mine, Cara's, Paul's. If the Captor asks, I'll say the light was stopping me sleeping. I can still move the pillow if I need to, when I'm alone, to look out. For the girl. Or for anyone else.

And the other pillow—well, its case can hide the letters from Cara. Two missions accomplished.

Escape plan A put in train, I can now face Cara again. I pick up her letter and reread it. Why wasn't I there at the school gates to pick her up? The Captor must have already got me. Did he do it in two journeys then? Or was one of us in the boot? Or was there an accomplice? I want to tell her I'm sorry I wasn't there. But it wasn't my fault.

As I pick up the pencil, my stomach rumbles. I look over at the granola. Healthy, nutritious. Not that I need to watch what I eat so much these days. With the yoghurt it would be delicious. And give me energy to fight for Cara. Can I eat it? Who would drug granola? Surely if you were going to drug breakfast, you'd make scrambled eggs, or porridge, or something else sloppy and indistinct. Not granola. But I'm not dealing with a logical person here. I'm dealing with a kidnapper. So he might have drugged it. Best not to risk it.

I turn back to the pencil and paper.

'Dearest Cara,' I write.

Cara. Beloved. I remember choosing that name, with her father.

People asking whether we're giving her a name, just now. Of course we need a name. Look at her. She's beautiful.

I wanted to call her all the names that summed up just how glorious she was to me: Cara Joy Aimee Hope Star Rose. In the end, I was persuaded just to go for Cara Joy. A name cannot sum up that much love anyway. The love that came just holding her in that little bundle, staring into her eyes, feeling her little lips at my breast, one finger wrapped up in her tiny hand. A magical day. I wonder if her father still remembers it. Remembers her. Fourteen years is a long time with no contact.

My stomach rumbles again. Love does not conquer hunger apparently.

I look at the breakfast tray. I could just eat half of everything. That way, if it really is drugged, it won't hit me with its full strength. I might just be caused to flutter my eyelashes a bit, not invite him into my bed. And I would have the strength to give my letter to Cara the full attention it needs. Plus me starving isn't going to help. I need the strength for a fight, if it comes.

I put down the paper and move to the tray. Cutlery this time, although plastic. Does he trust me a little bit then? To arm me with two (blunt) pencils and a plastic spoon? Or has he just risk assessed the situation—a happy well-nourished kidnappee is less likely to attack than a soul-starved hungry one?

If so, he's made a miscalculation. Because if my window sign doesn't get me and Cara safely out of here, then something else will.

ELEVEN

The other side of the door

I MAKE TWO identical lunches, on two identical trays. I add the ground-up powder. Perhaps I should feel guilty. Perhaps I do. But, in the bigger scheme of things, it's nothing, is it? And it will get us where we need to be. They don't always realise it, do they, when they most need your help? That your goal is their goal. That they should eat up and await dessert.

My mobile rings in the next room. Should I answer it? I know who it will be. Him. There used to be lots of calls, from other people, but now I always know who it will be. He's been phoning every day since... Well, obviously. Since then. I knew he'd read about it. I read about it. Maybe I shouldn't have. Maybe it's not healthy. But there's something about seeing the names of people you love in the papers. And more photos. I devour the photos—add them to the ones round the wall. But he couldn't be satisfied with that, could he? He has to phone. Demanding an audience. But why should I give him one? If Suze had wanted him, she would have asked for him, wouldn't she? Says it's about the girl, of course, not about Suze. And not about the money. That the money is just an extra concern. But I know what they're like, how these negotiations work. He'll wheedle his way in on the pretext of the girl, and suddenly it will be about Suze. I'll lose them both. And the money, which I need for our perfect future life. I can't let that happen.

Maybe just sit here. Don't answer the phone. Have a drink. Large glass of wine, maybe? Hah. No. I got rid of all that, didn't I? Tea then. But just sit here, ignoring him? I can. For now. He doesn't know where I am, where this place is. I think. I pray. I've done my best to hide this sanctuary from him. But maybe he'll find it. He found me, after all, out in the world, tracked me down. For the time being, his resources have failed him. Maybe someone's advised him against it, tracking down the postcode. More harm than good, perhaps he's been told. Doesn't want to put himself in jeopardy, when it comes down to it.

But he's bound to track us down eventually, if he's frustrated. Which would never do.

So I answer.

'Hello?' comes a voice at the other end. 'Is that you?'

'Yes,' I say. 'It's me.' Because who else would it be?

'I'll come over then, shall I?' says the man.

'You know I'm not going to agree to that.'

'I just want to talk,' he says.

Yeah, right.

'We can talk now,' I retort.

'Face to face.'

I don't say anything. If we were face to face, as he wants, I might not be able to conceal fear within hostility. I'm not sure I'm managing it now.

He continues to push.

'Where can we meet?'

'So that I leave the house empty? I don't think so.' I know his game.

'You're not helping yourself,' he tells me.

I don't need any help, from myself or anyone else, so I hang up.

Just imagine he found out where I live—he'd turn up on the doorstep immediately. In darkness, I can leave, if I go out the back entrance. Like this morning. No evidence of anyone staking the place out, at least not from the back. Maybe he hasn't told anyone what he knows. Maybe the big guns aren't out to get me. I can reach the woods easily from the back, take a shortcut to where I need to be. Because I have to go there, to that spot. That mound of earth so carefully packed into place. Remind myself why I'm doing it all. What's gone before. What's still to come. And keep my resolve. Because I've got to do this. I've got to stay strong. So I move away from the phone, back to the trays. And perfect the feeding time offering.

TWELVE

IT'S ALL VERY well lying to your mum, but lying to the headmistress takes extra skills, Alice thinks, as she exits the interrogation room aka the headmistress's study. With your mum, you know all the levers and buttons to pull and press. All the points to cry. And you know that she loves you. The headmistress doesn't love you. The headmistress pretends to love you, but really she is that very rude word that Daddy uses sometimes. And she can see into your soul.

So how was Alice supposed to resist? It was Mr Wilson's fault anyway, not hers. He shouldn't have read her English homework so suspiciously. Just because a few characters in a composition have a conversation about truth and secrets and best friends, it doesn't mean that she was talking about her own truth, secrets and best friends. Doesn't he know what fiction is? OK, so, in this case, it wasn't totally fiction, but it was so out of order for him to report her to the headmistress. *Mrs* Wilson. That's what she and Cara would have gigglingly called him if she'd been there, his voice was so high-pitched. But she wasn't there, was she? That was the whole problem.

So Mrs Cavendish had called Alice into her study and talked in very airy-fairy terms about truth and how helping a friend isn't always by doing what they ask you to do. Sometimes you have to tell people everything you know about a friend in order to be the best friend you can. Mrs Cavendish's eyes did not stray from Alice's for one syllable. By the end of the lecture, Alice was sure that Mrs Cavendish could hear her brain, and that there was little point in keeping the secret because Mrs Cavendish must already know it.

'OK,' said Alice, nodding bravely. 'I'll tell.'

Then in came Mr Belvoir with his questions. What had she seen? What had she heard, smelled, believed? What had Cara told her? Would she swear on that in court? Did she know where the man could be found?

All these questions, she'd understood. They reminded her of Monsieur Poirot and Mr Holmes, whose stories she'd listened to on Audible.com with her parents in the evening when homework was over. Non-police male detectives asked odd, detailed questions and achieved miraculous results, often changing the world with the results—reappearing the missing, making dead people live. But then there were questions that she didn't understand at all, even in the Poirot/Holmes world. Questions that left her a little uneasy. Questions about Cara's mum. About Cara's mum's husband. Personal, private questions, about habits, ways of living, that left her feeling dirty. And perhaps Mrs Cavendish felt dirty too. Because, after a while, she asked Mr Belvoir if he was quite done, as she felt sure Alice must have classes to attend.

And so Alice left. Now, on the way to History, which was hopefully all about Francis Drake and the Armada, and not about best friends and cars and peculiar gentlemen, Alice thinks she might have made the wrong decision. Perhaps she shouldn't have told. Although she didn't quite tell, did she? Because she didn't have the address. Of where to find the man Mr Belvoir seemed to be so keen to find. She just had the mental picture. From when Cara had taken her there. Because that was Cara. She shared everything. So Mr Belvoir can't really use the information, because he doesn't have Alice's mental map. Although she thinks she described it pretty well.

This isn't all Alice is thinking though. She also thinks something else. She thinks that on a second meeting this man, this Mr Belvoir, is very like the secret man that Cara had described to her. The man Cara used to meet. And who she'd gone to meet that day.

THIRTEEN

Dearest Cara,

So, so wonderful to be communicating with you. Not in ideal conditions. I know. And I'm sorry. I am so, so sorry. But such a relief, such a comfort, to know you are through there.

Yes, I am hoping Dad will come and rescue us. I'm hoping that even now there is a police sniper outside with the Captor in his sights.

But, in case not, we need a plan B. And I've got one. I don't know about your room, but in mine there's a small window. Don't get your hopes up—I didn't mean we can climb out of it. It's high, locked, small and unsmashable. BUT there's a girl who uses the grass outside to skip on. So it is possible that I might be seen. And so I've made a sign, telling the world that we're in here. It's not much, but it's a start.

I PUT THE pencil down. It's so not much that it feels almost futile. I'm counting on a small girl (a) maintaining skipping as a hobby, and not discovering skating or TV or even books (b) keeping up the discipline to practise regularly (c) practising in the same spot (d) looking at her surroundings (e) caring about them (f) seeing the sign

(g) distinguishing it enough from her own play world to think it worth telling her parents about it (h) not seeing a small pony or an ice-cream truck on the way home, which makes her forget about the sign entirely and (i) her parents believing and caring about what she said.

So yes. A lot to rely on. Or not. And a lot to ask Cara to put her faith in. So we probably need a plan C as well, at least. I force myself to continue writing.

> How about you? Do you have any windows? Could you do a sign too? Or perhaps there is a chance of getting through your windows. If you have them. Tell me. And tell me if you have any other ideas too.

Please let her have ideas. Please let her be able to escape whether she can take me with her or not. But please let her not forget me when she leaves. I won't be able to manage this without her.

> I think he goes out occasionally, the Captor. So we can make use of that, maybe? I don't know how?
> I want to go over again how you got here. Anything we know about the Captor could be useful. You said you remember a car. Try getting your brain back to that place. The model of car even. Who was driving? Was it him?

It means nothing, asking these questions. Why play detective? How will it possibly get us out of here? But at

the same time, it means everything. If we have knowledge, we have the tiniest bit of power. Power to analyse
our adversary. Manipulate him maybe. Or at least we
shake off that horrible ignorance of such a fundamental part of our lives.

But will I damage her? Cause her to revisit something her brain is saying should be firmly cordoned off?
She can only be what she is, remember what she can.
The pencil doesn't have an eraser though. I would have
to start again, which would waste precious paper, or I
would have to cross out in thick strokes what I'd written, which would make me look indecisive. And Cara
doesn't need an indecisive parent right now. She needs
someone strong and positive.

Like Paul. We both need Paul. I wonder what he is
doing now. Thinking of me, for sure. And of Cara. How
he can get us back. I wonder where he is. Outside, in
a stake-out? Or on our sofa at home, wrapped under
one of the grey fake-cashmere throws, exhausted and
emotionally drained by his search, by his anger, by his
staved-off grief, catching a compulsive hour of sleep?
I shake my head. That would not be like Paul. Paul
is strong, emotionally and physically. Strong, proac-
tive and capable. Look at how he helped me bring up
Cara. Always there in a crisis—not that there've been
many—to keep us safe. Even though she's someone
else's daughter.

Anyway, focus. Must finish the letter. Otherwise
Cara might think she has been forsaken. That I don't
have a plan. That she should escape by herself—oh

joy—and leave me still trapped—oh horror. I need to say something nice, something that will make her smile.

Remember when we went shopping that time, about a year ago, and for a joke we were trying on matching mother–daughter dresses? When we came out of the changing room to parade and after we'd twirled round in the mirror out front, you came face to face with that guy—Benny wasn't it? You thought you wanted to hide behind the mirror—I was only too aware how muttony I must look to him compared with your dazzling youth! But we managed to escape back into the changing room. Even if your escape was short-lived and you ended up in a McDonald's having a milkshake with him. But that ended well, you see, and we managed it together. We'll manage this together too. You'll see.

I sign off the letter with love and kisses, a nostalgic smile on my face. Tears in my eyes but not on my face. Because they're happy tears. Tears of love for my daughter. Who I will see again soon. Please, God. Please, Paul.

I sit and wait for a response. I wait and I wait and I wait.

Is there something wrong with my letter? Have I missed the mark? Is my treasured memory of our shopping trip an irrelevance for her? Have I over-glossed it? Was I the one who pulled her into the shop, picked out the dresses and dragged her into the changing room?

She doesn't even like high street stores, always customises her own clothes. When she went for that milkshake with that boy, was she just desperate to get away from me, and spent the whole time bitching about how embarrassing I am?

Is she even here, still, the daughter that I know? Is she safe? We haven't communicated since last night. A lot can happen, overnight, in the dark.

I wait some more. I can't hear anything at all from next door. Maybe she really isn't there? Maybe I need to find out, and do something to save her? Act now, quickly, before it's too late.

I'll give it one more minute then I'll knock. No, maybe that will be too late.

Tap. Tap-tap. Tap-tap, I go.

Nothing. No response.

Where is she? What's going on? Please, come on, knock back.

Nothing. Nothing nothing nothing.

I need to get out of this room.

I need to see the hallway, her door, see if there's anything unusual. Just to know. Just to see. Even if I can't help.

'Hey!' I shout out. I pummel the door of my room, louder than the knocks. 'Hey!'

And there it is. The key in the lock. I've done it. He's coming. I'll get out of the room somehow. A shower! That's it. I'll say I need a shower!

He stands in the doorway. As ever, between me and freedom. Between me and knowledge of Cara.

'Shower time,' I say. I try to make it sound natural. Not so urgent that he'll suspect it's a ruse.

He looks me up and down.

I shiver. I'd forgotten, in my hurry, what the shower would involve. Him looking at me. Like that. At the very least. And me with my clothes off.

It's for Cara. It's for Cara. It's for Cara.

'Fine by me,' he says.

He gestures to the open door. I take a step towards it.

And then comes the tap-tap. On the wall. From Cara.

I freeze mid-footstep. Has he heard it? Has he noticed me hearing it? If I had that moment again, I wouldn't freeze. Of course I wouldn't freeze. It highlights the noise, gives it a significance. But it was my daughter, communicating with me—how could I not react. Even though her knock, which I solicited, puts our whole communication in jeopardy. Maybe even herself. Stupid, stupid me, selfishly checking up on her, not being strong enough. Again.

He's looking at me, the Captor. Questioningly? Or desirously, looking forward to seeing me naked?

I don't know. I feel sick. At least Cara is safe. At least she is there.

She knocks again.

What? Is she expecting a return knock?

Stop it, I whisper to her in my head. Stop it! Find that earlier caution. It's lovely, wonderful, glorious to know you're alive and safe, but keep quiet, just now!

I look at the Captor. What has he noticed? What has he heard? I would smile at him but then he would know something was wrong. Plus I'm not sure I can bring myself to smile at the man who has separated me from my family.

Can I change my mind about the shower? Or will that look suspicious? Yes, probably. It will. I have to go through with it. I have to distract him from the sound of Cara. Of our communication. Our knowledge.

'Well, let's go and have this shower then!' I say. And I try to lead the way out of the room. Suddenly there's a scent of escape. But no. He's too sharp for that. He's in front of me again, clamping my arms by my side. I'm led out of the room. Past Cara's closed door—behind which, for now, she is safe, thank God—down the meaningless corridor. What if one day her door was open? Would that be a good thing or a bad thing? Right now, she is in there, reading my letter. But maybe one day I will be ushered past and the door will be open. She will be gone. Spirited away somewhere by the Captor. How absurd, how cruel, to keep mother and daughter so close but not let them see each other. Psychological warfare? Or does he want us both? Think we won't possibly yield with each other in the room? Needs us to feel isolated, alone. Well, we have a hidden strength, a unity, that he doesn't know about. I hope. Unless he has worked out the knocking.

I try not to think about what will await me in the bathroom. Not a long hot soak in the bath, like I used to enjoy, when I could find a quiet moment. No. The quicker option. But not quick enough. A very public shower. The toilet visits are bad enough. I've counted them—I need something to do other than write to Cara and stare out of the window for the little girl—

and crosschecked them with the sunsets. Twenty-one toilets. Even given my current levels of dehydration—I can't drink all the drugged drinks all the time—I must be going three times a day. Six sunsets. But I may have missed some. Sometimes I wake up and have no idea where time has gone, or where I am. I have to remember all over again. That I am not with my Cara, except I am.

But at least the toilet visits must be almost as grim for him as for me; him watching over me while I do my business is a security issue more than anything else. I hope. And at least I am partially clothed. A shower though. That is different. I will be naked. Slippery. Defenceless. I'll be worried every time I bend over. I will not come out feeling clean.

I try to keep that strength up as he orders me to take off my clothes. When I refuse, he moves towards me and rips them off for me. Or maybe, to be fair, it is more gentle than that. Slides and teases them off me. I think I'd prefer if he ripped. Less like he was trying to seduce me. Less sinister. Now I feel not only naked but coveted. Has my bare flesh always been this bare, this vulnerable? It shames and sickens me, with the knowledge of what he wants. I become a true Eve outside the garden—an ashamed hand over the breasts and one over the genitals. He is not going to get the view he wants out here.

'Get in,' he says, nodding his head at the shower cubicle.

'Aren't you going to open the door for me?' I ask, playing the coquette. Anything to put off turning around.

He doesn't reply. He just gestures again with his head. Of course he isn't going to move forward to open the cubicle—to do that would leave the exit to the bathroom unguarded. I could try to flit naked from captivity.

So, slowly, with as much posterior dignity as I can muster, I turn. I catch sight of myself in the mirror as I do. I look away again. I'm thinner than ever, but not good thin. Ribcage and thigh-gap thin. If only he wouldn't drug my food and I could eat it all. Or if I could have one of my own cupcakes. Or Paul's peppercorn steaks.

I pull open the door of the shower then shut it tight behind me. I turn the temperature up as high as I can to generate steam. I have my back turned to the door but—or maybe so—I know he will be watching me.

'Go on, love. Have a shower. Wash it all away.' It? Her. They mean her.

As the heat and steam build, and infuse my skin and my hair, I feel myself start to relax slightly. Does Cara use this shower? I wonder. Am I sharing her space? Is this another link we have forged in captivity? I will ask in my next letter. Eyes closed, I reach my hand out for some soap. Instead, I feel flesh.

I scream and open my eyes. It is the Captor's hand. Above the noise of the water he opened the shower door without my hearing. What does he want? Is this it? Is this the rape scene? Does he murder me in the shower now, à la 'Psycho'? I cower into the corner.

'Shampoo,' he says, holding out a bottle. 'Looks like you're washing your hair.'

I stare at him for a moment, my heart beating fast,

in heightened threat mode. I wonder if I can surprise him, push past him, or strangle him with the shower cord. But my hands are frozen across my breasts and genitals in defence, while the water runs on.

He waves the bottle at me again. 'You can't use soap. Makes the scalp itchy.'

I reach out a hand and take the bottle. Then he shuts the shower door.

Yet he is obviously watching. Because he knew I was washing my hair. I want to curl up in the corner of the shower enclosure and cry. Become invisible. But he would see my tears. Each one would probably arouse him. Give him a sense of pleasure in defeating me. However vulnerable I feel I cannot let him see me that vulnerable. I must remain calm. The tears must wait until I get back to my room. Just focus on the fact that Cara, too, must have survived this experience. Or is about to have it. Use the shampoo then place it on a ledge, at head height, so Cara will not have the indignity of having the shower door opened on her. Or having to bend over to pick up the bottle, observed by the Captor. I want to scream at him, over the noise of the shower: perv on my daughter in this way and I will kill you. Somehow. But I can't. Because he cannot know that I know she is here. That I have an ally. We each have an ally.

So, instead, I just perform a perfunctory wash of my hair and my body. I pretend I am one of those women in the bathroom commercials, advertising shower suites or shampoo. Except they always seem to have a towel in the shower with them. When my shower ends, I will have to emerge dripping, cold and naked. I will need to beg the Captor for a towel. While he watches me. I shiver, even though the water is still warm.

The shower door opens again. Not a surprise this time. But not a treat either. He reaches past me, turns off the shower.

'Don't want to run out of hot water,' he says.

Why? Is that an acknowledgement of Cara being here? Or does he want a hot and steamy shower after me? Enjoy himself where I have been?

He moves back from the shower unit again.

Is he going to do this every time? Reach over me like this? Can I bite his arm, really hard? Will that get me past him, out of the unlocked bathroom, to freedom? Shall I practise, later, in my room, how hard I can bite?

I adopt my new customary hand-to-breasts-to-genitals and wait for him to tell me what to do next.

He beckons me out of the shower. 'We need to get you dry,' he says.

He picks up a towel from the towel rail. It is worn, faded-looking. Years of use on him? Years more to follow?

I put out a hand, expecting him to pass the towel to me.

He doesn't.

Instead, he envelops me in it.

Then he is rubbing me, all over, through the towel. He pinions my arms to my sides so I cannot resist. If I squirm, he will surely break an arm, a rib. He is close enough for me to headbutt. Could I do it, suddenly? Perhaps I could. Perhaps this is my chance, one I won't get again. I can headbutt him and then rescue Cara.

I stand on tiptoes and thrust my head forward. I come in contact only with the air next to his skull. Before I can try again, he has grabbed my hair, pulled back my head, and has the other hand round my neck. The towel falls away.

'None of that,' he says.

I feel the pressure of his hand on my neck. Any tighter, and I'd say I was being strangled. That I'd die here in this bathroom. That Cara would never know why I was silent. Or that the Captor would come and make her shower in the room with my dead body still in it.

He pins me against the door and leans down to pick up the towel.

I have no choice but to stand there while this man that I hate rubs me down. And he seems to hate me too, because there is no sexuality to this drying. He is drawing the towel over me in a way that one might wipe a cloth over a kitchen cabinet to clean it, when really you are only cleaning it to avoid talking, avoid having an argument that would happen as soon as you unclenched your hand from the cloth and your teeth from your jaw. There's that restrained anger in every movement. All I can do is stand there silently, hoping his hand will not come back to my neck.

'Back to your room,' he says. Like I am some kind of naughty child. Like I can somehow make my own way back. But, of course, that is not allowed. I am led, naked, down the corridor. Past Cara's room. I pray she is not looking under the door, cannot see my humiliation. We arrive at the threshold of my room. It's like a strange date, the Captor escorting me home. Except this is not my home. And he is the one with the key.

He opens up the door and pushes me into the room. Then he closes it behind me, separating the two of us. I am left alone. Naked.

FOURTEEN

I SHOULD KNOCK on the door again, shouldn't I? Demand some clothing. Say it's against the Geneva Convention, the Human Rights Act, basic dignity, to keep a captive with no clothes on. But then, I suppose, none of them apply if you're doing something illegal in the first place. If your prisoner isn't a prisoner of state, or of law. Just a kidnappee. Alone, isolated, and now clotheless.

Maybe now it's just a waiting game until he comes and defiles me.

Or maybe it's another game. Like the bathroom game. To break me down. Maybe I'm meant to have my spirit destroyed. Maybe I'm meant to hammer on the door, demand some clothes from him. Cry, wail, plead, beg. So he can come back and 'comfort' me. Or laugh at me.

Well, I won't. I won't give him that satisfaction. I'll just stay here, horribly, horribly alone and naked in a room in a house I know not where with my husband apart from me and my daughter separated from me—but there, thankfully still there—when what I should be doing is deciding whether Cynthia and Harriet and their hen party would prefer a Strawberry Frost or an Oreo Wonder as the centrepiece for their cookery class. I should be buying eggs, cleaning whisks, chiding Cara for stealing spoonfuls of icing sugar. Sitting daydreaming at the counter, wishing I could afford a separate studio rather than pretending that my kitchen is that studio. I should be wondering if I have time to go to the loo before the clients arrive, whether I should cook steak fajitas for Paul and Cara later or whether I should just have a glass of wine after the clients go, and schedule in staring mournfully into the bottom of the glass, wondering how I can appear on the lists of those free magazines, so that everyone in London will read about my business and want to order from me, so that I can start doing corporate events and set up shop in Soho. And then I should look up to see a picture of me, Cara and Paul together and realise that this is all that matters, and then hear the doorbell, heralding the arrival of my hen group clients, and snap out of my reverie and carry on, business as usual, happy happy happy, like we're all meant to be.

I should be living my normal life.

I should not be standing shivering in the centre of this room. I should grab a sheet and wrap it round myself. I should definitely not be sinking to the ground, crying and crying and crying like that's what I've been designed to do. It won't help me. It won't help Cara.

Pull yourself together. Don't cry. The baby isn't crying, is she?

I should supress the sobs, in case Cara hears me, and stops writing to me, because who would want to write to a sad old mum who bursts into tears simply because she has nothing to wear?

And yet here I am.

And here I still am.

Still.

Cara, Cara, Cara. I'm letting you down. I'm sorry. Forgive me. Pity me. Please send me another letter. Don't make me just rely on those knocks. Beautiful, sweet and dangerous as they are. I want your words. I want your voice. Write to me, if you can bear to.

I don't hear the door lock turn. I just see him there. Standing, in the doorway.

He is holding something.

'Clean pyjamas,' he says. 'I forgot to give them to you.'

Forgot? How long did it take him to remember? How long have I been sitting here? Is it seconds or days? My eyes have a sting that says hours at least. But my skin is still wet. Sweat? Or shower water? Hot, or cold?

I don't know. I stand. I flick my eyes to the grate, just in case. As I always do when he is there. As I always do when I am here. Present.

There should be nothing. Cara should not have wanted to write to her broken mother. Yet there is. There is a letter coming through this very minute! Cara, my joy, she is writing to me. But the letter, waggling away, drawing attention to itself. He will see, he will see, he will see!

I do the only thing I can do that will distract him.

I stand up, walk towards him and press my naked body against him. And I kiss him.

FIFTEEN

FLABBY SLIPPERY LIPS on mine. I instinctively shut my eyes. Then I open them. His eyes are staring wide. Is that a hint of an alien tongue in my mouth? The touch of fingers on my hips?

I draw him into the room, towards the grate.

He pulls back. 'Are you sure?' he asks me.

I nod. Despite the grossness of being naked against the clothes of the Captor, despite the scratch from his cruel stubble on my cheek, the undesired of fact of his breath on my face, that I want to tear out his eyes for seeing Cara against her will, I nod. I pull him further towards the grate.

He kisses me this time. And this time, there is no doubt about the tongue, or the fingers. They are there. Does he taste the bile that rises in my throat? Does he detect the stiffness of my limbs? I force my own tongue into action. As it slides over his tongue, my insides crawl. It's for Cara, I tell myself. It's for Cara.

Are we at the grate yet? We must be. I break away and make as if I'm staring demurely at the floor. Yes. The grate. And there is Cara's letter on the floor. I cover it with my foot.

And then I push. I push the Captor away from me.

And I spit out the bile that has been gathering within me. I spit it out into his face.

I want to charge at him, to claw and to scratch and to tear. But I mustn't, because that would reveal the letter to him. So I stay where I am, curling my toes round the edge of Cara's letter. If he moves back towards me, if he tries to take me forcibly, then I will unleash my anger. It is the anger that makes me shake. The anger that this man, who has separated me from my beloved Cara, would think he has some kind of privileged access to my body. It is this anger, not fear.

But he doesn't try.

When the bile hits, he just sighs. A big, weighty sigh that forces out his nostrils, raises his chest, closes his eyes. Then he scrunches up his lips in a kind of wry scowl-smile, nods his head, and turns to leave the room. He doesn't even wipe himself clean.

'That's it?' I shout after him. I want to taunt him, call him a coward. But I'm not that brave. He's hit me before, after all.

As he gets to the door, he turns. His silhouette fills the doorway. He could obliterate me as easily as he obliterates the light.

'One day, Susan,' he says. Then he leaves and locks the door.

So. I am alone again. Except I am not alone. My skin crawls with a thousand little creatures. More than a thousand. Maybe a million. They've been waiting there since I began to kiss this man. Now suddenly they are released and, with them, the tears and the sobs that I have been suppressing. But still I must supress them,

I must keep them quiet, for Cara. I am not allowed to be audibly unhappy. I must appear calm, composed. I press my hand across my mouth to stop the sobs. But they will not stop. I lean both palms against the wall and place my forehead in between them. Breathe, breathe, breathe. Bastard, bastard, bastard. Can I not push the wall down with my head? Can I not get to my Cara that way?

'Mummy, Mummy,' she is calling me, throwing caution to the wind. 'What's wrong? Are you crying?'

There, you see, I've failed. I've failed her. She can hear my anguish. Button it up. Keep cool. Reply. Keep voice level. Whisper.

'Shh. Don't worry, I'm fine. I've got your letter. I'll read it now.'

Sing my little baby a lullaby. Rock her into a peaceful sleep.

Because I am. I'm fine. Really. Her voice has calmed me. The deep breaths actually bring oxygen to me now. We will escape, we'll be back with Paul in no time.

And the other feeling, apart from the bile, apart from the hate and the fear, that came when the Captor kissed me the second time—well, nobody need ever know.

SIXTEEN

Mum,

I'm sorry I didn't write for a little while. I felt so tired, so drained. And I just didn't want to write again until…until I didn't feel like it would rip me apart. The acknowledgement of where we are. How we are. It's really sinking in now. Don't you find?

But hey, let's be positive.

The window sounds great. No, I don't have one, just a skylight I can't reach, so we'll have to rely on yours. Has anything happened yet? Has the girl you saw come back? But yes, we can totally use the fact that he goes out. What if we just scream and scream as loud as we can. Or we ram all the furniture as hard as we can at the doors, so he won't hear the noise? Or could we even somehow put a piece of paper between the lock and our door so that it doesn't quite shut, then, when he is out, we can just escape? Or—maybe this is best—when you're having a shower (never have I felt so dirty after getting so clean—I wanted to scrub myself again so I could wash away his eyes from all over me) I can start screaming really loudly and then you can run from the shower out into the open (put some clothes on first) and get the police or Dad and come back for me.

Or we can just stab him with the pencils. If you break one in two. Stick it right in his throat.

I mean don't get me wrong, Mum—I'm not a sicko or a psycho or anything. But we'd be justified in killing him, right? Whoever the hell he is. Who is he? Why us?

Really. Why us?

Let me know what you think of my ideas. We'll get out of here by tea and you can make us cupcakes (mine's a sugar plum fairy one)! Or something.

OK.

I think I'll try to sleep again now. I haven't quite managed that yet.

C. xxx

I COULD WEEP. But I mustn't. Mustn't get all misty and mumsy. Must just focus on her ideas. Such as they are. Because the furniture one won't work, will it? No. And nor will the paper between the lock and the door. Otherwise the whole of the security industry may as well just retire now. The screaming maybe. Heaven knows, I would happily just spend my entire time screaming. But the house is semi-detached at the very least, so the view from my window tells me. If it's detached, no one will hear us. Or, even if they do, it will take a lot of screams to make them stop ignoring what is going on in their own backyard. Much more likely to ignore the screams with classic British non-interventionism, letting the man do whatever he likes in his own castle. 'Oh, probably just someone having fun and screaming in jest,' they'll decide, too easily.

But maybe there is something in the shower plan. I can't let her be the one to cause the diversion though, can I? I can't leave my daughter, my Cara, in the house by herself once I've fled, to face the consequences of my actions. No. She must shower and run and I must scream. But what if he gets wise to what she's doing before she's out of the house? What if there is a chase along the corridor, her running as fast as she can, him behind her? What if the towel she has hastily clutched round herself falls away and, as she bends to pull it up, he catches her, grabs her and strangles? punches? rapes? Floors her in some way? She would be defence-less against him, she would—

And breathe. Susan. Breathe.

Stop imagining the worst.

It is a viable plan. The bathroom door has no lock. We know this. She could easily make a run for it, if I give her a chance to prove herself, prove her plan. And I must, mustn't I? Let her prove herself. She's at that age now where I don't own her. I can't just bend her to my will like I used to (or did I—she seemed to know what she wanted when she was even a day old).

Because the other option is the murder option. And there is something horrible about your daughter want-ing to kill. Yes, I would gladly kill the Captor. The bile is rising in me even now. But could I love her again if I knew she had pierced someone's jugular? Been covered in their blood? Perhaps had an animalistic glint in her eye while she did it? I would have to do it, of course. And I will, if I need to. Of course I will. For me, for Cara. But I'd rather not. I'd rather he was locked up, away from everyone, like we are. I'd like him to suffer, in a way he won't in death. Although he'd have to wait until he bled out from the pencil wound—slower than a knife wound, I guess. So he would suffer. And then he'd go to hell.

But perhaps we should try to run first, before we kill. It's not that I'm reluctant. Although what if we need to convince a court we'd done all we could before we tried to kill him? And if he were the one on trial, we'd understand more about what is going on in his sick mind. And know who he actually is. Because as Cara rightly asks, who is he? Does it matter even? He is the bastard who brought us here, to this situation. Does it matter which bastard he is?

Possibly. But not right now.

Cara would need a weapon if she were to flee. Could she smash the mirror in the bathroom, get a shard of glass to use as a dagger if he catches her up? But what if she cuts that precious skin of hers while she is trying? No. If anyone is to do that it must be me.

Of course, none of this will matter if the window girl has seen the sign.

I go to the window and climb onto the chair. I look through the crack of available window left by my sign.

There!

She is skipping, the girl, outside. Facing away from me. But there nonetheless.

Turn! Come on, girl, turn! She's doing an ordinary

jump skip at the moment. Surely she must soon begin
the more complex steps. The whirling, twisting ones
she was doing last time that make her face towards
me. Surely this is just her warm-up act. I ready myself
with the sign.

And yes, here we go. The footwork becomes fancier.
She does kind of a mid-air trot then swings the rope
to the side. Then, then, here it is, she turns in a circle
while holding the rope. And she is facing me. I wriggle the sign as much as I can and bang on the window.
Nothing. I wriggle and bang again. Come on, please.
For me. For Cara.

Is she looking? Just keep facing this direction, that's
it, that's it. Now just look up, come on, let your feet do
their own work.

Trip, stop.

Oh.

And her attention is on her feet again.

Not on me.

The little girl is clearly well brought up; rather than
give up the step that caused her to fumble on the rope,
she earnestly does it in slow motion again and again.
Then she speeds up and finally, finally she is confident
enough to lift her head. And she looks straight at me.

Or at least, in my direction. Does she see me? She is
too far away for me to read the expression on her face.
An even if it is one of wonderment, of the engaged interest and trust with which Cara used to look at me when
she was that age, it may not do me any good. She's probably been told not to wave at strangers. But I waggle
the sign as much as I can. Is that a slight inclination of

the head? A nod? A shake? Even just an acknowledgement? That would be something.

She turns away from me and continues to skip with her back to me.

I slump against the windowsill. Fine. Be like that. Ignore me. A bit like Cara in her early teenage years, in that borderline between childhood and pretentions to adulthood. When I came into her room to say goodnight when she was little, she would throw her arms round me, kiss me goodnight and beg me not to leave. I often had to sit holding her hand until she drifted off to sleep.

But then, other nights, when she was older, she would remain turned towards the wall in her bed, pretending not to hear me. She knew that I knew she knew I was there. I can see her now. Hair—with purple strands, to match her latest customised outfit—lying over her pillow. The hallway light revealing her eyes wide open. The duvet not disguising the fact that her limbs were stiff, not sleep-filled.

Just lying there. No response. Am I somehow to blame?

I'd say, 'I know you're awake really.' But she didn't reply. Didn't utter a sound.

It was the intention to hurt as much as the ignoring me that was as painful. This little girl doesn't intend to hurt me; there is no spite in her turning her back. She either didn't see the sign or doesn't trust me. Maybe I have to win her trust somehow? Like I won Cara back when the 'parents are gross' phase passed. Or maybe the hormones won her back for me. But the Cara I know now, the fifteen-year-old version, humours and loves her old mum as much as she did as an eight-year-old. So I didn't lose her for ever. How did I do that? I made myself available, but didn't press myself on her. I made myself interesting, cool, a purveyor of all things sweet. I was the witch in the gingerbread house without the witchiness (and, to be fair, without the gingerbread either—I had cupcakes). She tells me everything. That's the beauty of the mother–daughter relationship we have.

So maybe I need to do the same with this little girl? Maybe I can draw her in through drawings. Little pictures, or little comments, on my piece of paper. Not 'Help Me' phrases. As a modern child she is probably used to phishing scams. Probably has her own email account—*skipping_girl@whatevermail.com*. Probably already sees things she shouldn't when the parental block system breaks down. Anyway, I need to intrigue her, interest her, cajole her into helping me.

So. A dialogue. Oh God, perhaps this is crazy. She probably can't even see the bloody sign let alone what's written on it. But I have to try something. I have to have another plan for Cara. An option B. If Cara's proposal—modified by me—doesn't work. So that we don't need to go for option C. The grizzly one.

What do I know about this little girl? What did I know about my own little girl? That the best friend at that age is a playmate. Someone to hold the other end of the skipping rope. Plus someone they can look up to, someone who can wow them with their own stories of the past. The child will watch, incredulous yet wanting to believe.

I tear out some new pages of my so-called diary.

I draw a picture of a little girl with a rope. She is smiling with a big cartoon grin. Then I write 'I skip too!' in as bold lettering as I can.

A lie, of course. I've never used a rope in my life—Cara was more into roller-skating and I liked hula-hooping when I was a kid. But what's a little white lie if it might reunite me with Cara?

I put the paper up on the windowsill in the place of the 'Help Me' sign. The girl still has her back to me. I stare at her a while, willing her to turn round. Then I get down. She can probably feel my eyes on her back. If I were that age, I would wait until I thought no one was looking before I went to examine a sign. It's less threatening yet at the same time a more daredevil adventure—grandmother's footsteps, will you or won't you be seen.

I turn my attention back to Cara and her plan A. Good start, perhaps. But it needs modifying. Because most important of all is that she should get out of here alive.

SEVENTEEN

The other side of the door

IMAGINE, DRAWING ME into the room, kissing me, arousing my hopes and expectations, and my relief—yes, relief that finally finally after all this effort it was working! All this, only to reject me. Yet again. Actually spit on me this time. Oh, darling. Darling Suze. I can't call you Suze to your face, of course. I have to repress that too. Like everything else. If only you knew the lengths I'm taking. If only you understood that it's for your own good. Somewhere within you, you must know that. I wish you'd acknowledge it. That way, I wouldn't have to make you understand. The hard way.

And all that sodding knocking on the wall between the rooms. Why do they think it's going to help them one little bit, these people? It was all I could do not to comment on it.

Well, I know what to do. It's food tray time again. I'm taking Cara's cherished instrument along to her room as well this morning; it belongs there, with her, even if she can't play it. Open up her door, balance the food tray and—

The doorbell rings.

Shit.

I nearly drop everything.

Come on, man. Pull yourself together. The cover stories have been given. You've been going out, looking normal. Nobody suspects anything. Apart from him. But he won't be here, will he? He doesn't know where you are. Right? He can't. After all the efforts you've made to keep it from him. Nobody's coming to arrest you. Although maybe I deserve it for what happened. For what I did. What I'm doing.

No. No. I'm not to blame. I've only ever done what's right. I must remember that. I must.

But still, who is it? And what should I do? I edge along the corridor from Cara's room until I'm round the corner and can see the front door. I should approach it. I know this is what viewfinders are for, that you're supposed to be able silently to vet the people who appear at your doorway to see if you want to admit them. They know, though, don't they, the people on the doorstep, that you are looking at them. The letterbox speaks, shares your footsteps, and the casting of light betrays you.

Ding-dong.

Perhaps I should just lie on the floor, play dead. Or dare to tweak the bottom of the curtain, lift it open a flap, see if I can see who is there without them seeing me.

Ding-dong, ding-dong, ding-dong, knock, knock, knock.

Oh Christ. Next I'll be told to 'open up', won't I?

An insistent postman or meter-reader? Could be. But are they really so diligent? Wouldn't I just have got a hastily scribbled chit through the letterbox by now? And I'm not expecting anything, am I?

Oh, wait. Yes. Yes, I do need to open the door. There was one thing I ordered. Something for her.

I rush to the door and take off the chain. Unlock, deep breath, then swing open.

Thank God.

It's not him. It's a delivery guy.

'Sorry about that,' I say. 'I was in the bathroom.'

The man crinkles his face slightly. He avoids touching my hands when he passes over the parcel. He can think what he likes about what I was doing in the bathroom. The important thing is that he has my coveted delivery.

I'M INSIDE AGAIN, ALONE.

Should I wait to unwrap it? Check that it is what it claimed to be, that it will be what we need (I may not be thanked for it yet, but people will be glad when I can finally explain)? Or carry on preparing the food regardless? No. The time it takes to unwrap, it will be worth the delay. Rumbling stomachs never hurt anyone.

I don't know why I've been so anxious. This is easy really. Much easier than anyone would ever think. Sit down maybe. Take a minute to relax.

And then I get the text message.

It's from him.

And it describes the outside of this place, my hidey-hole, exactly. From the crazy-paved path to the yellow front door.

I drop the package on the floor.

He knows where I live.

He knows about Cara, he suspects about Suze, and he knows where we are.

Christ.

And there's hammering on the door.

It's him!

But no. Listen properly. It's another door. Inside.

Suze's voice wafts along the corridor. 'I need the bathroom!' she's yelling.

I shouldn't have given her all that tea. Just stop yelling for one second. Please. Let me digest this news, let me clear up this important package, let me just have a moment to myself. Yes, of course, I know I brought you here. But please.

She won't stop shouting though.

So I've no choice but to leave the phone with it's horrible message, leave the crucial package on the floor, and hurry along the corridor to Suze's room.

I open the door quickly—anything to stop that awful shouting.

It's not until Suze is out of the room that I realise my mistake.

When the doorbell rang, I left Cara's door open. And I haven't shut it since.

EIGHTEEN

As soon as he unlocks the door, the Captor darts back into the corridor.

Something's up.

I'm going to rush him! I'm going out there!

He's at Cara's door. And it's open! He's pulling it shut, getting out a key to lock it—but look!

'Cara!'

There she is! I can see her!

I run forward.

Cara! Her hair, the slightest glimpse of her cheek.

But the door is shut again. He turns the lock.

I grab his hands, his arms, anything I can. I abandon my pretence that I don't know she's here.

'Open the door! Open the door!'

He fends of my blows with his forearms, propelling me back into my room.

'I saw her! I know she's in there!'

I'm inside again and the door is locked.

'Cara!' And then to him again: 'What can you possibly gain by keeping us apart? I saw her, I saw her, I saw her!'

I scrabble against the door, but that's not enough, so I slam my hands and my forehead and my torso against it. I'm sliding down the door, but I won't sink. No. Because I saw her.

But what's going on? She must have known that her door was open. So why didn't she try to escape?

I stand staring at the grate, as if it's Cara.

What are you doing, girl? Your door was open? Why didn't you run?

It's unfathomable.

Forget that for a moment though. There's a sort of golden glow spreading through me. My daughter, the sunrise.

Because I saw her. Just that little peep. It's enough for me, in this moment. I want to grin and dance and clap my hands. I allow myself a little smile, then a big one, then I hug myself. What a privation it's been! Fancy, a mother not seeing her daughter! I'd almost grown used to it, the obscenity of being separated by a wall. But like a bright light suddenly shining in, I'm aware of how dark it must have been before.

And, gradually, that light is fading again now.

Because I need to ask her, don't I? Why she wouldn't try to escape?

What's going on with you, Cara?

So I get out the pencil and paper and I ask her.

The reply comes in what must be about ten minutes.

Dear Mum,

What must you think of me? I know, I missed a golden opportunity. I'm an idiot. I can see myself now, running away from wherever we are, calling the police, getting them coming to rescue you, getting the Captor put in prison (or torn limb from limb by police dogs). But no. Because I messed up.

Of course I saw the door was left open. He'd brought my tea, and he didn't shut me in again. I don't know why. Perhaps he was distracted. He went out and left the door open. I sat staring at it expecting it to shut again. But it didn't. And I waited another minute. It was still open. So I got up from the bed, oh so quietly, and I opened the door a bit more. Nothing. Then I put my head round the door. The corridor was empty. My heart was racing. This is it! I thought. I put a foot out into the corridor. Then another. And I told myself to run. I couldn't. I'm sorry, I'm sorry, but I couldn't.

I just didn't know what was at the end of the corridor. It could have been anything. But most likely it would have been him. And I would have had to fight him. He's a big guy, right? I was frightened. I hadn't expected it; I wasn't prepared. It was just me, alone, in that corridor. It seemed so big, suddenly.

I still might have run. Or yes, gone to a different room, anywhere with a window, climbed out. But then I heard a noise from along the corridor. And I bottled it. I ran back into the room and closed the door over a bit as he'd left it, and I stood exactly where I'd been standing. Just thinking about what an idiot I was, trying to pluck up the courage to go out again, and I was just about to—and then I heard you and he shut the door and that was it. All over.

I'm so sorry, Mum. I know that doesn't cover it. And I promise, I really promise, that when we put a proper plan in place, I'll be all over it. I'll be ready. And I'll run, and I'll get us out of here. Because we'll be doing it together then.

There's nothing more to say, right? I messed up.

C. xxx

I reread the letter then fold it in on itself. Poor Cara. I can imagine being in that corridor, that she must have felt alone. And is that some slight maternal pride, or satisfaction, that she would have felt happier if I was there? That when it came to it, she couldn't do it alone? Maybe. I try to close it down. It's not a good side of me.

What there's most of, though, is a dull feeling of disappointment. Come on, Cara. This is not who I meant for you to be. Couldn't you just have done it? Couldn't you just have run? Couldn't we even now be outside, hugging each other, laughing, toasting our escape?

It's one of those sour regrets. When you know that however splendid the event could have been, you've got to be bigger than the loss. You've just got to screw up your heart and move on.

Oh, Cara. My poor love. I understand you. I just can't write back right now.

We'll find a way. I know we will. But it will need to be a plan that caters for the real us. Not some heroines in a late-night movie, all bold and feisty, who take any opportunity to run—and then find their captor waiting for them. No. It's about real Cara, and real me, getting out of this together. With all our flaws.

And then I want to take back all my selfish thoughts of regret. Instead, I want to hug Cara. Stroke her hair.

Poor baby. Tell her everything will be fine. Even though it won't.

NINETEEN

The other side of the door

SHIT.

Such a basic bloody error.

If I'd just realised one moment earlier—one little moment—I could have shut it, couldn't I? Bloody parcel, bloody delivery man. Totally understandable, my distraction. I see why I failed and I therefore have to forgive myself. Like with everything, every failure—totally understandable. For once, though, I'd like to succeed.

But for that I have to be the one who thinks about absolutely everything, don't I? I have to be on each little detail, every day. And sometimes I just want to sit down with a large glass of whisky and say sod 'em. Sod the plans, sod all the preparation. I'm having a drink, putting my feet up, forgetting all about the other end of the corridor until morning. Let them eat cake! Hah!

Instead, of course, I'm not drinking anything. And I'm sitting in the corridor, on the floor, outside Suze's room. Have been since I locked her in again. Because everything nearly came crashing down. That look on her face when she saw into Cara's room! You could see she thought, This is our moment, the moment we escape and report this bastard.

No. That's not how this story ends, I'm afraid, my love.

My loves.

I lie down, stretched out between the two rooms. Who would have thought I would, could, do all this? They'd have asked me why. Sometimes I ask myself why. But then the image of the two of them—the three of us—floats back into my head again. And I could almost levitate here in the corridor. Their two smiles calling me upwards.

But at the same time, dragging me back down. To the stark reality of it. The food trays. The staying indoors, each day, every day. The crippling boredom of playing the long game. The even more debilitating fear of discovery—before the journey is complete. If I can just get through, if I can just get that mirror mist to clear, we'll be fine. People will even be grateful.

Unless…

Unless this.

The mobile rings in my pocket.

My jaw clenches round my heart.

I bet it's him.

I want to ignore it, but that's not safe any more. Not after this morning's text.

So I pull the phone out of my pocket.

And yes, it's him.

'You will have got my message, then?' he says. He sounds pleased with himself.

'So you know what the place looks like. Well done.'

I'm not going to give him the satisfaction of my fear. Not yet, anyway.

He doesn't care. He knows he's winning. 'A little bird told me,' he says, playfully. 'A little bird named Alice. Familiar?'

I grunt. It's as much acknowledgement as I want to share. It's enough—he continues.

'Not as difficult to get inside a school as you'd think, when they're in a bit of a flap—flash a badge, forge a letter of instruction when you know the people who've "instructed" you won't answer the phone to deny it.'

'What do you want?' I ask him. Because I'm sick of hearing about how smart he thinks he is. And there's no point playing his silly games. I can't hide, now, can I? Literally or figuratively. Unless I move them. All the stuff that goes with them. Cara and Suze. But no. That would be too much. It's only him that knows. I think. Only him I have to deal with.

I can hear the smile in his voice. 'You know what I want to discuss. I thought I could pop over, see you all…'

'You're not coming here!' I say. Because he's not. He cannot come in. He cannot disturb this delicate eco-system.

'Let's be quite clear. I can do what I like. Knowing what I know. Unless, of course, we're going to agree on the ins and outs of that little incentive arrangement.'

'Fine,' I tell him. My teeth are less gritted, more hewn in solid granite. 'We can meet. But I want to be in view of the house at all times.'

'You don't fancy letting me in then?'

'No,' I say, because I don't. He knows that, but it won't stop him pushing.

'Good. Eleven a.m. tomorrow, I'll be in the Toyota Auris across the street.'

I repeat the arrangements out loud, more in horror than wanting to confirm. I feel like I'm in a bad cop movie. Without the good cop to help me.

'You won't regret this. It will be good for us both,' he tells me.

It won't be though, will it? It won't be good for me. Which means it won't be good for anyone in this house. No good at all.

TWENTY

Dearest Cara,

Did you hear him?

OK, I'm sorry. Backtrack.

My darling. You mustn't blame yourself about the non-escape. I was so desperately sad for you—how dreadful it must have been for you to have that opportunity and not feel able to take it.

But, sweetie, it's totally understandable. It wasn't a real opportunity. As you said, we didn't have a plan.

THIS NEXT BIT, I don't want to say it, I don't want to push her. But I've got to, haven't I? After what I heard this morning. I know I've got to be sensitive, but I'd be a worse mother if I didn't have her well-being at heart. And her well-being means the two of us being together again, out of here. So I carry on.

Cara, that wasn't a plan. It was a moment, you could have seized it, but it didn't feel right. And it wasn't right—as you say, you had no idea whether he would have been waiting for you at the end of the corridor. But listen. I think we now have something to base an actual plan on. The two of us, together.

Did you hear him this morning? My God, he must think sound doesn't carry in this place. In case you didn't hear, the Captor is meeting someone opposite the house at 11 a.m. tomorrow. Which means two things. At 11 a.m. tomorrow there will be a witness. And that the Captor will be flustered trying to get ready to meet someone.

So if one of us runs along that corridor, we know that at the end of it there won't be a captor. Because he won't be here. Do you see? You don't need to worry about the end of the corridor because it will be sorted.

I bite my lip. Am I pushing too far? No. I've got to go on. Cara has to see. She has to get out, whatever state she's in. I've got to push.

Cara, I think you should be the one who runs out onto the street. I know you'll be frightened. Believe me, I'm frightened. But I can't bear the idea that I would run and you would still be trapped inside. And you'll have someone to run to, out on the street. Because it must be a good guy, mustn't it? Whoever the Captor is meeting. If it was a bad guy, someone the Captor was in cahoots with, they would just come into the house. It might even be your dad turning up.

By which, of course, I mean Paul. Because, God help me, the truth is not something Paul and I feel she needs to know. One day maybe. But when she's sixteen. Or eighteen. Or when she graduates, when her exams are

all over. Or maybe when her actual father is dead. So
she never has to meet him. And I never have to see him
again. Now is not the time.

Your dad might be there to pay the ransom.
Pretty strange for the Captor to let on where he's
based. But maybe he's just stupid. A stupid sicko,
who doesn't know how to run a kidnap.

Anyway, look, the point is this: you can do this.
I know you can. I know you're strong enough.
Just take that courage inside of you and break
out. You'll get outside, you'll raise the alarm, and
someone will come back for me.

I know you can do it. But if you don't know it,
and you're too scared, tell me. I'll understand. Tell
me and I'll go out instead. But I hate the idea of
you being alone in the house with him. I hate the
idea of you staying in here and never getting out.

Here's what I think we should do. When he
comes in to give me the next meal, I'll ask him
the time. And then I can count. I can count the
hours until 10.30 tomorrow morning. Then I can
waggle the grate, and you'll know it's time to demand a shower. Just bang on the door; he'll hear
you. The genius is the 10.30 a.m., you see. He'll
think he has long enough to shower you before he
goes out. But then I'll start screaming, screaming so loud he'll think I'm dying or that someone
will hear, and he'll come running to me, so that
you can escape. Just grab the towel round you,

and run. Don't think of me until you're out of the house. I need you to be safe, you see.

That's OK, isn't it?

And then, when we're both free, we can find out who this man is. We'll find out and they'll string him up. You're sure you don't know anything, anything, about who he is? I know they happen, these random snatchings—that it's not random to the captor, they've obsessed over the people they kidnap for years—but you'd think we'd have some clue. That one of us would know something.

Anyway, never mind. It plays on your mind, doesn't it, what got you into this position. Sorry. Darling—is that plan OK? Write back as soon as you can, so I know. There's no pressure. We'll think of something else if you're not happy with it. But we have a plan now, sweetheart. A real actual plan. And just think, by tomorrow we could be free!

Your loving mother always always always xxx

We can do it. The big escape. She'll be OK. I feel like a general on the eve of a battle, rallying the troops—but troops that aren't just a number or a name in history if the going gets bloody. Like a general who knows the battle must be fought, but if it's lost he'll lose himself.

If I understand my daughter at all, that letter will have been just enough to convince her. Years of persuading—put on your coat, do your homework, switch out your light—gives you the knack. Right from the first moments you pay attention to every detail, get acquainted with all their characteristics, their ups and downs, understand how to use those to be the best mother you can.

Get to know her. Stroke every contour. Drink in all of that little person. Then keep her locked away in your heart for ever.

We'll get out of here. It just needs a little bit more strength.

And then we'll always be together.

TWENTY-ONE

DOWNSTAIRS IN ALICE'S house there are whispered conversations.

'She seems a bit withdrawn, don't you think?' Alice's mum asks Alice's dad.

He shrugs. 'I don't know. Maybe.'

Alice's mum nods emphatically. 'She is. I know my daughter. She's just…off, somehow. Ever since all this Cara stuff. I thought she was doing OK, but…' Alice's mum gets teary.

Alice's dad supresses a sigh then leans forward and strokes his wife's hand. 'I'm sure she's OK, sweetheart.'

Alice's mum clearly isn't so sure. 'It just makes me think, you know, there but for the grace of God, with Cara, and Alice.'

'Shhh, darling. Come on.' Alice's dad gathers Alice's mum to him. She cries quietly on his chest.

'I just want her to be safe,' she manages, in between the weeping.

'Me too, sweetheart. Me too. Do you want me to talk to her?'

Alice's mum looks up, smiling tentatively. 'Would you?'

Alice's dad nods. 'Of course.'

UPSTAIRS, ALICE LIES tummy-down on her bed, absently picking at the bedspread. The room is silent, but she'd be surprised if you told her that; her thoughts feel loud enough to fill the whole house. She replays all those final conversations with Cara, before Cara went off to meet the man.

'What will you do if your mum starts asking questions?' Alice had asked, wide-eyed.

Cara shrugged. 'Lie,' she said. 'Say I'm with someone else. Or say I didn't know who he was, any of the history, I just thought he was some guy. She'll believe me. She'd freak out, but not as much as if I told her what was really going on. It's fine. I'll make something up.'

But Alice noticed her friend's fingernails were bitten all the way down. She wondered if that was the worry of already having deceived her mum, or the thought of more lies to come. Of keeping her mum in the dark always, of letting her mum think she knew the truth, but never really knowing anything.

'Do you want me to come with you?' Alice had asked, on another occasion, more out of curiosity than concern.

And she'd wanted Cara to say no. Expected her to. That she'd give her a look and say, 'Don't be silly, Alice. What would he want with both of us?'

But then Cara had surprised her by saying yes, sort of. 'Could you come round, after? You know the way.'

If only she hadn't waited until 'after'. If only she'd gone with Cara every step of the way. Maybe it would have made a difference somehow.

Or maybe she would just be with Cara now. So better perhaps to have stayed behind. Although perhaps she now wouldn't miss Cara quite so much if they were together.

Alice puts her face into the bedcover and draws small arcs with her arms. What wouldn't she give to be sitting on this bed with Cara now, like all the happy times before. Plaiting each other's hair, putting on eyeshadow, sharing secrets and jokes. Why couldn't they just be laughing until their tummies ached, rather than Alice feeling her tummy ache with quite different feelings? Or maybe not quite aching. Kind of an empty gnaw, like hunger. Hunger to see Cara again. For Cara to say 'Don't worry, you haven't betrayed me. You needed to tell Mr Belvoir. You did what you thought was right.'

A knock on the door disturbs Alice's thoughts.

It's coupled with the words 'Knock, knock,' as if it's the start of a joke. But it won't be. It will be serious. It always seems to be these days. She rolls off her tummy and sits up on the bed facing the door, waiting to face her dad.

He puts his head round the door. 'Hi, sweetheart. How are you?'

She shrugs, à la Cara. 'Fine.'

Alice's dad shifts from foot to foot, like he needs the loo. He should have gone before, she thinks.

'Can I sit down?' he asks, indicating to the edge of the bed.

She shrugs again. Maybe if she acts like Cara, Cara will somehow be in the room with them.

He sits down. He doesn't seem to quite know how to sit. He tries with both feet on the floor at first then he swivels round so that he's facing her and puts his legs sideways on the bed. It feels like the facts of life talk all over again. Except they both came in for that. Embarrassing.

'Your mum and I are a bit worried about you, sweetheart. About how you're dealing with the Cara situation.'

'I'm fine,' she says. Because how do you explain to someone like him what it's like not to have your best friend with you? She bets he's never had a best friend. Or even a friend. Not like her and Cara.

'Are you? Really? Sweetheart?' he gives her a long hard look in the eyes and puts one hand on her knee.

She flinches and pulls away. Because she remembers what Cara said about that initial conversation in the car. That Cara knew from then on that knee-touching meant things were going to get bad.

'Sweetheart?' he asks again.

'Dad, I'm fine. Honestly.'

He gives her another long look. Maybe he needs glasses, if he can't see her properly without. All old people have glasses, right?

'OK, sweetheart. But if you ever need to talk, you know where we are, right?'

She nods. Of course she knows. And of course, night after night, when she has her pyjamas on, she longs to go and curl up on the sofa with them, or on their bed, like when she was little, and tell them everything. But she can't. Because they'll tell Cara's mum. If anyone ever sees her again. It was different telling Mr Belvoir; he won't tell anyone. He said so. If Alice's mum told

Cara's mum, she'd be sad and angry at Cara for always. And Alice will have betrayed Cara yet again. 'Cara, why did you have to be so secretive?' she asks her absent friend. 'Why couldn't you just have gone to your mum? Why did you have to put me in this position?'

Just before he leaves, Alice's dad turns to face her. 'You know you couldn't have stopped it, right?'

Alice stares at him a moment. Then she nods because it is expected.

But when her dad goes back downstairs, Alice curls up on her bed, legs drawn up to her chest. Only her sobs break the silence of the room.

TWENTY-TWO

THE SUPPER TRAY, that's what this will be, this turn in the lock. The door's opening now. Our first encounter since he closed the door on Cara. Since he knew I knew she was here. And our first real exchange since I kissed him then pushed him away.

His eyes. I look at them first. There's nothing in them for me. I can't read them. I could say angry, I could say pleading. But they're just eyes. Staring at mine as intently as I stare at his.

'I got you a cupcake,' he says.

I look at the tray.

And yes, there it is. The cupcake.

What fresh game is this?

It's plainly shop-bought, the cupcake. Featuring a blue colour in its icing that does not exist in nature. But what does it mean? Is he trying to show me he researched me before he brought me here? My cake business. He must have seen that picture of me and Cara. Is he trying to endear himself to me, trying again to make me want him?

I shrug at the tray. He looks hurt; that emotion I can read. He would hurt more if I let rip fully. If I tore up the cupcake and threw it at him. If I shoved it into his mouth and kept it there so that he couldn't breathe, like I can't breathe without Cara.

But there's a bigger picture now. There's a plan. So I can't throw the cupcake at him. I may even eat it, when he's gone. I can't worry about whatever crazy rationale he's working to; I'm working to a deadline.

'What time is it?' I ask. Because that's what I told Cara I'd do. Ask the time so I can count our way out of here. She hasn't replied yet to say she agrees to the plan, but I'm keeping my side of the bargain. Perhaps I pushed too hard. Perhaps she's distressed—in there, away from me. If only I could see through that wall, know how she was feeling. But I have to plan for success. I have to think positive.

And he blushes. Why would he blush?

'Sorry…it's a bit later than usual, I know, but I, well…something came up. Sorry.' He turns his gaze to the floor.

I can be magnanimous. When it suits me. 'I forgive you,' I say.

He looks up quickly, regards me keenly.

'For the delayed supper,' I say.

'Oh.' His face sags slightly. Perhaps he thought I was forgiving him for something else. Hardly.

Then he seems to remember himself. He lifts his chin again. Tenses his body. The armour, if it had a chink in it, is restored.

'Eat up,' he orders me.

I make a show of pulling down the cupcake paper.

'But, really, I'd like to know. For my sanity. What time is it?'

He looks at his watch. A really nice one—wide brown leather strap, a gold face with lots of little intricate whirring bits in it. The sort I'd choose if I were a man.

'It's seven p.m.,' he reports.

'Thank you.'

One, two, three…and so continues the constant ticking in my head. Because I must count, so I know exactly when it's 10.30 a.m., and our plan has to start, before his 11 a.m. meeting.

'About what you saw,' he says.

I look up at him.

(Eighteen, nineteen, twenty…)

'I saw Cara,' I remind him.

He nods. 'Right. So. About that.'

(Twenty-seven, twenty-eight, twenty-nine…)

'Are you releasing her?'

'Not really, no.'

'Are you releasing me?'

He shakes his head.

(Forty-three, forty-four, forty-five, forty-six…)

'There's a lot to do, Susan. A lot you have to understand.'

I understand already. I understand you've locked Cara and me away from each other. I understand you are between me and my daughter and our liberty.

But we also have a plan—I hope, if Cara is on-board. So I'm not going to waste my energy.

(One minute plus two, three, four…)

I clench my fists until my nails dig into my palms. 'Sure,' I say.

'I'll see you in the morning,' he tells me.

(One plus eleven, twelve, thirteen…)

I shrug.

I see his jaw tense.

He walks towards me again, until his face is only an in inch away from mine.

'You should care, Susan. You really should. Because this is the only way we both get what we want without you getting hurt.'

I'd shrug again but I don't know what he'd do. And I can't help but heed his words. So I nod, slowly.

He steps back.

'Goodnight, then,' he says. 'Enjoy your cupcake.'

When he's left the room I fling the cupcake at the door.

Don't cry. Don't cry. Just count.

(One plus twenty, twenty-one, twenty-two…)

I CAN'T HELP staring at the cupcake though. It lies in the centre of the floor, where its shop-bought rubberiness sent it bouncing. (One plus thirty-one, thirty-two, thirty-three…) I can't figure it out, what it means. I reject him, I spit in his face, and he tells me to enjoy my cake? (One plus thirty-seven, thirty-eight, thirty-nine…)

Maybe it's poisoned. (Forty-four, forty-five, forty-six…) Maybe he's moved on from doping me. Maybe he just wants to kill me, but he's too conniving, too cruel just to strangle me or beat me to death. (Sixty. Two plus one, two, three…) The sicko wants me to die by the very thing I've made my profession. (Two plus fourteen, fifteen, sixteen…) Or does it contain a sedative? If I eat it, will he rape me? Is that what he means about getting what he wants without me getting hurt? I'm not taking the chance. The cupcake can go in the pillowcase, along with the letter stash, and he can think I've eaten his drugged offering, and then he won't suspect we're about to escape. (Two plus twenty-two, twenty-three, twenty-four…) I scoop it up from by the door.

What time am I on? Must keep counting. Three minutes now? Yes, it must be. Just keep feeling the pulse. (Three plus one, two, three…)

I start to slide the cake into the pillowcase. It will go mouldy. Smell. Alert him. Or poison me another way. Maggots in my ear. Perhaps there's a better way. Yes, I know! The girl! Not Cara, the other girl. The outside girl. I can tempt her with the cake. It doesn't matter if it's poisoned because she'll never get it. I can put it on the window ledge, next to the skipping sign. Climb the chair and there, done, it's on the windowsill! Progress! (Three plus twenty, twenty-one, twenty-two…)

But only up to a point. What is Cara doing? Why hasn't she replied yet, about our escape? It was too much, wasn't it, me asking her to run down that corridor she fears? Too pushy. (Four plus thirteen, fourteen, fifteen…)

Or maybe she's just having her supper. Building her strength for tomorrow. She probably assumes that I assume she'll go along with my plan—her plan, really, with my simple revisions. I should eat too. Because look at the rest of the food on the tray. It looks so unappetising that it must be safe. Who would poison an overripe avocado? Or a grizzled pork chop. And, do you know, I might even treat myself to eating the whole thing for once. The cupcake was the danger zone. This must be safe.

And it feels good. It feels good to eat this full meal. I actually start to feel normal. (Four plus forty-seven, forty-eight, forty-nine…) My hunger is starting to be sated. Would be nice if there was a glass of wine to go with it, Chablis perhaps, to celebrate my last meal in captivity. Because tomorrow will go well. Tomorrow we will escape. (Four plus fifty-eight, fifty-nine, sixty—or are we on five already? I must continue counting. Yes, I must. Eyes drooping a bit, but I must, I must, five plus one, two, three…) And we can find out who this sod is, this sod who would take my daughter away from me, only to give me poisoned (five plus one, two, three…) food. Yes, tomorrow, tomorrow. I'll just rest my head on the pillow a bit, now it's not poisoned, and I'll be closer to Cara's letter stash. Yes, there we go. That's really—oh gosh, these yawns!—nice. (Five plus two, three… Plus three plus four…)

TWENTY-THREE

ALICE LOOKS OVER her shoulder as she hurries along the pavement towards school. Night has become day, but it feels like she's still in a nightmare, a crazy chase dream. Another two streets to go. He's still following her. The bright green car is leaping along the road towards her like an overzealous frog. Why won't he stop this? She keeps telling him that she's told him all she knows. She's done her bit. Described exactly the place he asked for.

Suddenly, the car is level with her.

'Hop in, Alice,' he says, like he knows he's driving in a frog.

She shakes her head and carries on walking.

'Come on, get in,' he says again.

Doesn't he understand? You don't get into cars with strangers. Who brought him up? Besides, she'll miss registration, and she doesn't want a black mark.

She starts to run. She stops looking where she's going and runs as fast as she can. She's told him about Cara, everything she knows.

But it was like he wasn't listening to what she said. He was only interested in his own questions: 'So did her mum usually drop her at school?' 'Have you seen her mum recently?' 'Did you ever see her with her mum and her mum's husband together?' 'What were they like?' 'What did they have for supper when you went round?' 'Did they ever have alcohol?' 'Did they drive you home afterwards?' And before she'd even answered one question, he'd start on another. Weird. Totally weird.

As she runs, she wishes she had told Mrs Cavendish. Mr Belvoir said he'd told Mrs Cavendish that they were meeting outside school, and that she'd said it was OK, because it wouldn't distract her from lessons. But that it was best to keep the content of their discussions secret, because he didn't want to prejudice the investigations. It sounded very grand at the time. But now she bets, she just bets that Mrs Cavendish didn't know about it, and that she shouldn't be keeping anything to do with this man secret. That's what Cara did and look what happened to Cara.

Look! Here's the street with bollards at the end, so cars can't get through. If she runs down here, he can't catch her. Turn in! Run a little bit more. Then stop. Catch up on breath. Phew.

But no! What's this? In the opposite direction, from the end of the street without the bollards, the green frog car. Coming closer and closer towards her. Until it's almost touching her. Engine still running. Window wound down.

'Why are you running, Alice?'

Should she stay anything, or keep quiet? Even if he didn't make Cara disappear, there's something not quite right about him. Maybe if she tells him she doesn't like him, he'll go away. That works at school.

'I don't like you,' Alice says.

The corners of his mouth turn down. 'I don't think little girls do like me.'

'Cara said she didn't like you. She said you were weird. I know she was on her way to see you. And I've never seen her again. So no, I don't like you.'

And then he's getting out of the car. He's taking hold of her arm. She's struggling. Surely someone must see her. He pulls her into the car. Help! Help! The door is shut and there are those stupid child locks that mean she can't get out. She bangs her hands against the window. He's going to drive off! He's going to vanish her like he vanished Cara! Even though... Oh, even though nothing. He's somehow to blame. She knows he is.

But the engine stops. The car doesn't go anywhere.

'Alice,' says Mr Belvoir. 'Calm down. You can trust me. Let me tell you what I know. Then you can see who you think the villain is. You've described where he lives. Now you can take me to find him.'

TWENTY-FOUR

The other side of the door

IT'S NEARLY TIME.

Just over half an hour to go. Breakfasts done, trays delivered—even to still sleeping recipients. No distraction there. Perhaps I should have shaken her awake. Used some of that force, that tension, that is building and building. That I must do something with. Before it explodes. Because we know where that can end up. The danger it can cause.

I pace back and forth, like the pendulum of a clock. Keep the adrenaline up. Come 11 a.m., I must be out of this door. I must be cool, composed and in control of the situation. And there's no reason why I shouldn't be. I know I'm in the right. Because I'm trying to help. I really am. I'm trying to keep us together under this roof. That's where we're meant to be. I know that's what Suze wants, if only she could see that.

Perhaps she will, soon, now. That's the hope. What with the other delivery I took yesterday. It's got to work, hasn't it?

Which is why I'm not going to let him, this man, pry into our affairs. None of this has anything to do with him. This is my sanctuary, and I have a right to treat the people here as I see fit. And I'm doing well. Very well. I have to meet him. To hear what he has to say. Because otherwise he might start to talk to others, if he hasn't already. Start a process. Blue flashing lights. As if I'm doing something wrong. But I'm not. I have right on my side. And, as for the money angle, well, I know what I need. What we need. But it looks like he doesn't agree that's the necessary sum. He's greedy, that's what it is. Wants to hang on to everything, keep it to himself. That doesn't work. It doesn't work. He must see that. He must do. Otherwise…

I must keep my head. Must keep calm. Keep the overall objective in mind. Don't let him get into my head, twisting a little scalpel around, seeing what my trigger points are. Exploiting them. I do enough of that to myself. At night. In the dark. Replaying all the images, the decisions, the choices. Reminding myself about consequences.

I go over to the window and flick the curtain. Perhaps he's early? No. No car parked on the corner. That is, there are cars, of course there are, here in the not-quite-suburbia-because-it's-London-so-it's-a-'village' belt. Just not his car. I wonder if he'll actually be in the car, or whether it's all a trap. Whether it will be full of police. Or just threats.

Perhaps it will be a nice exchange. He tells me what works for him. I tell him that's no good. We agree to differ. Then we part due to artistic differences.

Unlikely.

I check my watch again. Nearer and nearer draws the time.

Maybe I'll just see if all is in order down the corridor. It's quiet. Too quiet. Suze was breathing, I think, when I deposited the tray. I'm pretty sure I got the dosage right, last night. That I haven't over overdosed her. There's not even any knocking, though, this morning. All that knocking, on the wall, between Suze and Cara's room. I'm not stupid. I know what it means. It's what they do, isn't it, in this situation, when they think they've learnt something important? But it won't do any good. Almost breaks your heart, such futile behaviour. Almost. If something else hadn't broken it already. 'Something else'! Hah! Me. Me. I was the one who shouldn't have done what I did. But I didn't know that when I did it. You never do. It's only with hindsight. Hindsight screaming at you from the road up ahead, 'Stop! This will end badly. Choose some other route, quit this journey now, while you can.'

Perhaps my heart is not quite broken though. Just very badly fractured. And with a little assistance from the other end of the corridor—voluntary or not—perhaps that heart would heal. And so he, that other man, that man outside this spectacular heist I am attempting, must not be allowed to spoil my chances of recovery. I must show him that. At 11 a.m.

Because if I can't make that work, I'm going to have to create a new plan. In a hurry. And I don't like to think about what I might have to do.

TWENTY-FIVE

'SUSAN! SUSAN! BREAKFAST!'

I fling my eyes open.

There's a tray. Sunlight. Day.

Before that, night.

I've been sleeping. Which means I haven't been counting. Which means 10.30 a.m., 11 a.m., could have come and gone. Our plans destroyed by my neglect.

'What time is it?' I cry, swinging my legs over the edge of the bed. As my feet hit the floor, full awakeness hits me and I want to claw my question back. Who arouses suspicion on escape day?

The Captor stands back and looks at me.

'Why, you due somewhere?' he asks.

I shake my head. Damn, damn, damn. Think!

'No. I just want to keep a body clock. For when I get out of here. Because I will get out, you know.'

'Sure.' Is that a smirk? Is he laughing at me, the bastard, for the thought of being out of here? Well, let him laugh. He doesn't know what we have planned.

'So?' I ask. 'The time?'

He looks at that watch again, the pretty yet masculine one. I wish I could smash its face against his, both of them destroyed.

'Quarter to eleven.'

Damn. How could you, Susan? Indulging yourself—
sleeping—when Cara needs you! Bad mother. Bad, bad
mother. I want to hit myself, but manage not to. It might
seem odd. I pinch away the guilt instead. But look—
stop regretting too early. We could still push on with
the plan. I'll need to take a risk. It's only fifteen minutes out.

'How's the shower this morning?' I ask.

'You're not usually keen for a wash,' he says, with
an eyebrow raised in surprise.

'I didn't say I wanted a shower. I just asked how it
was. If the water's warm. Been tested yet today?'

'Not by me,' he says.

Damn it. Does he know? Is he playing with me,
with such an equivocal answer? I want to shout Has
my daughter used the shower today?

But I can't, of course.

I flick my eyes as fast as I can to and from the grate.
Nothing there. Still no reply to my letter. Is she down
with the plan or not? Can we even carry on?

I'm going to assume yes. We have to go for it.

'Why?' he asks me.

Ah yes, of course. Why.

And I don't have an answer. So I shrug, and take a
sip of the orange juice on my tray. It's like being at one
of those baking 'master class' functions again, drinking
cheap juice out of plastic cups. Or more likely, Char-
donnay. He looks at his watch. Is that the slightest tap
of a foot? Yes, it is. So, he's still in a hurry. Agitated.
Our plan can still work.

'Don't let me keep you,' I say. 'I'm sure I can manage breakfast without killing myself.'

I've got to plant that, you see. That seed of doubt. Make him wonder if, when I scream, that's what's happening. That I'm trying to kill myself. That there is something worth coming running for.

He frowns.

I look at him full square. I do open and honest but slightly troubled eyes.

He keeps frowning. Like he's not going to leave. Like one of his two prized possessions has suddenly developed a fatal flaw, and he wants to safeguard them.

'Figure of speech,' I tell him.

He nods, still frowning. I've reassured him enough for him to leave the room. But it should be enough to make him reappear once I start my screams. How easy it is to manipulate him—how well you come to know a stranger in these surroundings.

Door closed, I put down my orange juice and run to the grate. I rattle it as per my letter. Has she heard? I don't know. I'll have to risk a gentle tap on the wall. Still nothing. But then—yes, what's that! Do I hear a knocking from next door? Yes, yes, I think I do! Not on the wall, but on the door. Then I hear music—Cara's voice, I mean, my version of music—as Cara demands a shower.

This is it then. Will he come? He must. He must. There's the banging again. And that's her door being unlocked, is it? I can hear his voice. So unless he's talking to himself, he must be talking to Cara. I hear footsteps outside the door, heading in the direction of the shower.

Right. Give enough time for her to get into the shower room. For her to take off her clothes. To begin a long, leisurely rinse. For him to get increasingly agitated as he looks at his watch again and again. And then...

'AHHHHHHH! AHHHHHHH! AHHHHHHHH-HHHHHH!'

Everything goes into the scream. All the pain, the worry, the fear of being here.

Again.

'AHHHHHHHH!'

Black dots in front of my eyes. My hands on the sides of my head. The room swinging away from me.

The Captor standing in front of me.

'What? What's wrong?'

'AHHHHHHHHH!'

Spiralling now, the room is. And I'm physically sinking, I can feel myself, to the floor. The scream becomes a groan. I can't stay up. I have to lie down. My legs buckle. I crawl to the bed.

'What's wrong?' he asks again, standing over me. Or at least I think he must be standing over me. He might have moved into the doorway. He sounds very far away. Someone's hands are on me, shaking me, though.

I manage to look up.

Then I pull back. Yes, there he is. Leaning down, right next to me. They must have been his hands. In fact, yes, they are still on me. I look at them. He moves them away. For a second, I feel like putting them back again.

'Why were you screaming? Susan, what is it?'

Because I'm here, of course. Because I'm not where I'm meant to be. Because of what you've done to me. Be-

cause I want to be with my little girl. Because I can't bear,
I cannot bear, the thought of not seeing her. Because I
want to see her again now, now, now and for ever and—

Oh. Yes. That's right. I'm screaming so that Cara
can run.

Pragmatic.

The room rights itself again.

Even now, she must be running out of the house!
Even now, running down the corridor, away, away, to
freedom! Or is she still standing on the threshold of the
shower room, hesitant, unsure whether she should run?
Has he even left the door unlocked? Or is she trapped
in there now, away from me?

I need to think positive. And I need to buy her some
more time.

'Oh, it was just so awful, I was…' I trail off. Story
half-untold, but more for the telling.

'What, Susan?'

'No, no. I can't say.'

'Yes, you can. You can trust me, Susan.'

I look at him. I try to imagine a world in which I can
trust this man who I hate, this man who brought me
here. Or a world in which someone who has kidnapped
you and your daughter can hold himself out as a figure
of trust. It is only a warped world, a madman's world.
Which is what I am dealing with.

I shake my head. 'You wouldn't understand.'

'Try me.'

I shake my head. And I keep on shaking my head.
Then I pull my knees up to my chest and continue, just
sitting there on the floor, shaking.

He tries to put his arm round me again, but I flinch, so he lowers his arm.

I don't know how long he stands there, just looking at me. Perhaps he is wondering if this would be a good moment to rape me. Perhaps it would. I could lie back and think of freedom. I look at him, then I have to look away again, quickly. Just in case he can tell what I'm thinking.

I stop the head-shaking. Cara must be out by now, surely?

So as soon as he is out of the door he'll be back, won't he? He'll know then what I was up to.

Unless Cara hasn't escaped. And he has to punish her. Then I might hear nothing. Or her horrible screams.

How will I know?

I need to know.

Every moment he is in here with me is a moment of not knowing whether Cara is free; whether I will soon be free too to be with her. I need him out now. I need to know how he's going to react.

Why aren't they telling me? I've done my bit. Why won't they tell me—is she OK?

I smooth myself down and stand up.

My legs shake a little bit. The Captor puts out his hand for support. I see him see his watch as he does so. His brow crinkles a little. I see the time: 10.55. So. Almost late for his meeting.

'I'm fine,' I say.

'Are you sure?'

I nod. 'Just sometimes gets on top of me. All…this.'

He closes his eyes. 'One day you'll understand, Susan.'

He puts his hands on my shoulders. I wriggle to move them out of the way, but his grip is too strong. He kisses the top of my head.

I'm almost comforted by that kiss. It feels soft and pleasant. So I jerk away. This man is not my friend.

'I'll be back soon,' he says.

But will you, my captor? Will you? Because will my daughter have escaped? Go outside, go outside now, and let events unfold.

TWENTY-SIX

SILENCE.

There is still silence.

It is filling my head, my soul, this room. I can't imagine there being any noise anywhere in the world, unless I make it.

Nothing from the corridor.

Nothing from next door.

Why?

Am I suddenly alone in the world?

Has there been a sudden nuclear apocalypse, which somehow only this room has withstood?

Has Cara escaped only to find our world no longer out there?

I stand on the chair and look through the window over the now stale cupcake. I see trees blowing in the breeze. There's still a world out there then. But there, it makes a sound. Wind in the branches. A whistling or a rustling maybe. But in here, silence.

Think of all those Cara noises there used to be at home. Crying, early on—she refused to be comforted by that small sheep toy. Perhaps she knew it hadn't been meant for her. And then when she was older, those flute scales wafting through the walls. I hum a little scale now. It falls flat.

I climb down from the window again.

Should I rattle the grate?

Should I whisper, or even speak a hello?

Has she done it? Has she got away?

Where's the baby, Susan? Why haven't you brought home the baby?

Perhaps in his hurry to get to his meeting, the Captor forgot about Cara being in the shower. Perhaps he just left my room, left the house and still hasn't come back. So perhaps the drama will come on his return. Perhaps there'll be swearing and stamping and storming. Perhaps he'll drag me out of the room by my hair. Perhaps he'll hit me. Perhaps he'll finally rape me.

Which would be wonderful. Because it would mean that my Cara was free.

So I'll give it a bit longer.

How long do you give them? How long do you wait to see if they'll breathe?

TWENTY-SEVEN

Still just these four walls.
These, four, silent, walls.
White, or are they cream? Or even yellow?
Magnolia. They'll be magnolia.
Perhaps if I put my back against them, they'll
expand.
No.

TWENTY-EIGHT

I'VE REMADE THE BED. It didn't take much, just unrumpling the duvet. I reread and refolded all the letters from Cara in my pillowcase. Paper makes a nice noise when you fold it. A noise, anyway.

Why doesn't time tick? Why should we be reliant on clocks?

I smell the potpourri. It smells the same as it has every other day.

What's happened, Cara? Where are you?

I don't know if this was a good plan. I don't know if it will work, being without you.

Time, just passing.

Nothing.

Here I am.

Still here. Sitting on the bed, hands folded. And unfolded. Folded again.

Hello? I ask the room.

Silence.

I should—

Bang!

I jump up.

There we have it! A noise! A noise, outside this room! A door, slamming, it must be.

Now, now we have it. Now, I'll know.

TWENTY-NINE

The other side of the door

HE'S NOT IN his car when I go outside.

He's on the doorstep.

I know him from one glance. It's hard to miss that bulk, and the authority that comes with heft. Leather jacket, too, a rough texture worn by age. The perfect poster boy for the world of murk in which he works.

Once I'm over the initial shock, I quickly step outside and shut the front door behind me. He mustn't see the pictures. No one must see them. They reveal too much; they almost scream, Lock me up and throw away the key.

'We said we'd meet in the car,' I rebuke him.

He shrugs. A leisurely shrug, that says, Yeah, what you gonna do about it? so that his lips don't have to form the words.

'We'll go there now, shall we?' I ask.

In reply, he leaves the porch and walks along to the living room window. He ducks his head as if to look in. Casually, but with threat.

The blinds are down, of course. They're always down. Before I know it, we'll all be living in condensation-induced mould. And then the pictures will go mouldy too. I really ought to take them down. Like I took down the ones in the hall. Erase all traces of what's gone before.

'Shall we go to the car?'

I don't want him walking round the house. There's that window, outside Suze's room. Too high for him to see in, but if she sees him… Well, that could make things happen, couldn't it? If she sees him walking round the outside of the house, inside the fence or out, she's going to have a reaction. And she's probably going to wave, and dance, and anything she thinks will get his attention. And because he suspects—I know, you see, that it's not just about Cara for him; I know it's about Suze too—he will look up. And he will see. And then we'll be in game-over mode. I don't know whose game. But someone's.

So I do a bold thing. I walk round to his right-hand side, putting myself between him and the house. And I gently take his elbow so that I can steer him away, towards his car.

He looks at my hand.

If he sees the blood, he doesn't comment.

'I don't have a lot of time,' I say.

I put my hand behind my back.

He raises an eyebrow. 'No?'

I think of the mess I left inside the house. The shower room, in particular. That will need sorting out. Before Suze can use it again. Before anyone can use it again. Those questions she was asking, you'd think Suze knew what was going to happen. What I was going to do.

'No,' I say.

He does his nonchalant shrug again. We go to his car.

But we don't get in. Because there's a girl in there.

For a moment I think it's her. I even look back at the house to check my sanity. Then I look at the girl again.

Of course it's not her.

But that same uniform. And the face vaguely familiar. She's staring at me with big frightened eyes. Yes, I know fear when I see it. Her seat belt is still done up. Like that would somehow offer her protection.

'What's with the girl?' I ask him.

'We've got a little arrangement. Helps me out. Doesn't help you.'

I don't understand. I don't think I want to understand. Is he being deliberately cruel, showing me this vision? But that can't be all he wanted to see me for.

And then we have it.

'Why did you get her into the car with you?' he asks me.

Bam, the first question, collision force. No messing about, no warming up the engine first. Just straight to the accusations, the assumptions.

I look down at the kerb. Now is not the time to acknowledge guilt. If 'guilt' is the right word for it. Because you can redeem anything, can't you, by what you do later? By what I'm doing in that house.

'With your record, you knew where it would lead.'

I look up at him.

He smirks. 'Oh yes, I know all about your record. Did you think I wouldn't? Do you think that when it comes to prosecuting the shit out of you, I wouldn't know your past?'

The world freezes, as it will do at times like this. My brain only thinks that it should be thinking. The rest of the world moves on though. It isn't frozen.

'Because I am going to prosecute you, make no mistake. I've got the connections. I'm going to put together a case, get all the evidence, and I'm going to take it to the right people, and they're going to show you for what you are.'

He doesn't need to tell me what I am. Because we both know.

'Unless, of course...' he says.

And here we go. Here's the bartering. Here's what he's come here to ask me. To threaten me with.

I listen, and then I very calmly walk away from the car.

He calls after me. Tells me not to be stupid. That this won't be the end of it.

But I'm not being stupid. Because it's not just the money that we disagree on. It's Cara. He wants me to give him all that is Cara. That's just not something I can do.

So here I am back inside. And I need to sort out the shower room.

THIRTY

THERE HAVE BEEN no great cries. No hysterics, no screaming, no weeping. On the other side of the door, that is.

I press my ear against my side of the door. Footsteps.
An internal door opening. The shower room? There's
a faint sound of running water. What's going on? Did
he install a lock? Just keep her in there while he was
away? Or is she going in there now? Did I go to sleep
again? Or is she dead in there? Is he washing away the
traces? The traces of my daughter?

I must know. I must know.

I hammer on the door.

No response. Maybe he can't hear me over the sound
of the water.

I hammer again. 'Hey!' I cry. 'Come and open up!'

The water sound stops. Footsteps coming nearer.
The key in the door.

I look for the time on the Captor's watch.

But his watch is covered. He's wearing rubber gloves.
Those latex disposable ones, the type doctors and forensic teams use. And, of course, murderers, and rap-
ists. When they need to leave a scene clean. Hide the
evidence.

Cara.

But in his own home, why wear gloves? His DNA

is everywhere. Cara's DNA is everywhere. Why the gloves?

I must get out into that corridor. Into that shower room. To see what's happening.

'I need to piss,' I say.

'Well, you'll have to wait a bit. I'm busy right now.'

'I really, really need to piss. I'll have to piss all over the carpets otherwise.'

He frowns and sweeps the glove over his brow. Bad move—DNA transference guaranteed.

'Fine,' he says. 'Just let me—'

'I can feel it leaking out now,' I say.

'All right, all right. Come on.'

It has the easy petty familiarity of a domestic argument. But then he frogmarches me out of the room. The latex of the gloves rubs on my bare skin. I have a sudden longing for them to be off, just to feel skin-to-skin contact. But the longing goes—I must focus, look around me in the corridor.

There's nothing to say what has happened. Cara's door is still shut. There's no hint of wet footprints or discarded towels in the corridor. No blood, which is what I feared. In the bit of my mind I shut down there are handprints covered in blood adorning the walls. Cara's blood, spilt. Here, there are just the same bland empty walls. Looking closely, I can see there were pictures there once—there are slightly lighter squares of wall here and there. They've all been taken down, if they were ever there. Vanished with just a teasing trace. Like Cara. Except now there is no trace at all.

Finally. We are in the shower room.

'Go on, then,' says the Captor, gesturing at the toilet.

As I squat over the toilet bowl, I survey the room. Nothing out of the ordinary. Not even any steam on the—oh wait, the mirror has gone. Significant? I don't know. Everything else is in place. It just looks like a shower room.

It's when I get up to wash my hands that I see it. A single shard of glass, in the sink. And on the glass, there is blood.

THIRTY-ONE

'WHAT HAVE YOU done with her? What have you DONE with her?' I can't hold back. The blood. The glass. My child?

He takes my arms, pinions them. 'Calm down,' he tells me.

'But what have you done? What have you done?'

I wriggle and I wrestle and I twist, but he holds me. He keeps holding me. He's destroyed my daughter and still he keeps holding me.

'Where is she?' I ask him. Maybe she is here still. Maybe he's hidden her. Maybe she's lying somewhere, bleeding out. 'Where is she? Where is she? What have you done?'

What have you done with my baby? Why can't I see her?

He's just shaking his head at me.

'I can see it! I can see her blood in the sink! You've murdered her, you child-murderer, you—'

And then there's a stinging in my face. He's slapped me! The force of it sends me to the floor. It's not like that warning slap he did before; it's a proper slap.

But I must know!

'What have you done with her? What have you done with her?'

He grabs me from the floor.

'What? What are you doing?'

'Back in your room.' He is dragging me.

'But you have to tell me! Please!'

He's not answering though. He's just dragging. His jaw is set and his eyes are staring dead ahead. When we get to my room, he pretty much throws me in there, and slams the door shut behind him.

I slam my hands against the door, claw it with my nails, as if I could whittle away the wood.

'What have you done with my daughter?'

I shout and I weep and I cry because what has he done? And why the silence? I can't bear it, I can't bear it, I can't bear it.

'I can't bear it,' I whisper. But no one can hear me.

THIRTY-TWO

The other side of the door

NEARLY LOST IT THERE. Again. Shouldn't have smacked her. But I could have done more, I could have… That would ruin everything though. Death is not the plan for her. Unless it has to be. What she was saying… There's only so much provocation a man can take, isn't there? Particularly when he's been trying so hard for so long to care for everyone.

And I shouldn't have left the piece of glass in the sink. That's what it comes down to. Stupid, stupid, stupid. But I thought I'd cleared everything away. I have now, of course. All gone. I did that as soon as I'd locked Suze back in. I felt like doing it all again, when I'd locked her up. Reprising the earlier shower room scene. And the blood.

I deposit the black bin bag in the living room and sit on the sofa. I put my hands to my face and just sit. I didn't know it would be this difficult. I just thought that if we were all under this roof, it would be easier. To do what I needed to do. To help. Because that's all I'm trying to do. Help.

Help me.

A pitiful cry.

I put it back in the box it came from. There's no time for that. I need to get on.

I look up from the sofa. All the photos, all over the walls. I must take them down. It's not safe for them to be there any more. If he sees them, if he forces his way into the house, then he'll have them. Maybe not for his prosecution. But he'll have them. And with them he'll want her. But he's not getting them, any of it, either of my two girls. They're mine, and I'm keeping them. What I've got of them. Because I know, at the moment, I haven't got much of her.

It's not like I even need the photos anyway. I remember every moment. They're stored, agonisingly close, in my mind. I remember when I first saw the two of them. Of course I do. You don't forget a day like that, a day that changes three people's lives for ever. There's another day I won't forget, too, of course. Although I wish to God I could.

I turn away from the photos. Like she turned away from me back then. But I knew we'd be together again, the three of us. I swore I would make it my life's ambition, for as long as it took. The photos hold too much hope. If I look much longer, it will turn into bitterness. Towards Suze. Even the girl. Which is wrong. Of course it is. I know that. And dangerous. Look at what happened earlier. That was bad. I shouldn't have done that. But, sometimes you just can't help yourself, you know? The anger gets in the way. Then people suffer. Sometimes they deserve it. Sometimes they don't. But I don't deserve that treatment from Suze. That name-calling. I don't. Do I?

I remember when I first locked her in the room. The names she'd been calling me. She didn't understand who I was. That I was her saviour. Or why I had to do what I've done. There was no other option, if we were to get to where we needed to be. We will still get there. I know we will. So I'm sorry I had to sedate her. I wish it had helped more. With her hostility. Or her comprehension. Oh my Suze. We'll get you there. We'll get us there. With or without Cara. You just mustn't push me beyond my limits. I have some self-control. Clearly. Or I wouldn't be taking all these baby steps. But I'm not an angel. We know that. He knows that. It's just a question of what he's going to do about it. And of what I'm going to do about him.

THIRTY-THREE

'ALICE, DO YOU know the answer to the question? Alice? Alice? Alice?'

'I don't know the answers to your questions! Stop asking me your questions!'

'Alice, how dare you talk to me like that!'

Suddenly, Mr Wilson's face is in hers. She jerks back. She sees the eyes of the rest of the class on her. Hears their giggles. Feels her cheeks turn red.

'Mr Wilson, I'm sorry, I thought…'

'I don't know what's wrong with you, Alice. I don't care if you do know the answer. I don't want to hear from you again until you've learnt some manners.' Mr Wilson turns to the girl next to Alice. 'Hettie, let's have the answer, please!'

Hettie shoots a smug glance at Alice before answering Mr Wilson's question.

The lesson continues. Not wanting to attract attention, Alice sits up straight and silent in her seat. But she cannot stop her hands going to her mouth so that she can bite her nails. Soon they will be as bitten as Cara's were. Alice hasn't been able to stop chewing her fingers since Mr Belvoir put her in his car and told her what he knew. Or rather suspected. And made her take him there. And see him. The other man. The villain.

Then it was her turn to ask questions. For a bit.

'But what are you going to do? Are you going to tell the police? How can we stop him? And rescue her?'

He was working on it, he said. But he didn't want to involve the police. Not yet. And she mustn't either. She must just keep it between the two of them. He didn't need to say 'or else'. But she understood, now, didn't she, why he needed her help? Why he needed her to answer his questions?

And then they started again. So many questions. More than the everything she'd already told him about Cara and her family. One line of questioning in particular.

While he'd bombarded her with questions, she hadn't had time to think about what he'd told her. But afterwards, she had. She had thought and thought and thought. And she was still thinking about it now. How could anybody do something so wicked and terrible? What had Cara endured in that place, even before all this happened? Alice shivers and rubs her hands up and down her arms.

This is too much for me to know, she thinks. I just wanted to come to school and live my life. Mr Wilson, going on about his verbs and grammar. What do they matter? Why don't any of these teachers teach about the world? About the horror and the cruelty and the sadness? Why even bother coming here? Why bother staying? How can I sit here when over the other side of town… She shivers again. Well, I won't. I won't sit here and just accept it. I'll stand up, I'll run, I'll shout about it. I'll tell everyone.

But, as Alice puts the balls of her feet more firmly on the floor, the bell rings for the end of the lesson. Chairs are scraped back, Mr Wilson shouts out the homework deadlines, and her classmates whirl out of the classroom. In a few moments, there is nothing left. Alice is all alone. With her thoughts. And her images. And her imaginings. About what is going on in that place.

THIRTY-FOUR

Perhaps the blood belongs to him. Not my daughter.

Perhaps we haven't botched the escape attempt.

Perhaps we can still save her.

Perhaps Paul is about to come charging in with the cavalry.

I hope so. I hope so, I hope so, I hope so. Because otherwise…no.

THIS IS THE longest we've ever been apart. The school ski trip was the other time. I didn't want her to go; I had horrific premonitions of her careening off a slope into a snowy abyss, or ploughing into a set of trees, limbs and skull smashed. Or just forming an illicit Alpine liaison and coming home too delicate to ski for nine months. That delicious fear reserved to parents.

But of course you were fine. More than fine. You were glorious. The pictures showed me that. My gorgeous, confident, blonde one. Much cooler than I ever was.

That was nine days. And I don't even know how long this is. Plainly, counting is not what I'm best at. If I'd been any good at that, we wouldn't have botched the escape attempt.

If we botched it.

And why should I be apart from you? Why shouldn't we be always together? You were part of me for, oh, much longer than nine months. Even after you were born, I couldn't tell us apart. In those exhausting nights early on, when I caught a rare moment of sleep, I would awake thinking I was you. I thought my hands were your hands; I adopted your foetal position; I felt so small. And you, you cried out to be in me again. No Moses basket placated you. Your father didn't understand. He just moaned that you couldn't be put down. (Did he want, all along, to 'put you down', like an inconvenient pet? Is this all somehow his doing? Was leaving, agreeing to leave, whatever, not enough?) But I knew. I knew because I felt it too. We are one and the same. Which is why you must be able to hear me thinking, mustn't you? When you looked up smiling from my breast, I knew you could read my thoughts, my love for you. And, ever since, all these fifteen years, you've known, I'm sure. How much I love you.

How much I've failed you.

Because I have, haven't I?

I've failed you.

I let you become a separate person. I let you leave the house. I let you talk to people I hadn't vetted. I let you get here. I should have kept you at home, wrapped in cotton wool, too precious to leave. I as good as brought you here by my neglect.

And I made a plan that put you at risk. We could have waited. We could have waited for a rescue.

I'm to blame. I'm to blame for all of this.

I just thought, somehow, everything would be OK. Against the odds we'd get through this, together. That we were unbreakable. And we'd go home to Paul and be happy, for ever, the three of us.

I realise I've been staring at the grate, willing a letter to come. But why would it come?

Either you'll be there, bleeding, cursing me (and you won't write).

Or you'll be free. Free. Praise the Lord, thank you thank you thank you. But you won't come back to me. You'll run as far as you can.

Or you'll be...

No. Don't think it.

So I mustn't wallow. Unbearable, horrible, horrible though this is, I must—

But what? What's that?

It is, isn't it?

It's a letter.

Through the grate.

You're there!

Quick, quick! Tear apart the pages. Kiss them. Cara, Cara, Cara, my darling! What do you have to say?

Mum,

It didn't work. Let's just leave it at that, OK?

I know you will have been wondering what happened. I'm sorry, but I couldn't write. I just couldn't. I'm sorry. I just wanted to be alone. After... Well, after what happened. I love you,

Mum. I love you. The only thing keeping me going is knowing, as I sit here shivering after… well, after we failed…was knowing you were so close. I wanted more than anything for you to hug me, like you used to when I was small. I've been going to that happy place, I think from when I was about eight, I remember sitting on your knee on that old brown sofa, after I'd fallen over or something while you wiped away my tears, put on a plaster and made everything better.

Some things run too deep for a plaster though, don't they? So please, pretty please, let's just not talk about it. It's in a box. I've shut the lid. Maybe, later, we can talk about it. But I'm not writing about it. I tried. There's another draft of this letter, all scrumpled up in a ball. I couldn't finish it. I cried too much. I needed your hug too much.

So. We still need to get out of here. Which means a new plan. How's your skipping girl coming on? Because if she hasn't seen your sign, we need to use that other plan.

The killing plan.

Cara xx

THIRTY-FIVE

She's alive! Oh my Cara! Alive, well, happy…

No. Perhaps not happy. Or even well. But alive! And next door to me again. She never left me really. She was always there.

But oh, how have I made her suffer? Look at that letter, read the gaps between every word again. What has he done to her? I notice my fist clench round the letter, crumpling the paper. I smooth it out. I mustn't let the Captor or my anger at him destroy anything belonging to Cara ever again. Because what must she have gone through? And what wouldn't I have given to be there, on the other side of that wall, with her, giving her the hugs she needs.

The blood, then, might still have been hers. What kind of a parent am I to allow that to happen to her? I should never ever have let her play any part in that plan. It was all my fault. Saved from the crumpling, the letter now faces the onslaught of my tears. The paper could dissolve in front of me. Cara washed away by grief.

Stop it, Susan. She is next door. She is alive. Don't waste your tears. Be a mother to her, don't wallow in your own darkness.

And it's clear what being a mother to her now means.

It means killing.

Unless…

I climb onto the armchair and look out of the window. No little girl. No skipping. No clue that she has seen or acted upon the sign.

I can't hold out hope for that. We need to go the death route. Cara's asked for it, so I have to give it to her.

I don't mind. Of course I don't mind. Just conjuring up the Captor's face creates a hatred so strong in me that bile rises in my throat. He has driven us to this. The only question is how. How do we do it safely (for us)? The plan mustn't fail again. I must do better than that for Cara.

We'll need a weapon, of course. There's always the pencils. I could take him by surprise; hide behind the door when he comes in. Then slam! Into his jugular with the broken wood. Watch the blood seep out, then step over his body to the outside world. But I'd have to be strong. Stronger even than him. Because it requires quite some jabbing, a pencil, I'd imagine. I prod my finger with the graphite. Nothing. Not even a grey mark on my finger. It might be better with the broken wood. I snap the pencil in two. Or, at least, I try to. It's harder than it should be. I try again. If I can't even snap the pencil, how do I shove it hard enough into the Captor's throat to kill him? Come on. Put some strength into it. Some fire, some passion, some we-need-to-get-out-of-here energy.

Snap! The wood splits neatly down the middle and I'm left with two half pencils. I run a finger over the ends of each. Not nearly jagged enough. I would have been better with just the point. But that's blunted from writing to Cara, and her pencil will be blunt too.

Something else then. What? If only I'd been able to keep that shard of glass from the mirror. That would do the trick. Could I get another one? Will he have replaced the mirror? Could I somehow distract him, smash it, then...no. This is the first plan all over again. I need something new. Something more unexpected.

I won't be able to do it with my bare hands. That's for sure. He'd knock me flat then probably kill me. Then Cara.

Cara. I need to write back to her. I need to let her know I agree, that I'm here for her, that I'll do what she says. Think of her, my poor darling, sitting in the next room, wondering if I've got her letter, wondering if I hate her for refusing to share or plotting to kill. How we end the Captor is a detail. What is more important is that we will, and that Cara knows this. Besides, she may have some ideas.

I take up what remains of my pencil.

Darling Cara,
Darling, darling Cara.

I'm so sorry. It's my fault; I should never have let you do this. I will not push you to tell me what happened. You're a big girl now. I respect your privacy. But if you ever want to tell me, you can. And if not, I will pay for the best counselling we can get for you. When we get out of here. Because we will, we will get out of here.

Of course I'll kill for you. Consider it done. I don't know how; I've never killed a man before. Any thoughts welcome. I don't think stabbing him with a pencil will work.

Anyway, we'll think about it. And we'll work

something out. I just wanted you to know that I love you, and I'm here for you, even if I can't sit you on my knee and cuddle you like I used to. How I wish I could.

Mum xx

Just pick her up and cuddle her. Craving her breath on your cheek. Your little girl.

She probably will need counselling, won't she? I've probably got a permanently damaged daughter. Something I can't cure with cupcakes (although, no doubt, I will try). We'll probably both need counselling, once I've killed him. It has to be me. She can't do it. I won't put her in that position again.

I look round the room. There's nothing I can use. Potpourri has never killed anyone, to my knowledge, and the bowl it's in is plastic. The sheets, for strangulation? Possible. But I'd have to make some kind of crazy slip-knot lasso. Plan C, or X, maybe. Pillow, for suffocation. But how would I get him in a position where… Oh. Well. That's possible, I suppose. Plan Z, perhaps.

There must be something, there must be—

The key turns in the lock. The Captor sticks his head round the door. His eyes seem softer than they did earlier. Maybe he's got over being called a child murderer. Or his disappointment at not being one. I don't know. I don't know anything about him except his vileness.

'I thought you might want some coffee,' he says, holding out a mug.

And bingo. There we have it. The mug is ceramic. Smashable ceramic.

THIRTY-SIX

As I TAKE the mug from him our hands touch.

There's a frisson, like an electric shock in my spine.
I jerk my hand back. The mug slips from our grasp, towards the floor. His hand darts out to catch it. Good
reflexes.

'Careful,' he says. 'You don't want coffee spilling
everywhere!'

He looks at me like that is supposed to mean something.

'Sorry,' I say.

We try again. I take the mug. I'm careful to avoid
touching his hand. I don't understand that frisson. It
was like a physical connection, as if…

As if nothing. Excitement, that's all. Excitement that
he's handing me the tool for his own death.

I expect him to go again, to leave me to drink it in
peace, but he lingers at the doorway.

'Go on, then,' he says. 'Drink up.'

I look down into the mug. It will contain some drug,
some doping agent, I know it will.

'I'll save it for later,' I say. 'I like my coffee cold.'

He raises an eyebrow at me. He doesn't go away. Instead, he leans against the door frame.

'I'll wait,' he says.

So. There must definitely be something in the coffee. Otherwise, why so adamant? And if he stays, he'll take the cup back with him too, won't he?

Maybe I can placate him. Maybe I can drink half now, pretend I'll drink the other half later.

I take a sip. It's hot and sweet. Is there an undertone of something else? Something noxious? Something that will see me wake up tomorrow morning, sore, in tangled sheets?

'It's too hot,' I try again.

He shrugs. 'As I said, I'll wait.'

Damn. I take another sip. It tastes good. It would taste better with a cupcake. I have a sudden yearning for that melting of buttercream in my mouth, the breaking away of moist yellow crumbs, the satisfying licking of the blue and red patterned cake liner. I think of the 'hundreds and thousands' or brown and white crumbled Oreos, or little silver balls I could put on top. Running my hands through them beforehand in their little jars, feeling their texture in my fingers. Smelling the sweet luxuriousness of the sugar. Or perhaps the citrus scent of some candied orange peel.

I realise my eyes are shut. I open them to the stale beige room. And the empty whiteness of the mug.

I've drunk all the coffee.

'Finished?' he asks.

'There are still some dregs,' I lie. I clutch the mug to me, like I'm enjoying its warmth. Which I am. But that's not the point.

He doesn't inspect the mug. He inspects me, though. He looks me up and down. Like he's trying to sense something. Some change. Some sudden bedability. Extra vulnerability.

I keep my poker face. Or at least, I think I do. But maybe I've betrayed something. Because there's a slight upward turn of his mouth.

'Sleep well,' he says. Which is odd. Because it's not night (I don't think). And caffeine isn't renowned for its sleep inducing properties.

But, of course, that wasn't just coffee. My soppy reverie about the world of senses outside this room has done for me; whatever was in that drink, I'm going to succumb. Let's just hope I'm not going to sleep like the dead. That my potential murder weapon contained a murderous brew. Why, though, would someone like him waste that brutal strength, by drugging me to death? No. There must be something else. Something I'll find out to my cost.

I feel a chill spread over me. I want him gone. I feign a yawn. He smiles again, then he leaves. I'm alone. Alone with whatever now awaits me. But at least I have the mug.

THIRTY-SEVEN

The other side of the door

I HOPE IT WORKS, this stuff. It's new. A new contingent, anyway. I've upped the dosage a bit. Not overdosed. That would be dangerous. And that's not what I want. I want her to be safe, well, happy. With me. It was a bit brazen, I know, with the coffee. Even though the act itself—imagine it almost spilling, the surreal romance of that!—might trigger some recollection. I have no choice but to be brazen now. I might be running out of time. Because of him. And then where would all my plans be? He keeps telling me what he needs. 'I need this from you, otherwise the next knock at the door will be the police.' 'Think of the money as a reverse ransom, mate.' 'I'm going to need you to give me everything.'

What he needs is a hole in the head.

Huh.

It's a new thought. One I haven't had before.

Could I?

Or is that too many moving parts?

What with Cara, then Suze—do I really want to add that to my list of misdeeds?

Not that Cara and Suze are misdeeds. I can't be held responsible. All I've ever done is try to help. He should know that. He should understand. Perhaps I haven't been clear enough with him. Perhaps there'd be more clarity if I held a gun to his head.

I could get one. A gun. The same part of the Net I had to go to for Suze's special brew. In fact, maybe I should have got one before. As soon as I knew he knew where we're hiding. He thinks he has a right to meddle with me. That the law is—broadly—on his side. That he's smarter than me. So he has this bubble protecting him. Or thinks he does.

Perhaps I need to burst that bubble. Forcibly. Because that's what he's trying to do to me, after all. Burst my bubble. Take everything away. And now he knows where we are, now that Alice person told him, there's nothing stopping him, is there?

And a gun. A gun would do that bursting. He'd back off, then, wouldn't he? Take his malicious little threats and messages back where they came from. Call off the pet policeman or private detective or law books whatever it is that he's got at his disposal.

And if he doesn't...well, I could pull the trigger. I could buy a silencer. Shoot him in the middle of the night. Bury him in the woods. It's the right place, out there. Fitting, really, when you think about it. He might appreciate it, if he knew.

It would complicate things, of course. And I'd have to do it right. Be slick. Forensic. Make sure I don't leave a trace.

Maybe this is all a fantasy. Maybe I'd never pull the trigger.

But it would be handy, wouldn't it? A gun in the

house. I don't know why I didn't think of it before. That way, if what I'm trying with Suze doesn't work… Well, it's another route. Not my desired one. But it's better than the alternative. Because I made a promise, didn't I? A promise I intend to keep. Even if it means an end to all of us.

THIRTY-EIGHT

I WILL NOT SUCCUMB. I will not succumb. Whatever this is, I will not succumb.

Think thoughts. Paul. The kitchen. The white oak dresser. The rhododendron bush outside the kitchen window. Cara's rosebud lips. Keep them safe in your mind. Whatever he's given you, don't go there. Don't go to that dark unknown place.

Resist. Think of the future. Cara passing her GCSEs. Cara giggling over one permitted glass of celebratory champagne. Her cheeks will flush slightly. She'll rake one hand through her hair, parting it with her fingers, flipping it over the other side. Like it makes her look grown up. But really it will just show in a beautiful wannabe gesture her enthusiasm for life, continuance, happiness. Think how you'll give her that, the happiness. She can still have it. Driving lessons, house parties, university, a wedding. Oh, she'll look so beautiful in a wedding dress. No veil though. I will not have her behind a veil. Who could pull a cover over that glorious face? And perhaps she'll have her own children. A beautiful gurgling little mini-Cara, so small, so precious, so we can once again watch her grow. For me, once again. Not for Paul, obviously.

But even before that wonderful, wonderful future—

which no Captor, whatever he's made me drink, whatever he's made her do, can take away from us—even before that there will be so much joy. Setting foot outside with Cara, even if we're both soaked in Captor blood. Hugging Paul, my Paul. The three of us, together. We'll cry beautiful tears of relief and joy that it's through, it's all over, we can carry on. Paul will take us home. I'll sink into the soft grey cashmere throw on our beautiful double bed. Cara will collapse with happy exhaustion onto her own bed. Paul will join me on our bed and we'll lie together side by side, staring upwards, knowing we are all safe. Paul will take us for a deliciously casual pub lunch the next day. We'll briefly help the police with their inquiries, then Paul will say, 'Surprise!' And from his pocket, he'll pull out tickets for a world tour. Everywhere we've ever wanted to go: Florida, Vietnam, the Seychelles. Think of those blue skies, the sandy beaches, the sounds of waves, of life. Of Cara laughing as she runs into the sea, turning her face back to us. Oh, how lean and gorgeous she'll look in her swimsuit. Oh, how handsome Paul will look in his trunks. Imagine being able to run a hand through that matted chest hair, the firm but not formidable torso. To feel that Paul pink skin. To know he's there, always. To know that after a swim in the sea, we can all three of us head back carefree to a café, have a cheeky beer while the salty water dries on our skin in the sun. Maybe Cara can even play her flute to the waves. Oh, I can see you there, Cara! I can see the blue and white halter straps of your swimsuit! I can see you, Paul, as you smirk and laugh beneath your shades!

I can see all this. I can have all this.

Don't cry, don't cry. Be strong. It's out there—the world, your family. Keep planning, keep dreaming, don't let this man bring you down. This man, with his bloodied bathrooms, his strange foods, his obvious lust. With his horrible awful temerity and cheek to bring us here. And why? Why? He wants me for sure. But why so coy? Why us? Who possibly has been lurking out there, so keen and eager to decimate our happy family existence, then, once he has us, so backwards with us? Just little flashes of desire here and there, danger lurking beneath. But then otherwise to keep us trapped here, like two pedigree goldfish, in our tanks, longing for air.

I'll kill him. I'll not succumb. I'll kill him, then I'll find out who he is. I'll turn this place over and over until I find out every last thing about this horrible sordid man who would take my Cara from me.

THIRTY-NINE

The other side of the door

I WISH YOU could get bedroom doors with little grilles in them. That like a state jailor, I could just look through and check for progress. But instead I'll have to go in. I'll have to check.

So I do. And, as I open the door, I immediately wish I hadn't.

Because when I go into Suze's room, she is standing in the middle of it, crying. Wringing her hands together and crying. Her eyes are shut, but her lips are open. She's mouthing something. A prayer? I don't know. But whatever it is, it's not pretty. It doesn't end in a big hug for me.

I start to retreat. She didn't notice me come in. Maybe she won't notice me leave. I take a step backwards. I misjudge it. My boot collides with the door-jamb. Thud.

Suze's eyes flash open.

I see her see me.

And I almost recoil.

There is no warmth in her eyes. They are cold and blue. They remind me of those horror-film staring eyes plastic dolls have; eyelids flapping open to reveal a sinister empty stare. Cara had one of those dolls with her, I remember, years ago, the time I bumped into the two of them. I remember thinking that I would buy her something so much nicer, more comforting, if I had the chance.

Suze glares at me. 'I'm still awake,' she says.

'You're not', I want to scream. 'You're asleep. You've been sleepwalking, dreaming away, ever since I did what I had to do'. I want to shake her, slap her, make her see me and appreciate me with real eyes.

But that's not the plan.

So instead I just say, 'I can see that.' I want to leave. I can't stand the hate radiating towards me. But I should say something positive, something loving. Something that may, somewhere in her brain, move us forward. 'Try to get some rest, though, hey, Suze?'

As soon as the word is out of my mouth, I wish I could take it back.

FORTY

'Suze.' It's slightly drawled. He hasn't called me that before, has he? Or maybe he has, and I somehow haven't spotted it. Because there's a familiarity to it. Not difficult to become confused in here. There's an easiness to the way he says it, like he's been trying it out to himself for years. Which I'd guess he has, as some masturbatory thrill before he turns out the light each night. But if that's right, he must have known me somehow, right? To use my name like that? Otherwise, why pick me? Us?

And that's what I mean about the familiarity. It's not just that it seems familiar to him. It seems familiar to me. I feel like I've heard my name said that way before. Before we came in here. That particular intonation. The lilt. Perhaps it's just déjà vu. Perhaps the tiredness and anxiety are making me see memories where there are none.

Or perhaps I do know him? Or have at least encountered him before?

I think back over the men. Surely there haven't been that many? Surely I'm not that much of a slut that I wouldn't recognise a man I'd romanced, who'd romanced me, at such close quarters? OK, so I'm no saint—there were a couple of randomers in nightclubs, way back when. And I'm pretty sure they were as drunk as I was; they wouldn't recognise me without their beer goggles, up in the realities of daylight. All the serious ones—Andy, Callum, Joe and, of course, Cara's biological father, Craig—they wouldn't have changed so much as to be unrecognisable. Would they? We're not into James Bond super-villain territory here, of face transplants and plastic surgery to be able to pass undetected, surely?

Then it must be someone more casual. Just a passing acquaintance. Some dad outside the school gates—no, come on, a dad couldn't behave in this way, separating a woman from her child! Some husband of a client then? Or just a postman, a bank manager, a taxi driver? One of these myriad men we come up against every day. Did I randomly flirt with any of them, let them know my name? Did I go for a quick coffee with someone I've long forgotten, but who has remembered me ever since?

Or perhaps Cara's the link? Perhaps someone I know through her? Some chatty teaching assistant from when she was at primary school? One of those kids' club coordinators? The boyfriend of a Brown Owl? God, you meet so many people over the course of forty-four years! And it just takes one nut-job to covet you and/or your daughter, and you're done for.

Perhaps Cara will have some thoughts? Perhaps if I tell her the Captor is becoming familiar to me, perhaps it will jog some memory in her. Her subconscious may start to work away and she'll sit right up in bed one night—presuming she has a bed through there—and say, 'Of course, it's X!'

It shouldn't matter, of course. Because, whoever he

is, I'm going to kill him. But it does make a difference, somehow, doesn't it? If I'm killing someone I've known, spoken to, had some connection with, I'd like to be aware before I plunge in the dagger. Or, in this case, the piece of mug. There could be a conversation, Cara or I could reason with him. Find out how he ticks. Or perhaps he doesn't deserve that. Perhaps all he deserves is our hate. Because if he had some prior connection, some claim to know us, he would have told us, wouldn't he? Would have used it to try to snake me into bed. Unless he's made himself known to Cara? Perhaps she knows him and wishes she didn't? Perhaps he's some secret internet assignation, a virtual fourteen-year-old boy turned real forty-year-old man.

But then how the 'Suze'? The familiarity? That earlier frisson (because why try to hide it from myself?)?

Is this all just imagined in the name of cowardice? Is the reality I can't bring myself to kill, so this is some imagined excuse, a way to avoid my duty?

No. I can do it. I will write to Cara. Tell her about the mug. But I may as well ask for any thoughts. Just in case. In case it stops the niggling in my mind.

Strictly, it's her turn to write. But, as Mum, it's always my turn, isn't it? Maybe I'm one of those fussy helicopter mothers who—according to headlines—stops their offspring surviving in the real world. A 'non-coper', as the Sunday Times put it. But this is not just offspring; it is Cara. And for her to survive, for either of us to survive, at all in the real world, I need to get her back there. Out of here. With me.

So. I pick up my half-pencil again.

Darling Cara,
I have good news. I've found a weapon. Or rather,
the Captor found it for me. A mug. He brought it
in, laced I assume with some foul chemical that
is going to get me to do things with him.

Does she really want to hear about that? No. I'm sure
she doesn't. But I can't cross it out now. I can't show her
I'm hiding things from her. And I can't waste paper by
starting afresh. However soon I think we're now going
to be out of here, we may be in longer. I can't not talk
to Cara. So, it stays. Besides, I need to warn her.

I hope you aren't accepting any drinks from
him.

It makes it sound like he's plying her with champagne. I don't know, maybe he is. If it's really her who's
his prey.

I know something has already happened (and
don't worry, I won't talk about it, but whatever it
is, you don't want it to happen again).
Anyway, the weapon. A ceramic mug. I need
to find a way to smash it quietly. Then, one day
when he's not expecting it, I will lure him far into
the room and, hands around his neck, I will do the
deed. I will stab him and we can be free.

Do I need to tell her about my hands around his
neck? That I itch to touch him, I don't know why? I

will leave out that I think I may kiss him first. I don't
know why these nasty little thoughts keep coming to
me. The fact is, though, he doesn't make me as physically sick as he used to. Here we go, then:

> Silly question, but you don't see anything fa-
> miliar about him do you? The Captor? No reason,
> really. Let's just say I'm playing police officer.
> If—when, don't worry, when—I kill him, I want
> to know I'm clear of some motive towards a pre-
> vious acquaintance. That it's just self-defence, a
> necessity to escape. You'd tell me, wouldn't you,
> if you recognised him? Or even knew him. I won't
> be angry. I could never be angry with you.
>
> Just tell me, then the way is clear. And so is
> our way out.
>
> All the love in the world,
> Mum xxx

So there. Now she will either tell me or not. I push
the letter through the grate.

All I can do now is wait.

I walk over to the bed and lie down. I can't face
staring at the same beige ceiling any more, so I shut
my eyes. Paul and Cara fill my brain. Our house. Our
car. Our life. Then the tears fill my eyes. What must
I look like now? I haven't seen myself since the mirror went. Perhaps I am unrecognisable. Perhaps Paul
would walk in here with the police then turn round to
them angrily and bark, 'You told me this was my wife!
This is not my wife—look at her!' Because how faded

I must be. How purple my eyelids. How bitten my lips. But maybe, when I see him, he'll just kiss me. He'll know it's me. He'll know that where it counts, I haven't changed. I'm still me. If he just breaks away the layers that hold me captive here, we'll have a fresh new life outside, the three of us.

So away with the tears. Let the eyes rest. Let there be peace. Let me sleep.

Lips, pressing mine. The man has no face, just lips. I know them. I've felt them before. I take my clothes off, all my clothes, because I want more than the lips. But no, suddenly, they're horrible to me. And the lips are mine now—my own lips have gone. And I don't want them on my face, so I tear at them, I tear at them. No! No! No! 'But it's OK,' say the lips—they are in mid-air now, floating, a Cheshire cat of calm. 'It's OK, kiss me, kiss me. You know you want to.' 'But there's something I have to do! It's important!' I tell the lips. 'Kiss me, kiss me. It's what you want to do,' they say. 'Who are you, mystery lips?' I ask them. 'Who are you? Who are you?' 'It doesn't matter. Just kiss me, Suze, Suze, Suze.' And we do, we kiss, we kiss, and we…

My eyelids flutter open.

Guilt.

Horror.

Bliss.

Because in the dream, I know him. I know the Captor. I still don't know who he is, objectively, but there's this sense of knowledge in the dream, so that in the dream world I don't even need to question who he is.

And, because it is only a dream, it cannot hurt me. I

will drift back there for a while. I can allow myself to enjoy it, can't I? Even if it's immoral for what has gone before and will come next. Let time stop, just for a moment. And who knows. I might even learn something. The thing. The identity.

FORTY-ONE

Dear Mum,

OK, I have a confession to make. Please don't be mad. But I need to tell you.

It's not like I know the Captor. I get what you mean. There is something weirdly familiar about him. But I can't help you with who he is. It's the sort of face you always see around, so much that it becomes part of your daily life, but you can't isolate it enough to identify it.

So it's as much a mystery to me as it is to you.

But I have to confess something else. Something that may be relevant, if you're playing the police person here. Where I was that afternoon.

I was with a guy.

I know I said this was meant to be a confession. But I don't want to tell you who.

You'll be mad by the end of the story. And I don't want you to go looking for him (if we get out of here). But he was safe. I met him online at first—he liked some pictures of my designs on Pinterest (you know that scrunchy gauze and silk skirt, the jade one—well, that). Don't worry, he's not some kind of forty-year-old loser (no offence on the age). Though he did bring his dad with him when we first met up. Just in case I was a forty-year-old loser, I guess! But he was cool. My age. I hung out with him a bit. And we started going out. I went over to his dad's place a couple of times. Not to see Alice, like I said. Sorry. And that afternoon, we knew his dad would be out, so… Well, it was only English that afternoon. And I've read 'To Kill a Mockingbird' like so many times—I know how the story goes. I figured I could survive one afternoon without discussing its themes. Again.

So, yeah.

That's me.

It was a nice afternoon. The right place to be but, obviously, the wrong place to be.

Because if I hadn't been there, I wouldn't be here. I guess. Unless the Captor is some pervy stalker (actually we know he's that) who was following me wherever I went. Only a coincidence.

But I just wanted to tell you because it sounds like you're struggling through there. It's tough, right, being alone like this? You begin to think all sorts of things. Crazy things. Your thoughts kind of slide. Interruptions from nowhere. No one to talk to except the bastard who brought you here. Or yourself (but really, don't go there). So I wanted to give you something. And to show you I trust you, Mum. I trust you enough to tell you things. And that you will do the right thing by us. When we get out of here, we're going to have such an amazing time.

And my boy, he's really sweet, you know. So maybe, if he's waiting for me, I'll introduce you one day. If you're going to be cool about it. In fact, he's probably helping the police even now. My knight in shining armour. Except the armour—actually, no, let's not go there. Sorry. Really wish I had a rubber. Eraser. Anyway...

But basically, I love you, Mum. So stay strong. Don't worry about who the Captor is.

Just get us out of here. Use the mug. Smash it, as you say. Then stick it in his filthy throat.

Cara xxx

OH THE LIFE my daughter is living! She shouldn't be meeting people from the internet. How do teenagers still convince themselves they should do that? He could have been anyone! My brow sweats, my hands become clammy. It could still be that he is anyone. What teenage boy asks his dad to come along for moral support? Either a loser or someone whose dad has suspicious intent—'You've got a nice new young girlfriend, you say? Nah, you can't be sure, son. Let me come along and inspect her.' Grooming her on behalf of the father? Could any father really be that depraved? Convincing his son to meet a girl online—'Come on, son, all the grown-ups are doing internet dating, let's make a man out of you'—so that he can take the spoils? Admire those young firm legs, the proud yet chaste flaunting of the newly acquired curves, the short school skirts, the glowing skin, the 'come hither' eyes that don't yet quite understand what they invite. A lift home, maybe, in dad's car? A friendly hand on the thigh—'Call me Jim'—each time a little bit higher? Then maybe an 'accidental' arm across the breast as he reaches across her to open the door? Hot breath on her neck? Desire in his heart, in his crotch, in his hand, later that night?

Little black dots before my eyes. The world spinning slightly. My legs shaky.

Come on, Suze. Calm down. Breathe. I sit on the edge of the bed. You're overreacting. 'My boy is nice.' Cara is no fool. She knows what's genuine from what's not. Think of the banter she will have had with this guy online. Cutesy flirting. The sweet shyness of meeting up face to face. A fellow innocent in this boy, not a yob on the payroll of his dad. A lovely, happy time. Perhaps not even a full adult encounter in his room when they were supposed to be at school. Just some of the other stuff—second and third base, if they still call it that. I remember the gossipy chats at school. The girls with boyfriends would sit on the window ledge of the big bay windows before class started, and the rest of us would try to coax out of them news of how far they'd gone with their boyfriends. They desperately pretended to want to hide the information. Then they'd snap, whisper it to a chosen confidante (never me). The teacher would come into the room and so the rest of us would drift away, not knowing, only suspecting an intimacy we felt bound never to achieve.

So—good on my daughter. One of the cool girls. What I would hope for. Sacrifice an afternoon at school for a real-life experience. I can't condone it to her when I write back, of course not. That would be liberal parenting gone too far. And, of course, with a girl, there's always the pregnancy worry. But I have an inner smile, even an inner hug, at the thought of her enjoyment. It counterbalances the outer frown.

Can it really just be a coincidence though? That her afternoon of indulgence was the same afternoon that we were kidnapped? Someone must have known where she was going, otherwise they would have waited outside the school for her as usual. It can't be, even on my most paranoid theory, that the dad of this 'nice boy' was the Captor, because she would recognise him. Would the dad have boasted to someone else about what his son was up to? Someone who takes a prurient interest in the not-quite-sex lives of not-quite-legal girls?

But then where do I come in? How the familiarity of the 'Suze'?

I throw the letter down on the bed and clutch my temples. This is mad. I'm sliding, like she says. Like my fifteen-year-old daughter has to tell me. Why did I think I could be a good mother? Why did I think I could be strong enough for both of us? Oh, how I love her for her resilience, her empathy, her knowledge of just how I am feeling! Even when she was little, she could do that. When she was three, and my dad died, I remember her little hand in mine at the funeral. I looked down at her. She gazed up and said, 'Not sad, Mummy.' 'OK,' I replied. 'Not sad.' I was still sad, of course. I feel now like I've always been sad. But, at the same time, happy. Happy beyond limit to have produced such a treasure.

I need to get out of this room. Just for a few minutes. The walls, I'm sure, have shrunk, squashing my brain. There is no mental space left. The corridor and bathroom seem suddenly welcoming.

I bang on the door to summon the Captor. I'll endure an unnecessary toilet trip just for the mini-escape, a quest for logical clarity. He arrives, swiftly. Another opportunity to stare at him, figure him out.

But this time it's the corridor that attracts my attention. Not just the space. In fact, it too seems small. Compressed and narrow. Yet also unreal. That horrible sense of déjà vu you get when you're tired. Exhausted. It's like there's two of me walking along here. One woman who has been here before, at this very moment, which gives a calmness. Then another woman who is trapped here, can't wait to escape. Who feels unease at the sudden mismatch of sense versus reality. It's the same in the bathroom. I have sudden images of horror. I see myself, in the bath, naked. It's like that moment in 'The Shining' when suddenly there's an old woman in the bath, with no explanation, just everything inexplicably shifts. I shake my head and the image is gone. There are just the two of us in the shower room again.

I do what I need to do to convince the Captor the trip was genuine. Then I meekly let him take me back to the room and lock me in. Whoever he is, wherever I am, I'm a prisoner again.

I sit down on the bed, shaken. The walls haven't expanded any in my absence. If I don't act soon they will crush my mind entirely.

Cara's right. I need just to focus on getting us out of here.

That's what I need to do. That's what I'm going to tell her I'm doing.

But I'm going to find out. About the mystery of him. I want to find out. Before his throat is slit.

FORTY-TWO

The other side of the door

HALFWAY DOWN THE soft drinks aisle, I abandon my trolley.

I shouldn't have come. I shouldn't have left the house. I should have got Tesco to deliver. Or maybe Ocado; my soul could do with a lift.

But I was cracking in there. Spoiling things. 'Suze'. It's fine for her to be that in your own private world, but you'd vowed not to use that. Vowed to stick to Susan. Stupid, stupid, stupid.

And the nostalgia beat me. I wanted to be where we first met. All of us.

Years ago, it was. I was at the supermarket, getting my weekly shop, in the days when everyone still went out and did that. I'd got one of those trolleys that you can't control, wheels all skewed. No wonder they end up in canals, along with all the boots and dead bodies, detritus that no one else wants. Anyway, I ran my trolley straight into theirs.

I hadn't noticed them before the collision. I don't know how; two blonde beauties should have attracted anyone's attention. Everyone's attention. But, when we collided, her coffee spilled, and my world stopped.

Susan—as I later found her out to be, through enquiries—looked up with a scowl on her face. But then she felt the connection. I know she did. The look changed when she saw me. It was the look of someone who likes what they see. I saw her clock the muscles, the stubble, the good hair. Yes, I'm sorry, it's vain, but I'm attractive to women. Why lie? And I was even more attractive back then.

I told her I'd get her a fresh coffee to apologise. She shook her head—regretfully?—and inclined a gesture to the girl. Of course. Tricky to go on a date when you've got your kid in tow. But I wouldn't have minded. They were both so lovely. And it would have been a date. Because I was entranced already. And, of course, she was too. Even if she couldn't admit it at the time.

And I've been entranced all these years.

For all the good it does me.

But this nostalgia is self-indulgent.

I pull up my hoodie. I want to hide from myself. From the lapse in responsibility I've made in coming here, when I should be at the house, guarding my precious goods. I move into a sprint in the car park, onto the main road. I didn't even bring the car with me, that's how serious I was about actually buying anything. And I thought, to the extent I was actually thinking at all, that if I left the car, went out the back way, he wouldn't notice. If he's still out there.

Because I don't want a confrontation just yet. I've got a gun burning a hole in my pocket. They escalate, scenes with him. Over-provoked, I could pull it out. Mocked, I could fire it. I could justify myself to him.

Show my authority. My manhood. My right to have those Suze and Cara rooms inside. And he would go away permanently. Peace. Imagine that. Peace.

My run has slowed. I pick up the pace again until I'm at the back gate. Just before I slide in, I notice the girl.

FORTY-THREE

ALICE KNOWS SHE shouldn't go back. It's too dangerous. Who does she think she is, some kind of 'Harriet the Spy' character? She should at least have tipped off the police, or left a note for her mum and dad. So they would know where to find her if she doesn't return.

Mr Belvoir would know where to look. But he probably would never know she'd gone. Or if he did, he might not bother to tell anyone. For all his questions, he seems to be taking a very laid-back approach to this. She's not sure about his motives. If he genuinely wanted to help, he would have snatched that horrible man and dragged him to the police. He should be bold, like she's about to be. Is she?

It wasn't enough, showing Mr Belvoir where she thought the man would be. Where Cara had taken her. She needs to do more. At least, she thought she did. Now that it's almost dusk and she's there, across the road from that place, she thinks she might have been mistaken. This is real. Inside there, there are real things going on. Things that are not right. Things that Cara wouldn't want. And because it's real, there is real danger.

Because he is evil, isn't he? He has to be.

She could just go home.

But she owes it to Cara. Because like her own mum said, how can she ever think of herself as Cara's best friend if she doesn't do what she can to help?

So she crosses the road, takes a deep breath, and rings the doorbell.

And waits.

Let him answer the door, let her say who she is, let her shame him into confessing. Stay outside at all times.

Or just run. Now.

But she forces herself to wait a little longer.

With an unwilling finger, rings the bell again.

Nothing.

Such a disappointing relief.

Although, yes, there is something. From inside.

It's the sound of screaming.

And Alice runs.

As she runs, she thinks she sees a man. Through the back gate.

But she keeps running.

She runs until she's all the way home, up the stairs, and on her bed. Knees tight to her chest, she waits for the hammering of her heart to die down.

Cara, I love you, she thinks. But there are some things you can't expect me to do. This must be left to Mr Belvoir.

FORTY-FOUR

'GET DOWN FROM that window!'

His voice. Loud. I flinch. I didn't even know he was in the room. If I had, I wouldn't be up here. Wouldn't be shouting out. Shouting and waving. But I couldn't help myself. She was just there, looking up. A little girl. Not the skipping one. A different one.

Slowly, I turn.

And then I flinch again.

Because he's waving a gun.

I press my back firmly against the wall. And stay where I am.

He waves the gun again.

'Get down from that window!'

He's shouting. His face is red. He's still wearing his outside coat. Hurried in from somewhere, eager to kill me.

I'm stuck to the spot.

'Move!' he says.

I can't. All I can see is death pointing at me. Death from a man I know but don't know.

He can move though. He is coming towards me. Gun still in his hand. He seizes my wrist and pulls me down so that I'm sitting in my ladder chair.

'What were you doing?' he asks me.

I just sit and stare. The gun and the face. Foreign objects, yet one familiar.

He sighs loudly. Then he starts looking up at the window.

He'll see my sign, the cupcake, maybe even skipping girl, if she's there now!

I shoot up onto my legs.

'Nothing. I was doing nothing. Just looking at the outside.'

But he can't believe me. Because he's pulled himself up with his gun-free hand to see the window ledge. Upper body strength that I just don't have.

I try to pull him down.

'There's nothing to see,' I say. Too wildly. Too desperately.

The gun waves at me.

I sink back down.

'What's this?' He's seen it. 'Some kind of—Jesus, it's a sign!'

He's back down at my level now. Reading the sign on all those little bits of paper. Shaking his head. Gun casually cocked in one hand. Perhaps I could…

No. He's looking up at me again. Fully alert.

'Suze, this is crazy. Why can't you see how ridiculous this is? Christ, if you would just grasp—'

He stops himself. Was he going to say more? But no. He's at the windowsill again. He has the cupcake. It's covered in mould.

Again with the head-shaking.

'Suze, I need you to stay away from the window.'

'No one's there,' I say. Has he seen the skipping girl?

Please let him not have seen the girl. What will he do to her? My one other chance of escape. Should the kill, somehow, not come off.

'Don't lie to me, Suze.'

I slump down in the chair. Unless Paul comes charging in with a ransom or a police sniper, Cara and I are on our own. And I don't hold out much hope for the cavalry. They say the first twenty-four hours is the most important for a find. After that, you tend to be looking for a body. Two bodies. Our time is more than up.

He kneels down in front of me. I see him try to iron out his frown. It's replaced with what I suppose is a kind of smile. Grim, like the gun.

'You're going to stay away from that window now, aren't you, Suze? For everyone's benefit, hey?'

Everyone. Cara.

Mustn't antagonise him.

'I know you, Suze.'

Do you? How, how, how?

'I know you don't want me to use this gun.'

True. Hardly a personal insight though. Hardly substance for a claim to know my innermost thoughts.

He leans in towards me. The gun against my breast. His mouth against my ear. He speaks, low and soft. I feel the hot breath before I hear the words. My skin creeps and thrills at the same time.

'For Cara. Don't make me use the gun.'

Of course. The Cara card.

He leans back from me. His face close to mine. The gun between us. It could go off now. The end of me. The end of Cara. Would she still exist if I weren't here? The tree falling in the wood with no one to hear it. Soundless, lifeless? Of course not. You're sliding again. Stay focused. Your daughter is on the other side of this wall. Preserve her.

Preserve her, preserve her. We must preserve her. Just as she is today.

Look into his eyes and concentrate.

Not on his eyes. Not on the reflection of myself in them. Nor in the feeling that I've gazed there before.

He looks deeply into my eyes, his moving left to right, searching mine.

'Good,' he says. Silence to him means consent. He stands up and walks away, back towards the door, taking his gun with him. Here, I will be again, with my thoughts and my letters and my hope/despair.

'Wait!' I call.

He turns. Looks at me expectantly.

Wait what?

I clear my throat.

'We knew each other before, didn't we?' I ask.

He leans his head towards me. His lips curve up. 'Yes. Yes, Suze, we did.'

Triumph! Progress! Vindication! Now, don't antagonise him. Take it gently.

'I'm, um, I'm just trying to place exactly…'

He moves towards me again.

We stand facing each other.

He lifts his hand. His gun hand. Very slowly, he traces the barrel of the gun and his index finger along my collarbone. The suggestion is clear. The knowledge was carnal. I want to hate his touch. And I do. There is anger, anger, anger, deep within. But my skin remembers something of this touch. There's nothing alien here. Except the gun. The gun is new.

'You're making me so happy, Suze. Just being here.'

I nod. I understand, maybe.

'You and Cara, you…' He trails off.

The words are replaced by a light kiss on my forehead.

Then on my lips.

So soft.

So soft that I could almost ignore the gun that's still pressed against me.

A man who wants me. Who says he's been with me. But who would also kill me.

Who?

Who?

'Who?'

He smiles and shakes his head. Ruefully?

'It will come, Suze. I know it will. I'm not going to force it. Just take your time.'

And, with that, he leaves the room.

FORTY-FIVE

The other side of the door

A GOOD INVESTMENT, that gun.

Because it's the first time she's shown signs of re-membering. Of some recollection, of who I am.

I hadn't meant to threaten her with it. But then, she wasn't meant to be standing at the window shouting for help. And that sign! God, I should have spotted it long ago. Botched. The whole thing could have been botched because of that.

But yes, the gun. I owe it so much.

Seeing, feeling, Suze's look, when I touched her with the gun. Recollection. Empowered by the power of threatened bullets. And, of course, the other stuff. The stuff that she's been eating and drinking, know-ingly or not, since I started this whole thing. A heady combination.

Soon, now then, we'll be reunited. Properly. Cara, too, can come out of the woodwork. We'll sit down, talk it all through. I knew it could happen. I knew it could. Just a little patience. And the rest. But I mustn't be too meek. The gun has shown me that. Exhibit a bit of the old power. The old force. The old magnetism. That she loved. Loves. Deep inside. And—

Doorbell.

Why now?

What now?

Him?

Well, with the gun, I know what to do about that, don't I? If it is.

Creep up to the spyhole.

Oh shit.

Not him.

Worse.

Her.

Shit, shit, shit.

Not today. Not when I'm so close to the goal.

What to do? Open up?

Hide?

But what then? A return? With more of them? These bloody nosy people? I thought they'd bought my story. I thought they'd leave me alone. But no. They can't keep away. Think they've got an interest. Well, they bloody haven't. It's nothing to do with them. I'll do it all. I'll do it all alone, my way, and I know best. With my gun I am omniscient. Omnipotent.

Oh shit. Look at her, wandering round the outside of the house. Have to go out, invite her in, put a stop to it. She's driven far to get here. From her Home Counties middle-age comfortableness. Hair put up specially. She won't go away without an audience. Have to put the gun away for a moment.

Open the door. Stick my head out.

'Marge, hello there.' Look at her.

'Oh, hello, love!' She sounds surprised. Why surprised? It's my house; why wouldn't I be here? She's the one who turned up.

'I wasn't expecting you,' I say. Pointedly, I hope.

'No, well, you weren't answering the phone, so…'

Yes, you may well trail off. Admission of your nosiness, your temerity, your inappropriateness. Why should I answer the phone? When I know it will be him. Or the PPI robots. Both annoying, one dangerous.

'I just wanted to see. That everything's OK.'

'It's fine,' I say. 'Why wouldn't it be?'

I know why, of course. We both do.

I stand at the threshold of the front door. Arms crossed. Gun, my dear gun, in my pocket.

She'll want to come in though.

Invite her in, to allay suspicion? Or keep her out, to evade the truth?

Not mutually exclusive. Get her in. Hedge.

'Won't you come in, Marge? You'll have driven a long way.'

'Thanks, love.'

Stop calling me your love. There is no love here. Love means trust. It means what I have with Suze. If you trusted me you wouldn't have come.

'So…' she says, once she's in. Does she think that her one syllable will distract me from those roving eyes, scrutinising everything? I look round, seeing it as she sees it. The plain walls, thank God, after I took the photos down. And yes, she can see the mess. The half-empty mugs. The packaging from deliveries cast aside. The crusts of toast, abandoned. Her lips purse in disapproval. And, if we turn to the kitchen—the trays. Oh dear. The trays.

'Sit down there.' I point at the sofa. 'Let me get you some tea.' Whirl into the kitchen. Distract her with activity. Stick the trays into the sink.

'Oh, right, thanks.' She takes off her coat. No, don't do that. I don't mean I want you to stay long enough to get warm, for God's sake. Just to have a mouthful of tea then be off. Look at you, sitting so neatly and prissily. That same blush-pink anorak folded on your lap. Why don't you share its shame on your cheeks? Instead of the unnatural rouge you've applied for your big trip out?

Talking now. Words from your lips. The kettle is boiling, though, so you're obliterated.

'Sorry?' I say, hands cupped behind ears.

'I said, how's everything? How's…'

'Oh, you know. As good as can be expected.'

She nods. Like she knows. Something, everything. Nothing.

'Of course,' she says.

Yes, of course. Everything is obvious, isn't it? To you, in your simple little world, where $2 + 2 = 4$. No complex equations. No codes. Just straightforward cause/effect. Just sorrow, grief, cure. A natural flow. 'Piss off. Just piss off', I want to yell.

'I'll get back to that tea,' I say.

She nods.

Into the kitchen, turn my back. Lean momentarily against the wall. Give me strength. oh gun.

Stand straight again. Tea bag in the mug. No pot for

you. You're not a special enough guest. And it denotes leisure. Time.

Leave the bags in. Take the mugs over. Milk, still in its plastic bottle, alongside.

'There,' I say.

A frown of distaste. Looking at the tea bag.

'Is there something I can use to… ?' She indicates pulling out the tea bag.

I wonder what would happen if I offered her the gun for the purpose. Suggest that she fish it out with the muzzle?

Up again, I get her a spoon. Can't fob off this lady.

'So have you heard… Well, you must have done. But have you had much contact? Everything OK?'

I nod, slowly, seriously. 'From time to time,' I say. 'I think—Well. It's going to be slow, of course. But I think, you know. Getting there.' I duck my head. Give me sympathy. Suspect me not.

She copies my nod. 'Of course.'

What would it take to get her to stop saying that? My hands slide to the gun. There, just separated by the cloth of my trousers. So easy to pull it out. See what powers it will give me this time. But then, another body maybe. The last thing I want. Or next to last. Something bad, anyway.

'I just find it a bit odd,' she's saying. 'Just to go away so soon after it all.'

I shrug. 'Who can predict how people will react?' I say. 'Do you know what you'd do?'

Do you, do you, you bitch? Can you possibly imagine, in your small little world, the width and breadth of

human suffering and emotion? Over the years? Have
you ever been able to understand any of it?

She shakes her head. 'I can't imagine,' she says. No.
Thought not.

Looks into her tea. I slurp mine. It's too hot. I bite
my tongue. Against the pain and the shouting.

'Can I use the bathroom?' she asks, abruptly.

So. She wants to look around, does she? On a mission, yes? That stupid non-emotionally intelligent newt
of a husband sent her to gather facts? I'm surprised she
managed to keep him away. Maybe they agreed she
would be better at this. More sensitive. More likely to
cajole information out of me. Hah.

Can I escort her? Check she doesn't 'forget' where
it is, try to go into rooms that she shouldn't. Locked
rooms that don't concern her.

Let's try.

'Of course,' I say. She's got me doing it now. 'Just
along here.' I stand with her, and begin to walk with her.

She puts a hand gently on my arm. Speaks, quietly.
'I know where the bathroom is, love.'

I nod. Pass a hand over my brow. Feigning forgetful-
ness in the awfulness that she is still trying, but failing,
to imagine (but secretly thinks she can). She gives me
an 'understanding' smile.

Well then. We'll have to chance it. Off she goes.
Along the corridor. Watch her back. Gun slightly out
of pocket. She rounds the corner. I can't see her any
more. Strain to listen. A door opens. Good, not a locked
one then. What's in the bathroom? What will she see?

There's nothing to incriminate me now, is there? Think, think. Chew the lip, it helps the brain. I think I'm OK.

Toilet flushing. Right. Come back in an orderly fashion, then, please, Marge. No wandering off the route. Footsteps coming towards me. Slide the gun back in. Sorry, fella, false alarm.

Here she is, back into view.

What's that she's carrying? A towel, but—why?

'I didn't know which was the guest towel, love. Seemed to be so many of them. All a bit damp.'

Freeze in putting the gun away. Damn Miss Marple. Brought down by the towels? When I'm this close? No. No. No. Should I… The power of the gun… Not yet. Wait. Just downplay it. Try a little laugh.

'Yeah, sorry, washing isn't exactly top of my priorities right now.'

A blush. Finally, a blush.

'Of course. Sorry, love. Look, let me help.' She bustles off back to the bathroom.

Returns with the towels. 'Let me put these in the washing machine.' And she barges over there, into the kitchen, the kitchen with the trays, the washing machine with the—Oh Christ! The clothes! The clothes with the blood!

'Look, just leave it. Just leave it, OK? I'm doing fine. I can manage. Just…you shouldn't have come.'

And I feel the anger. I feel the frustration, the anguish, the stress of what I have in this house. How near success and failure. And I feel the gun. Oh God, I feel it. My hand on my thigh. Ready. Steady.

She stands in the middle of the kitchen. Hands droop with the towels. Lips quiver. Doesn't know what to do.

I should maybe defuse. Hug. Apologise. For what? Not shooting off her nosy little head?

I take a step forward. She takes a step back. Is there something in my eyes maybe? Something that suggests—

The doorbell. Again. Why so popular today?

She opens her mouth. Speaks, in a wavering voice. 'You'd better get that.'

I nod. Sure thing. Why not. What harm could it possibly do? NB Sarcasm.

Can't look through the viewfinder. Can't show I'm hiding from the world. Must just open the door the door brazenly. To find...

Oh Lord. Him.

'Hello,' he says.

And she hears his voice. Recognises the threat in it. She must do. Because she's dropped the towels.

FORTY-SIX

THE DOORBELL AGAIN!

The police. I know this time. I can see them. Right in front of me. As though it were me opening the door. 'We're here about Cara,' they're saying. I'm sure they are. I can hear them. At last, at last.

But then why am I so terrified? Why do I see myself sinking down onto a carpet, one of them trying to catch me. Why am I crying? Wipe away the tears—with a hand that's shaking. Why shaking? Stop it, Susan. Stop it. You're about to be rescued. This is it!

I rush to the door of the room and press my ear against it.

Listen.

A man and the woman.

But wait.

Surely not.

Is it… ?

No. It can't be, can it? Yes, it is. It's him. And, my God, that's her, isn't it! They've found us! They've come with the police to save us!

I shout as loudly as I can. 'Hello! Hello! I'm here! It's Susan! I'm here! Help!'

The voices stop. Where've they gone? Don't leave. I need you to help me.

'Cara, shout too! This is it, they've come to save us!'

Cara hears me—she must, because she shouts too. We both shout and scream at the top of our lungs. But still no one comes to beat the door down.

'Please!'

Still there are no footsteps.

'In here! Get us out!'

Still no sirens.

'Keep shouting, Cara!'

And we do, we do. Because, please God, let us out of here! This horrible, horrible place where we're stuck, trapped, deserted, so apart from the outside world, from light, from love, from happiness. Please get us out. Please let me and Cara and Paul be together again!

So I shout and I shout and I shout. And I shout so loudly that I can't even hear Cara any more, can't hear if the voices are responding, can only hear my screams. The whole world is my voice pleading for escape. I can see in my head a huge great big roof of my mouth, all the pinky-red grooves and ridges raised, and at the back the black hole with engorged tonsils and uvula, tongue flat, just screaming, screaming, screaming.

But not so loud to stop me hearing the gun shot.

Suddenly, I am quiet again.

All is quiet.

It's his gun, is it? Or someone else's? The police's? Are they armed? No, not in this country. Unless they sent the snipers. His, I bet it's his.

Has he… ? Surely, no, please, not!

All quiet except the Captor talking.

So he can't have killed them. Not if he is talking to them.

Unless he is only talking to one of them.

I can't hear what he's saying. I press my ear so hard to the door that you'd think it would melt through to the other side. Mumble, mumble, mumble. Speak up! I grab the cup. The lovely ceramic death cup. And I put it against the door, like they do with glasses in the movies, to try to help me hear. Still it's not clear. Still just indistinct words that I don't understand. And only two voices, those two voices that I know. The police don't seem to be saying anything at all.

Maybe Cara can hear? She is closer.

I scribble a quick note asking her and feed it through the grate.

No response. She doesn't know, you see, who those voices are. Well, she knows one of them. But she doesn't even know the other one exists in relation to her. So how can she worry? That's good. She'll feel safe. Be safe.

Even though I can't hear the words, I keep my ear against the door.

And then there they are—the others again. The Captor hasn't killed them. Thank God. Or thank the Captor. Maybe he is merciful after all.

More talking. More useless words. I daren't shout again. Bullets sound when I shout.

But oh—no, please! Oh, maybe I should have shouted once more. Because that's the sound of the door, isn't it? The front door. Slamming shut.

'Help! Help! Hello! Help us!'

But there's nothing. There's silence. They've gone.

They've somehow gone. Why? How? How can they do
that when they know, they know that we're here! And
what kind of police work is that? How could they not
check every room, every crevice, for Cara? And why
only call about Cara, not about me? I slam my hands
off the walls. Bastards. Bastards, bastards, bastards. I
don't care if it's not their fault. I don't care about the
gun. They should have found a way.

I close my eyes. I take a deep breath. I try to force
down the sickening failure of hope that I can feel like
acid rising in my throat. Swallow down the despair.
Make a meal of the regurgitated sadness and disappointment. Breathe. Just breathe.

Open my eyes.

So.

I'm still here.

We're still here.

It seems, perhaps, that we're doomed still to be here.

I shut my eyes again. It doesn't help.

What will help?

I tear another sheet of paper from the diary.

'I love you, Cara,' I write. Because that's the only
hope-giver, isn't it? In all of this. Life with Cara. I love
my little girl.

And I cry. I cry and I cry and I cry.

Yet part of me smiles.

A dark, wrong part. The recalcitrant rainbow, sun
through the rain. The part that is glad it wasn't the Captor who was shot. The part that is looking forward to
seeing him in here again. Because I know. I know, I
know, I know. That he is someone. Not someone whose

identity I actually, currently, know. But still, a person, known—formerly—by me. Once. And that something inside me is rediscovering him. And that something— well perhaps, perversely, it might quite…not hate him. Completely.

FORTY-SEVEN

The other side of the door

I KNEW THE gun would help me again.

That it would help them understand. Buy me time. Let them have a space to think rather than just react.

When I heard the shouting from along the corridor, I thought that was it. Done for. I was ready to point it at their heads, bang, bang, then at mine, bang, finito.

But the gun, the gun shone through. Some force within it compelled me to raise it immediately. Like it could sense my need. No hesitation, it came bursting with a life surge out of my pocket.

'Listen!' it said. I was its ventriloquist's dummy. My lips moved while the gun made me talk, kept them silent.

'Listen!' And because the gun was there, they did listen. They listened with wide, wild eyes. 'Don't second-guess me. Don't question me. What I'm doing here is completely necessary. It's none of your business, OK? So you think now you're going to be on some rescue mission? Well, hear this: you're not. You understand nothing. Nothing, nothing, nothing.'

They didn't speak at first. The gun helped me check

their hearing. Yes, they heard it click, as I took off its safety catch.

'You wouldn't dare,' he mumbled.

But oh, the gun showed them. That shot. It was beautiful. I loved the way it ricocheted round the room. How it made them duck for cover. Quiver and shake. Good work. Because they understood a little bit then, even with their lack of empathy.

And, when I explained further, told them everything, made them promise on pain of death—not just their own—that they would not summon the police, that they would walk out of here and leave us alone, they listened. They properly listened. It was my words that soaked into them then. The gun gave me the time, the opportunity, of course. Without it, I would be spread-eagled on the floor with the cops on top of me and my capture long gone. They wouldn't have bothered listening otherwise, without the gun; just have said what I was doing was wrong, have rushed past me along the corridor. But when I told them everything, explained it all, they began nodding. Agreeing. Marge's eyes even misting. Of course, she would always side with me in the end. Once she'd been given permission not to react conventionally.

He was more difficult, of course. He thought he could bargain.

And, in fact, it turns out he was right.

The gun may be good. Great, even. Such a crutch to a man who's frankly had enough of all this…shit. But you can't replace logic. Logic knew that if he walked out of this house without the things he wanted, he would still go on wanting them. Logic also knew that if I let the gun have its wicked way with him—boom! Everything would suddenly become a whole lot more complicated. And when already you're struggling to sleep, not knowing whether the next day will be the one when it comes right, to add to that the worry whether that day will be the one you are arrested for murder as well as everything else—I could do without it.

So we made a bargain. And may I rot in hell for it. Because it's against all my judgement, all my internal protestations, all my red lines. But I made it.

Suze for Cara.

Or rather Cara for Suze.

I gave him Cara.

On the basis that I can keep Suze.

Because what choice do we have? It's Suze that I need. Suze who needs me.

As we stood outside Cara's room, I felt the gun had somehow turned traitor. Like it was there, pointing at my head, making me do this unthinkable thing. I unlocked the door. I let her out. The light in his eyes sickened me. And then he took her. I just let him take her. No shouts. No screams. He's driving away now, the car full of Cara.

The house has never felt so empty. It's just me and Suze now. And the gun, of course. I haven't forgotten about the gun. And I doubt Suze has either. I'm assuming I'm still here anyway. Still a person. Still human, still morally functioning. Because you wonder, sometimes, don't you? Or at least I do.

Me, sitting on the sofa. So far as I can tell.

Suze, sitting, standing, who knows what-ing—I should have installed a webcam—in that room.

Empty.

Except not. Everything is so full. My mind. This house. Of thoughts. Of expectations. I'm so close now. I can feel it. Very soon, she'll know. And then we'll be together again. Not this separate life, in separate rooms, in separate beds. I'll have my Suze. And then I'll be able to retire the gun. But not till then.

FORTY-EIGHT

THE DOORBELL KEEPS me awake for hours. Ringing, ringing, ringing. When I try to sleep, it rings again. The police are there. So real I could reach out and touch them. I shut my eyes, put my hands over my ears, but they're still there. It's like tinnitus but with blue flashing lights attached. And each time I see them, I want to stop them speaking and I want to collapse. The fear is so great that I'm almost physically sick.

What is it? What is my subconscious doing? Why am I so frightened of being found that I imagine these saviours as enemies? And why didn't they look round properly earlier? How is this captor so convincing that he can turn the police away? Do I want to find out who he is so much that I would rather the police go away?

There they are again. Ringing and ringing and ringing the bell. I put my pillow over my head to stop them. Then I hear is the rustle of Cara's letters inside the pillowcase. As comforting as a lullaby. If only I could be through the wall with her singing her to sleep. Sing myself to sleep.

Sleeping, waking, sleeping, waking, dreaming, tossing, turning.

Man in supermarket.

Chestnut hair, lovely smiling eyes, dimples. Morphs—

fewer dimples, hair darker now. But still smiling, still happy.

Waking, now. Dreaming? Yes, go back there, mind, please! So nice, so clear.

Man in street, outside.

Man inside.

Waking, waking—no, not yet, not yet, stay…

Fight back—the man, the man, the lovely man. I saw his face so clearly, the Captor's face, of course, but I knew his face, I understood his face, I knew who he was to me.

And then—Christ!

'Good morning, Suze.'

There he is, in actual waking land. Face level with mine.

The face, the dream face, made real.

I could lean forward and I could kiss him.

I move fractionally towards him.

'Tell me,' I whisper. 'Tell me how I know you.'

He keeps his head level with mine. He opens his lips, made for words and kisses.

This is it. He will tell me. I poise myself, ready to know.

Then he stands up. He stands up and he grabs the pillow from under my head. I fall back onto the mattress.

'What the—?' I start.

Is he going to smother me? Is this it? I asked too many questions? I'm going to die? He's going to shoot me through the pillow maybe?

'Laundry day,' he says, loudly. Too loudly? Too abruptly? Or is my brain still fogged with sleep?

And he starts to take off the pillowcase.

The letters.

Oh Christ. The letters. All Cara's letters are in there!

'Don't!' I say, snatching at his hand.

He pulls his hand away. Still too strong for me.

'Why?' he asks.

'I was sleeping, let me sleep!' I protest.

'You won't get back to sleep. You never do.'

There's a chilling knowledge in his words. But there's more of a chill in him reading the letters. My private letters from Cara.

'Pillow fight!' I say. It's ridiculous. Of course it is. But it's the only reason I can think to grab the pillow back.

So I grab it.

But I grab the wrong part.

The pillow itself.

He still has hold of the pillowcase.

The pillow comes out. And, with it, the letters.

All of them, floating to the floor, like paper feathers. Love Cara, Love Cara, Love Cara carpeting the room.

I know what they are, but he doesn't. Yet.

I lean down and begin scooping them up, holding them tight to my bosom.

'My diary!' I exclaim.

He bends down to pick up the paper.

'Why've you torn the pages out of the notebook?' he asks, casually.

Then he passes an eye over one of the pages. The casual air goes. He looks more closely. I snatch the letter out of his hand. He mustn't know about the letters.

He mustn't know about my constant communication with Cara.

'Suze, these are letters, not a diary!' he exclaims.

'I write my diary like letters. You know, "Dear diary".'

I keep the letters clutched to my chest, my eyes lowered, hardly daring to look at him. Please let him have bought it. Silence. I can't read it without seeing him. I raise my eyes.

He is staring at me and at the papers. There's a frown on his face.

'Give them to me, Suze,' he says quietly.

I shake my head. I won't let him have them.

'Suze, the letters, please.'

Again, I shake my head. It's all I have of Cara. He can't take them. 'You'll have to fight me for them.'

He scrunches his face up. Then he produces the gun. 'Really?' he asks. 'You want to fight?'

No. I don't want to fight. I want to sink into the floor with these letters, fan them around me, caress each one. I want him to see me do it; I want him to understand how much they mean to me. Why he shouldn't take them.

'Please,' I beg.

He shakes his head slightly and puts out the palm of his hand to receive the letters, gun still trained on me.

Do I let him shoot me?

Do I let Cara hear the sound of her mother dying?

No. No, that can't be right.

'Why are you doing this?' I ask. 'You know me. We know each other. Why are you making me suffer?'

'Suze,' he says. His voice is low, but there's a hard edge to it. 'This isn't suffering. I know what suffering is for you. I could let you have that. But if you're good, I won't. I'm saving you. Now, the letters, please.'

My skin creeps.

But I must try one more time.

'They're my private papers. My diary. My confessions. My innermost thoughts. You mustn't read them.'

He keeps his hand outstretched, the gun aloft. But he takes a step closer to me. Again, that breath on me. Again, that tension. It's as though the force of it draws the letters away from me, magnetising me. With one final wrench, I separate my daughter from my bosom and I hand her to this man.

'Good girl,' he says. His eyes stay locked in mine for a moment, then he looks down at the letters.

'Don't read them,' I whisper again.

He takes the letters and leaves the room.

As the door closes, I remember. I remember that the letters aren't just about being close with Cara. They aren't just evidence of our communication, which he will now stop. They aren't just an excuse for him to torture Cara to make her surrender the epistles I've sent to her.

They contain the plan. The ceramic plan. The plan to kill him.

Because Cara repeated it to me, didn't she? She said that the plan to kill him with the mug was a good one. So he'll know. He'll read the letters and he'll know. Suddenly, the past few days since I had the mug seem like pure self-indulgence. All that internal whinging about 'Oh, I need to find out who he is before I can kill him.'

Idiot. I just needed to get it done. Look, now, what's happened! I've put him on alert. I've squandered the only remaining chance to free Cara. He'll read that letter, come back, take the mug, and that will be it. If I'm lucky. What if he comes back and kills me, then her, before we can kill him? Yet again, I've put my own indulgence over Cara's needs. Yet again, I've failed at motherhood.

I pace back and forth around the room. Each time I reach a wall it is too soon; I need a longer walk for my thoughts than this cage will allow. But one thought is clear. I must stop him reading the letter with the ceramic plan. If he hasn't already.

And then I must do it. I must just get on and do it. The killing. For Cara. Whoever the hell he is.

FORTY-NINE

The other side of the door

So MANY OF THEM. So many letters. How did I not see this happening? I leaf through them, getting the overall picture before I start in on the detail.

Although there's one key detail that springs out at me.

To Mum. From Cara.

Oh hell.

I put the letters down for a moment.

Just when I thought I was maybe making progress, this has been going on. Right under my nose. It wasn't just the knocking, then. I'm going to have to take action. Bring it to a stop. They're not dated—obviously, I guess, because how do you know dates if you're locked in a room with no way of telling days—but they must go back almost to the start. When I first put my Suze and Cara measures in place.

D'you know, I hardly even want to read them.

I sit staring at them.

What do I do next? Do I go into Cara's room and see if I can find letters from Suze in there?

There's shouting coming from along the corridor. Somebody wants something then. Maybe a postman—

looks like that's what needed. Well, they can wait a little while, for once.

I suppose I ought to read the letters. Find out what I've missed. Arm myself. Then I can figure out how to deal with it.

Are they in any kind of order?

Let's see. This looks like an early one. So pleased to have established communication, etc. Christ, I feel sick. I never should have given Suze the tools. Diary, my arse.

Some more. The business of living. Memories. What it is to be a girl in the world.

Then—Oh. Revelations. Is this about the blood in the bathroom? Such a chaste explanation, no details. But hints. All those hints. I realise I'm holding the letter so tight in my fist that I'm screwing it up. Screwing everything up.

The shouting down the corridor is getting louder. Suze. I should go. She's sounding a bit desperate. Just one more letter, perhaps. Let's see, what does this one… Oh hang on. That's interesting. That's very interesting indeed.

FIFTY

FINALLY, FOOTSTEPS. I've been shouting for weeks, months, years.

Certainly long enough for him to have read all the letters. The letter that matters.

And long enough for me to be prepared. For me to have smashed the mug. To have the fragments ready. Or rather, one fragment. A particularly sharp one. I should warn Cara that now is the time. But how can I? I mustn't knock. I'll arouse suspicion.

And then it's too late to warn Cara. The door opens. He stands there. He's got the gun in his hand. Of course he has. I inhale. This is going be difficult. Dangerous.

'Yes?' he asks. Terse. It's like me, when I've been interrupted mid-bake for something Paul or Cara thinks is important, but just isn't. How could anything be as important as getting the level of a cake exactly right?

Stupid me. Frittering away marriage and motherhood by staring into ovens.

'Come in,' I invite him. After all, this room is my home now. Or rather, dwelling place. It's missing the love of a home.

He comes in.

Both of us just stand there. Me with my hands behind

my back. Perhaps I should have concealed it somewhere better, the murder weapon.

Has he read the letter? Does he know Cara and I want him dead? More than that, that we have a plan?

He's not giving anything away.

'I want to touch you,' I say.

At the same time he says, 'I've been doing some reading.'

I swallow hard. He's read it then?

He takes a step forward.

'Quite the correspondence, between you and Cara,' he says. There's an odd note to his voice. Mocking?

'Never mind about the letters,' I say. Can you tell someone not to mind about their death warrant?

'Come here,' I say, gently. Seductively?

He doesn't move.

'It must be a relief for you, having communication from Cara,' he says.

I nod, because it is.

'Make the days here easier,' he says.

Again, I nod. I don't know where he's going with this. How much he's seen. But I can't disagree.

'And I trust you've been replying to all her letters just as attentively?'

'Of course,' I say.

He nods.

'But look,' I start. 'Don't worry about the letters so much. Just a teenage girl, venting her spleen. You can't read too much into them.'

He raises an eyebrow. Scrunches up his face again.

He doesn't believe me. I don't know what he knows.
But I have to get him over here.

'You'll have read in the letters that we were trying
to figure you out,' I say. I keep my voice light.

He nods.

'You know, what you want from us. Who you are.'

He nods again.

I clear my throat. I'm nervous. I mustn't mess this
up. I clutch the ceramic so hard behind my back that
I can feel it pierce my skin. Good. It's sharp enough.

'Come over here,' I say again. 'If I could just touch
you, feel your skin, I might know. I'm sick of not knowing.'

He looks hard into my eyes. He's trying to read me.
And I'm trying to read how much he has read. If he
takes a step forward, will it be to comply, or to kill?

He moves slowly towards me. He holds chin up
slightly. The move exposes more of his neck.

'Here,' he says.

What is he inviting? Me to touch him? Or try to kill
him, so he can beat me down? Shoot me down.

I move a step closer to him. Tentatively, I raise one
hand up to stroke his face, one hand behind my back.
I feel stubble. Rough, uneven, attractive. Its traction
against my skin makes my fingers tingle.

'Well?' he asks.

I shake my head a little. 'I'm getting something, but
not quite…' I say. I'm not lying.

'Come closer,' he whispers. 'I dare you.'

He knows. He must know. Or doesn't he?

I step closer. This time I place my cheek against his.

I close my eyes momentarily and inhale. What a scent. Wood, cinnamon and manly sweat. My nostrils rejoice. I open my eyes again. None of that.

'And?' he asks.

And I bring the other hand out from behind my back, loop it round his neck, and thrust the ceramic shard as hard into his skin as I can.

He pushes back from me, falling away from me.

'What the… ?' He has one hand to his throat. He takes it away and examines it. Blood.

'Suze, bloody hell, what are you doing?'

So he hadn't read the letter.

I lunge at him again with the ceramic shard, but, as I do, I see something between us. The gun. On the floor. He must have dropped it in surprise. He sees me see it. Both of us reach down to get it. I feel like I'm in a film. We grab at it. I kick it out of his grasp. He dives towards it, over the top of me. It's like a lethal game of Twister. For once, my size, my comparative litheness helps me; I slide fully under his legs then out the other side. Then I have it. I have the gun. And I dart back from the floor, training the gun on him, finger on the trigger. Ready, one two three, sque—

'Suze, stop! For goodness' sake—I'm your husband! It's me. I'm your husband. I'm Paul!'

FIFTY-ONE

THE WORLD SHIFTS.

I freeze.

'What?' I ask.

'It's me, Suze. It's Paul.'

All I can do is stare. I feel like there's a seesaw in my head. It's tipping between infinite glee and complete confusing despair.

How can he be Paul?

I laugh. Or rather, I do a laugh. There's no merriment in my larynx. Perhaps the noise will drown out the sound of bells ringing deep within my mind.

'Very funny,' I say. 'Pretty desperate attempt to avoid getting shot, isn't it?'

But the gun is limp in my hand.

'Paul' edges towards me. He puts his hand on the gun to take it. I start to let him. Then I seize it back.

'No! I… I don't understand. You're not Paul. Paul is…'

I try to explain what Paul is. That he is what this man isn't. But the two men slide together, two fuzzy images from disparate parts of my brain suddenly making one clear picture.

'How can you be Paul?' I shake my head and I keep shaking it. I don't believe him. It's not possible! How would I not recognise my husband? But I do believe him. Which still doesn't make this possible.

I'm still holding the gun, pointing it at the floor.

This apparent husband moves towards me again. Again, he tries to take the gun but I keep hold of it. It's so reassuringly solid in my hand. Alleged Paul stops trying to take the gun and instead, very slowly, propels me over to the bed and sits me down.

'I won't believe you!' I say. Even though now his Paul-ness is starting to flood back. His familiarity is explained. The draw towards him clear.

But I hate him. Why do I hate him? How have I not recognised him? What am I doing in this room? Why, how, what? Why, how, what?

I start to cry. And shake. I cry and I shake and I cry. He puts an arm round me to comfort me and I let him be there for a moment, then push him away. I retreat to the furthest end of the bed.

'No,' I say, shaking my head again. 'No. It can't be true. You've been drugging me, making me susceptible. It's a trick. I've seen the films. You're lying to me, taking advantage. Why wouldn't you have told me before? Soon you'll bring out photoshopped wedding pictures and claim they're real.' I try to inject some passion into my voice. But everything feels dull. Remote. Hunched at the end of the bed, I train the gun on him.

He is crying too. Not sobs. Just tears, leaking from the edges of his eyes.

'Yes, I've been drugging you,' he says.

The seesaw swings to confusing despair again.

'I knew it, I knew it, I knew it,' I say, pretending to myself to prepare to shoot.

'I've been drugging you with venlafaxine and olan-

zapine. For depression and psychosis. From your old
supplies, and online.'

Still I'm shaking my head. Now the rest of me shakes
too. I don't understand. I don't understand.

'After...' he starts. Then he stops. 'A few months
ago, you got pretty unhappy. You had an episode. You
stopped recognising me.'

I'm rocking, now, as well as the shaking. It feels true,
what he says. And he looks like Paul. He feels in my
heart like Paul. I know he is Paul. But how can I trust
what I know? If it were true, it would mean... It would
mean that every day I've been sitting here not knowing
my husband. Thinking separately of Paul. That he is
someone else. And that, for some reason, my husband
has held me captive.

He is talking again.

'I'm sorry, Suze. I'm sorry I had to do this. But, after
what you've been through... And you'd made me promise never to let you go back there again.'

'There?' I ask.

'When you were committed. Fifteen years ago. The
worst experience of your life, you said...so far.' His
voice cracks.

This is unbelievable.

'So...what? You've been "treating" me? You've kept
me imprisoned in this place to stop me going insane?'

The question hangs there.

Stop?

'You're not insane, Suze. Never say insane. You've
had psychotic depression. But I've got you out of it, do
you see? I've saved you!'

'Why the hell wouldn't you tell me who you were? If

you are who you say you are? I don't understand! Why do this for—what is it—days, weeks, months?'

'Weeks. I didn't want to make you worse, I wanted to win you back, make you accept your life. I wouldn't have told you now, when you were so close, starting to recognise me, since I'd upped your medication. But, Suze, you tried to shoot me! I just reacted. I had to tell you. And I guess I'd got your dosage to the point where me telling you was the last piece of the jigsaw.'

He looks at me like his words should mean something that I can understand.

'Suze, you've been at home, with me, this whole time. In the spare room.'

I just… This room, my own house… ?

What do you do? What do you say? Do I…? Well, what?

What, what, what, what?

I shut my eyes. I need to think.

'Go,' I say.

'What?' he asks.

'Leave me. I need to… Just leave, OK?' I open my eyes to look at him. Paul. Paul. Paul. I have an impulse to throw myself into his arms, to hug him, but I don't. Something, everything, is holding me back.

He stands up. Then he sees I have the gun. He puts out a hand for it. I shake my head.

'Suze, I'm not leaving you in here with a gun.'

Oh, I see. Suicide. That's the implication.

'I wouldn't do that to Cara,' I say.

He freezes for a moment.

'Right,' he says.

There's something odd about how he says that.

And, before I know it, he's out of the room. And he's shut the door. Not locked. Just shut.

'Wait!' I cry. Because something isn't right. Something else. Something other than me apparently not knowing that I've been locked in what is allegedly my own home by a man who says he's my husband.

'Paul, come back!' I shout. 'I want to see Cara!'

FIFTY-TWO

'PAUL! PAUL!' I call out. He isn't coming back. I don't understand. Why won't he come back? And I'm panicking, and there are more tears pricking, and I'm standing and running to the door. Because deep down, there's something, something horrible that's starting to well within me. I must see Cara. I must see Cara.

I pull open the door to the corridor. And I see now that it is my corridor in my house. My home. The corridor in which I carefully hung pictures of our family. Of Cara playing the flute, Paul and me on holiday, Cara in one of her designs. Pictures that Paul has now obviously decided to take down. But there's still the skirting board for which I chose the shade of white paint, still the carpet we bought on the cheap from Carpetright. Our own particular beige. I see it now. How could I not see it before? For a moment I'm transfixed.

But only a moment. Because the important thing about this corridor is that leads to Cara's room. Paul is trying to take me in his arms, stop me running. But I push past him. I have to see. I have to go in there. I open the door to Cara's room. Cara, please, Cara, Cara, Cara—

It's empty.

It's empty.

There's no—

There's no anything. There are no posters. No pictures. No pink hearts round photo frames. No sheet music. No customised clothes hanging neatly on the wardrobe.

And no Cara. There's no Cara.

No. It's not true. Cara is in here. She's in here. I saw her!

'What have you done with her?' I scream to Paul. 'What have you done with her?'

'Suze, it's OK. Come on, Suze, it's fine.'

I'm vaguely aware of him continuing with these platitudes, of his arms trying to encircle me, him still holding the gun, and of my brain questioning why she would be writing to me if we haven't in fact been kidnapped, but I push on.

'But she's here,' I shout. 'She's been writing to me—she's here!' I yank the gun from Paul's grasp so he can't do anything to me—because how can I trust him now?—and I go over to where the grate must be. It's behind a chest of drawers. Cara's chest of drawers. She must have had to shift it every time. I push and pull the unit away from the grate. I almost can't see for tears but I'll still do it. I'll still pull it away. And Paul hovering uselessly, uselessly in the background. Finally, I manage it, finally the grate is revealed, and I see…

Oh help me.

I see all my letters. In a pile. Unopened.

This can't mean what it means. It can't, it can't, it can't.

I sink down to the floor and I put my hands to the

letters. And I see in one hand I have the gun, and it's
the only way now because this isn't what I wanted, this
isn't the dream at all, this isn't what I wanted. Where is
Cara? What has he done with Cara? Tell me, brain. Tell
me what is happening. Think, retrace, understand—letters, unopened, no Cara, how, why, what?

Paul, letters, Cara, no Cara; Cara, no Cara.

Oh, but no.

NO.

Stop it, brain! I take it back! I don't want to know!
Oh God. Oh God. Oh God. Spiralling down through
my mind, horrible, horrible recollections, realisations
that she's not here. Why she's not here. Why she's not
anywhere. Go away, memories! Go away, truth! How
do I stop this? How do I make the reality go away? I
can't bear it, I can't bear it, I can't BEAR IT! I raise
the gun, to my head, into my mouth and I gag and I
fumble and Paul, Paul he's on me and he's ripping the
gun away from me and tearing out the bullets, throwing them onto the floor, and I'm sobbing and I'm sobbing and sobbing in his arms and I'm broken now. I'm
broken and I'll never be fixed.

Because she's dead, isn't she? My beautiful, lovely
wonderful wonderful Cara is dead.

FIFTY-THREE

Paul

SUZE LIES PROSTRATE against my arm. I think she's asleep, exhausted from crying. Her eyes are closed. She may just be hiding from the world. I keep stroking her forehead, half willing her to open her eyes. What has it done to her, this shock of reality? What have I done to her? Will there be lasting damage? I'm an idiot. A meddling, idiot amateur. I should have sought help two months ago. Back when she started slipping away from me. The mood swings from exhaustion turning darker. The monosyllabic answers. The refusal to eat. The failure to sleep. The lies she began telling herself, and me, about Cara. About what I'd done.

And then, the worst time. The time she didn't recognise me. When she got so scared and angry that I had to sedate her. When she looked at me with such hatred and asked why I'd kidnapped her. A fantasy. A complete fantasy to block out what happened. Then of course she 'saw' Cara.

I just wanted to help. I couldn't send her back—she had such an awful experience the first time. I wasn't there; it was before my time. But she told me everything. Not over the coffee after the supermarket with

her and little Cara, to make up for the drink I'd spilt on
Suze by clumsily bumping into their trolley. But at din-
ners after that. She told me everything she could about
the institution. About the denial of her will. How she
was made to question everything she wanted. How she
was drugged so heavily she hardly knew if she was real.
How she became heavy, lethargic, distanced. How the
other patients—particularly the men—terrified her so
much she refused to come out of her room. How every
word she said was dismissed as a fantasy. How her mind
was bent to destruction. How she thought she'd be in
there for a week and came out three months later. How
things were never quite the same with her and Craig
after that, but that she had no one else, so she stayed
with him—until he left her, after Cara was born, and
the crying started again. How she went from being a
teacher to being an outsider, ostracised, with nowhere to
work, only a kitchen to bake in. And how she never ever
wanted to go back to that place. And so I promised her
that with me at her side she would never have to return
there. That she and Cara would be safe with me. That
was my mission statement, the manifesto pledge with
which I proposed marriage. Never ever again would
Suze be in an institution.

So we became our own medical experts. She took
her medication religiously. Lied to the doctors if ever
she felt sad, erratic, confused. Just said she was 'sta-
ble, thank you', and got repeat prescription after repeat
prescription. For the depression only. She didn't think
she'd have to contend with psychosis again. Thought it
was a one-off thing. A single episode, fifteen years ago.

If I'd known that was coming, perhaps I wouldn't have tried to medicate with wine and foot massages. Perhaps when my wife didn't recognise me, and I panicked, I should have panicked towards a doctor. Not drugs from the back of the cupboard and off the internet, God knows how dated and impure. But I'd made a vow, you see. And I couldn't break it. They would have taken her away. I couldn't lose her, too.

There was of course one other thing she'd told me. That it was Cara who had kept her going, when she came along. That despite the tears of exhaustion and hormones and whatever else, she loved Cara passionately. The mental health services team could see that and were happy. Cara was her one joy from Craig. Shared with me. And I…

What happened happened.

I was more to blame than she was. Of course. Although there was something, that when I think of it, makes me feel for her a fraction of the hate that she must have felt for me smouldering beneath the surface. When I first found out. Where she really was. What she was really doing that day, what she effectively made me do. I hated her then. I feel my hand tighten on the gun. To think that she… But no. Come on. That's in the past. I relax my hand again. She's been through so much. It's she who has to forgive me. For all of this. If I was misguided. Which it's looking like maybe I was.

Just as I'm wondering how I can face Suze and how she can ever recover from this, her eyes open.

There's a slight flash of panic, as she wonders how it is she's next to her captor. Then she remembers and

I see her relax. But the next moment her face contorts again. Fear? Hate? Sorrow? I press her to me and we stay like that for a few minutes.

Then she finds her voice.

'So I've been writing letters to myself?' she asks. 'Hallucinating them coming through the grate?'

I nod.

She nods too. 'And replying to them?'

I nod again.

'And the knocking on the wall?' she asks. 'I was hearing things, sending goodnight kisses to myself?'

Again, I can only nod.

'I guess, when she stopped writing, when she stopped knocking, when I started to remember you, get déjà vu about the house, that was the medicine kicking in?'

'That sounds about right,' I say.

'But what about when I saw Cara, in her room? That flick of her hair?'

He shrugs. 'I've thought I've seen her so many times in other people's faces, in a trick of the light. The mind makes its own ghosts.'

She sits silently for a moment, her head in her hands.

'How did I become this crazy?' she asks.

I'm going to treat it as a rhetorical question. She's not ready, I don't think, for the full facts. I'm not ready. I just don't know how she'll react. To me.

But she asks again, more insistently. 'Paul, please. I know... I know that Cara's, that she's...not here.' She can't use the real word, the d-word, and I don't blame her, not for this. Even after her euphemism, she has to pause to stop the juddering breaths. She can't stop them, so she continues anyway. 'But I can't… I can't place everything. I've spent too long thinking she's in this room. You need to take me back there. You need to fill in the blanks. All of them.'

Then she's silent again for a moment. She's looking at my hand round the gun. I look down too. I seem to have tightened my grip again.

'And, Paul, you'll hide the gun, won't you? I'll keep the bullets. You keep the gun. I just feel…they shouldn't be together. Neither of us should have them both. OK?'

FIFTY-FOUR

Suze

HE LEADS ME from Cara's room, along the corridor. I feel like an invalid walking outside for the first time. Or Bambi when he's taking his first steps. Before he loses his mother. Oh if only it were that way round. But at least there's a comforting familiarity about the territory now that I understand where I am. This corridor that I was frogmarched along to the bathroom so many times when I was 'kidnapped' felt so alien. And the only attraction of it was the hope that I might find Cara in it. There is no hope left here now. Just blank gaps where now-remembered family photos used to be.

Thank you, mind, for the brief respite.

Thank you, Paul, for sheltering me? I don't know. Do you thank a husband who keeps you a prisoner in your own home? Do you heap him with gratitude for putting you in fear for your life? For threatening visitors' lives—Craig, and Marge?

For keeping your daughter's death from you?

It's not the sort of thank you message that Hallmark cards were designed for. Or for which I'd bake a cake.

After the blank corridor, the living room. Yes, there has been life in here. The sofa, the fireplace, the curtains, all familiar. But there's a lack. It's on the photo frame on the mantelpiece. Paul, Cara and I. When Cara was younger. When we were all happy. When we were all, importantly, alive.

Paul sits me down on the sofa.

'Are you sure you're ready for this, Suze?' he asks.

I look at him. I can see love there. Nervousness. The moistness of the eyes, the wringing of the hands. I must reassure him if he is to give me what I need. I keep my eyes in his and nod repeatedly.

'I'm ready,' I tell him.

He seems unsure, so I go further. I put out one of my hands and squeeze one of his.

'And Paul?' I say. 'Thank you.'

His shoulders slump in relief. He squeezes my hand back. The moisture in his eyes escapes down his cheeks. Words don't seem possible for him immediately. He swallows a lot and bites his lower lip. Then he redis-covers his tongue.

'It's all because I love you, Suze. It's been tough, you know, lying to everyone.'

Sure, it's been tough for him. Me, I've had a walk in the park.

He continues. 'I was just so determined to keep you here. With me. For your benefit, of course,' he adds, hurriedly. 'After Cara... I just couldn't lose you too.'

'I know,' I tell him. Although I'm not sure I do. The bathroom approach, for instance? Why? We never went to the toilet in front of each other before; we're not that sort of couple. Did he need such emotional brutality?

'You understand, then?' he asks me.

I pause. Do I say 'yes' so we can get on to what is actually interesting to me? On to the thing that is making my heartache. To my beautiful, beautiful Cara. Or do I call him on the cruelty? The complete falling into the role of the kidnapper?

He seems to grasp the meaning of my silence. 'It was all for love, Suze. I know some of my methods were a little—I don't know, tough love. But I couldn't risk breaking your phantasy. You weren't ready. I hadn't fed you the medication for long enough; it would have damaged you and you wouldn't have believed me. I only risked a new, increased dose that time in your coffee, when I thought you could handle a bit of drowsiness if it brought you back. And I never actually hurt you, did I? I kept you clean, and safe, and fed, didn't I?'

He looks so desperate for my approval that I know we won't be able to move on unless I give it. And there is a sense in what he is saying. He didn't drug toast and water; he drugged cupcakes and coffee. I had fresh fluffy towels. I wasn't left to kill myself with mirror shards or strangle myself with a shower cord. Acts of love then, not brutality?

I nod and smile, because that's what's needed. 'You did. Of course you did.'

'And work, I ignored so many calls, I must be blacklisted by now. Didn't dare take on jobs, leaving you alone here. Plus our families, I had to lie to them about everything. Said you needed some alone time, went away, to Spain. For some sun. They bought it, at first. But you've no idea how hard it was. Some of them didn't believe me. My bloody sister came nosing around—

trust Marge to play detective. Craig, too. He didn't believe me. And he kept threatening me, threatening to
tell the police, threatening to take you from me, wanted
money for his silence, kept threatening to reveal—' he
stops himself, then continues '—things.'

'What sort of things?'

He pauses. 'Let's get on with it, shall we? I've got
some clippings about…it.'

I nod. I try to smile. To show my pleasure at being
about to come face to face with my daughter's death.

He pulls a box-file from under the coffee table. A
slight pause before he flicks open the lid.

And there we have it. The big black newspaper head-
line: 'Girl killed in car smash'. Girl. Girl! My Cara. My
own beautiful Cara. I'm not sure I can do this. I'm not
sure I can see in black and white this news, that isn't
news at all. But Paul takes another newspaper out. Beneath it there are more. 'We've lost our angel, says car
death mum'. Did I say that? I don't remember. It doesn't
seem enough. I can't imagine having a long enough
break between tears to say something like that. 'I feel
responsible, says car crash dad'.

I look up at Paul. Is that why I hated him when I
thought he was the Captor? Why there's something in
my gut that still tells me to despise him? Because he
was somehow to blame? He meets my gaze.

'I was driving,' he says. 'You were busy with…your
cupcakes.'

It's like a kick in the stomach. Guilt-flavoured fon-
dant. How could I have prioritised work over my daughter? What is the importance of teaching some banker's

wife how to frost when your daughter needs ferrying? My fault, then, not Paul's? Not a blameless crash, but a mother's failure?

I try not to dissolve. I guess there are tears on my cheeks but when are there not, now?

I continue.

The article tells me Paul was collecting Cara from school.

School? But I thought she was…

Oh, right. That was the Cara my mind invented for me, who I have to grieve too. The one whose letters I wrote to myself. Real Cara was being studious not hanging out with boys she'd met online.

And why wasn't I there, picking her up? I should have been, shouldn't I? That's what I did. Why was Paul doing it? I shake my head. I don't remember. As Paul says, I must have been busy with my cupcakes.

The blue Honda Civic crashed into a wall to avoid a head-on collision with another vehicle. Police are appealing for witnesses. The girl was taken to hospital in a critical condition. She never woke up.

I shut my eyes. Memories flood back. Yes, a bedside. Tubes, drips, bandages. Sitting, holding Cara's hand. Praying for her to wake up. Please let my daughter be safe. Please let my daughter be safe. What do you mean? No. No. That's just not possible, it's not possible, you don't understand—

'You spent a week at the hospital,' Paul tells me. 'I don't think you slept once. They wouldn't let us both stay, so I went home at nights. I'd come back in the morning and you'd be raw with nervous exhaustion, hyper with hope if you'd seen her eyes flicker under her eyelids. I tried to get you to leave, but you wouldn't.'

Of course I wouldn't leave. How would I leave my daughter? How could I hold back doing anything that would keep her safe, keep her alive?

'When the doctors finally confirmed that…she wasn't coming back,' Paul continues with his useless euphemism. Dead. Dead dead dead. 'You just—you wouldn't accept it at all. I guess the trauma, the lack of sleep, the grief, it just flipped you over the edge. Back to the old bad places.'

Of course. Bad brain. Bad mental networks. Bad failed resilience. History of poor mental health, susceptible to psychosis and depression. Not safe to be alone. I can hear what the doctors would have said.

'So I looked after you,' says Paul.

'There was a funeral, though?' I ask.

He nods. 'I took you, but I'm not sure you were… there.'

I nod as well.

'There's a grave, then?' I ask.

'Yes,' he says. 'Over beyond the woods. It's a nice walk.' His voice is dull, flat. That explains his visits out, coming back smelling of mould. Woodland flavours released by rain.

An image of Cara's name engraved in marble appears in my mind. I shake my head to clear it. No. I can't do that. I can't go there. Not yet. It's one thing to accept reality. It's another to see it carved on a headstone.

I continue reading the article. The reporters say we

are grieving. That Paul wasn't to blame. That Cara had great potential. Nothing surprising.

But wait. There is a surprise. Or rather an error. Because the paper says she was eight years old. So does the other one. And the other one. But my Cara was fifteen.

'I don't know who briefed them,' I say to Paul. 'But they've got her age wrong.'

He looks at me. There's sorrow in his eyes. When he speaks, his voice is quiet.

'No, Suze. They haven't. She was eight when she died.'

FIFTY-FIVE

Suze

I FEEL MY brain slide. I'm emitting some sort of noise. 'Wuuh uhhh,' I can hear myself say, but it's all I can do. I feel faint. I need to lie down. Now. Or everything will vanish, my mind will collapse.

'Suze? Suze!' Paul is saying. 'What's wrong?'

I pitch sideways so that my upper half is flat on the sofa. I bring my legs up and I curl as tight as I can into a little ball. If I could get back into the womb I would. Or Cara back into my womb.

Because this is…

It's…

Hideous.

I could just about accept that I wrote letters to myself from Cara. Some comfort, some escape to a parallel reality, where there was some explanation for our separation other than her death, that I could somehow keep her with me.

But to have written them from a fifteen-year-old Cara, when she was only eight?

Ohhh… I just…

How do you even… ?

But no, Paul is wrong. He must be wrong.

'Her date of birth,' I tell him. 'Her date of birth was 10 August 1999. You don't forget your daughter's birthday!'

He is shaking his head.

'I'll prove it!' I shout at him. 'We've got her birth certificate. I'll find it, I'll show you, you'll see!'

I'm on my feet now, about to head off down the corridor. Idiot Paul. What trick is he trying to pull?

But then he speaks again.

'Suze, that wasn't Cara's birthday. That was Belle's… not-birth day.'

Belle.

Belle.

Belle.

Oh my God.

I feel my hand at my mouth, holding back the retching.

This is Belle.

This is about Belle.

FIFTY-SIX

BEAUTIFUL, TINY BELLE. Belle who didn't make it past seven months inside me, but who came out anyway.

Little blue Belle. Stillbirth—the phrase that so horribly and yet so inadequately sums up the experience.

Fifteen years ago, my first little girl, dead before she'd even taken her first breath.

Please, just let me be with my daughter. Let me hold her close. So close I can almost hear her breathe. Almost, but not quite.

I still hoped I could love her to life. If I just held her enough. If they just let me hug her one more time, I could succeed where all the oxygen masks had failed.

Shh, little baby, don't you die, Mummy's going to sing you a lullaby.

But I couldn't.

So, me, back then. Broken, shocked, grieving. Rampantly grieving. Grieving more than Craig with his facile little brain could understand. So one-dimensional—a security guard, made good, but not as good as I originally thought. Working for a 'security enforcement company'. Everything black and white in his thuggish brutal mind. Couldn't understand why I wanted to cradle her, take her home, why I was so upset when they rushed her away for analysis—*my baby, my baby, what have you done with my baby?*—couldn't understand why I could hear my baby crying when she 'wasn't there'. But she was there for me. Some nights I could have reached out and touched the source of those cries, they seemed so real. Why did I have to give up the idea of her so quickly? Why was I supposed to focus on the positives, look to the future, have a nice shower, plan for another baby? Why did I have to be in an institution designed to suppress, repress, cancel out her life and my own natural inclinations? Because I was ill. Of course. Ill. Not unhappy. Not distressed. Not pushed beyond my level of endurance. Ill. A risk to myself. Maybe even others. So they decided, with Craig. So I was 'treated'.

And now…this… They must have been right, then, mustn't they?

Craig must have been right.

Because what I have done is, I have done it again. Except more so. I've made Belle and Cara real together.

And neither of them is real.

And this creation was never real.

It means I've really lost her then, haven't I?

Cara.

Because if that's what I've made her, this Cara of Belle's age, then I don't remember Cara. The real her. I don't have her most recent actual self in my mind at all. I might as well have invented her ever having existed.

All that I held dear as I was writing those letters, it was all a fiction? All about the boys, the shopping trips, the mother–daughter intimacy—all of it was untrue? I was reliving memories that weren't real?

'She's gone,' I manage. 'She's completely gone.'

And how mad am I? Did she die seven years ago? Have I made up the difference, counting her lost years? I snatch at the newspaper. It's this year's date. At least I think it is. Have I been here, in this false mental state for so long that I don't even know what year it is, how old I am?

'Paul, did she die this year?'

He nods.

So. I've just made up this life. Oh, poor horrible sad brain—to prolong Cara's life in that way. To give her the chances she missed. The boys she would have kissed. And to resuscitate Belle at the same time, the way she couldn't, I remember, oh God, how painfully I remember, she couldn't be resuscitated at the time of her non-birth. Brain, your motives were pure. Paul, your motives were pure. But I'm sick. I'm ill. I need treating. Call an ambulance!

But then, with a flash of remembrance, I see hospital gowns. I see male patients groping me. I see nurses patronising me. I feel the horrible powerlessness of being unable to make myself understood through layers of medication and prejudice. The inability to discharge myself. When I finally was let out, rushing back to Craig as if he was somehow a pillar of strength in my life, even though he instigated me going there. Because I was so shattered by that place, on top of everything else, that I had no alternative to cling to what I knew.

No. No. I'm not going back to that. Maybe it was fifteen years ago, but nothing moves on that much.

I must just stay here. I must stay here and I must try

to get back my daughter. My actual daughter. My Cara. I must remember her as she was when she was eight.

There's only one thing for it.

I stand up.

'I'd like to go back to my room now, Paul.'

'What?' he asks, clearly alarmed.

'I need to go back to my room. Where you were keeping me. I need to be with my Cara. My real Cara.'

FIFTY-SEVEN

Alice

'WE SHOULD HAVE done this a long time ago, Alice,' says Alice's mum. 'I'm sorry.'

They're standing, the three of them—Alice, her mum and her dad—in front of Cara's grave. Hand in hand. Each of them looks at the granite headstone. The dates between birth and death so short. 'C A R A' chiselled in spooky but solid white. 'A daughter, much loved'. Roses, withered. A card: Dad.

Alice wonders which dad. At home dad, or meeting in strange cafés dad. Mr Belvoir dad. Either way, it looks like they can't be bothered to visit too often.

Her parents didn't let her go to the funeral. They said it would upset her too much. She knew which day it was on, and sat in her room wearing black and wanting to be with Cara. Alice looks at the grave now. She no longer wants to be with Cara. Not there. Not now. It's too final. Not like the happy times in school corridors or each other's bedroom. Alice had thought for a while that heaven might be like that, full of whispers and giggles. But this grave doesn't show any sign of it. It doesn't show anything of her Cara at all.

If only Cara hadn't agreed to go on that car journey

to see her 'real' dad. And made Alice an accomplice. If only Cara hadn't felt the need to hide from her mum that she knew her dad wasn't her real dad, and that she was visiting the real one. Or maybe if only she'd lived with her real dad the whole time. Because what her fake dad had done was horrible. So horrible. Alice thinks back to when Mr Belvoir/aka real dad had first told her what he suspected, that time in his car. When he made Alice show him where Cara lived. Alice had such shivers and chills. The idea that someone would lock up their own wife in their own house, when their daughter had just been killed in a car crash! How could people do that to each other? Maybe it was a good job Cara was dead, if her fake dad was so crazy. Was Cara's mum still there, locked up, or had Mr Belvoir managed to set her free? Maybe she should try again—not just ringing the doorbell and running away.

Alice's dad squeezes her hand. She looks up. Maybe she doesn't need to do anything. It will all work itself out, without her. Even though she's nine next birthday, there's a limit to how much she can do. It'll be different when she's ten. When you're ten, you're practically a grown-up.

Poor Cara, to miss out on that.

For now, the adults will have to sort themselves out. But there's still one more thing for Alice to do. She breaks her handhold with her parents and puts a hand in her pocket. She pulls out a friendship bracelet. Pink and purple. Cara's favourite colours. Solemnly, Alice advances to the grave and places the bracelet down in front of it.

I didn't betray you, Cara, she think-whispers to the gravestone. I've helped. I helped Mr Belvoir. I told him what I knew. I told him where you lived. Where your daddy—or fake daddy—lived. And now your mummy will be safe. All will be well again. You can rest in peace.

FIFTY-EIGHT

Paul

I DON'T KNOW what to do.

She just stays in the room.

The door isn't locked, but she just sits there, on the edge of the bed, one hand pressed against her forehead.

I try to go divert her, go in and keep her company. Tell her stupid anecdotes. Remind her of when we first met. Sing. Cry. Shout. But she either ignores me, or just fires out random questions:

'Did she have pigtails?'

'Did she prefer maths or English?'

'What was her favourite colour?'

'How many of her milk teeth had she lost?'

'What was her favourite bedtime story?'

'We'd shown her 'Pinocchio', hadn't we? I love 'Pinocchio'. With that little cat, whatever it's called. But oh, the wooden boy, not a real boy…'

Then tears. Always tears.

I'm questioning now, really questioning, whether I've done the right thing. Because drugs alone, they can't handle this, can they? She needs proper medical and psychiatric help. Help that I can't provide. Five times a day, I'm this close to calling an ambulance, or a men-

tal health services team. I've Googled 'depression' and
'psychosis' and 'when does it end' and 'what the hell
should I do' innumerable times. Seek help, it tells me.
And then my search engine advertises self-help books
down the side of the page.

She takes food, thank God. I'm still making up the
two sets of trays, one for her, one for me. Doesn't look
at the food—I could feed her a processed Mr Kipling
cake and she wouldn't blanch. Takes the pills too. Possibly even sleeps—hard to tell, with her hand shielding
her eyes all the time.

But, what's worse is, I can't answer all her questions. I only came on the scene when Cara was four.
I don't know about 'Pinocchio'. I don't know whether
she had a red phase before the purple one. I don't know
whether she'd ever been to London Zoo. All I know is
that Suze is in agony.

Standing in the doorway biting my nails isn't going
to help. But what will? If I hadn't already punched the
bathroom mirror in frustration what seems like weeks
ago, reduced it to bloody shards, I'd do it now. Even
if it meant Suze calling me a child-murderer again.
Christ, that accusation hurt. Much more than the glass
cutting my fist. Our perfect mirror picture future shattered just as the mist was starting to clear. But the mirror was a better target for the punch than Suze would
have been. Bad enough I locked her up so roughly afterwards. Please forgive me, for whatever wrong you
think I may have done.

Wait, Suze is standing up! What's this? She's pushing the chair to the window. I rush to help her, or re-

strain her, whatever seems more appropriate. But she doesn't seem to need me. She's standing on the chair, looking out.

'What's up?' I ask her.

'Just checking,' she says.

I've no idea what she's checking.

'Anything I can help with?' I ask.

She looks at me directly, for the first time since I showed her the newspapers. Well, some of the newspapers anyway. Not the one with that accusation in it.

Suze seems to be considering her answer.

'Can you see her?' she asks, gesturing for me to stand on the chair.

I stand on the chair and look out. There's a little girl skipping.

'Yes,' I say.

Suze exhales and closes her eyes. 'Good,' she says. 'Just checking.'

Then she sits down on the bed again.

Did she think she had made up the girl? That she was Cara's ghost? I have no idea. But my answer seems to have cheered her up because she's not holding her head any more.

Oh, but less good—she's crying again.

I can't take much more of this. I throw myself at her feet. 'What can I do, Suze? Let me help.'

She nods, rubbing away tears. 'OK. OK. I thought I could do it all in here.' She taps her head. 'But I'm going to need external stimuli. Her clothes. Her toys. Her books. Her flute. Photos, little scraps of papers, mementos. Everything. Anything.'

I don't say anything. How can I? She continues, maybe thinking she needs to explain.

'I made up a new foreground. A teenage foreground. All her real life faded into the background. I need to bring it out again. Wherever you've packaged it up, can you get it for me?'

She looks me in the eyes.

I avert my gaze.

'The thing is, Suze...'

'What? What now?'

How can I admit this? How can I hurt her more? How do I tell her I gave every last thing her daughter had to Craig sodding Belvoir in exchange for his silence? That he took away all of Cara's belongings in that car of his, a long with the cash, the cash that would have been Cara's inheritance, our old-age security, in exchange for letting me keep my Suze secret. In exchange for him staying away from her—he knows the pain he would cause, for her, and for me. For not trying to expose me. He didn't need Cara's things. He didn't care about Cara. He just wanted to screw me over. Hurt me. Because that's what he does to people.

I can't do it. I can't tell her what Craig has taken. It will destroy her. And she'll hate me. She'll hate me for ever. So I'm going to have to call Craig. Explain. Beg.

'Sure,' I say. 'If that's what you need.'

She nods then goes back into herself.

I slip out into the corridor and take out my mobile. I press Craig's number. Let's hope to God he'll agree. And hold his tongue. About Suze. And about the other thing.

FIFTY-NINE

Suze

HE'S GIVEN ME access to my clothes again. Which is good of him. He suggested I might want to come back into 'our' bedroom and look in the wardrobe. But I don't. It's too full. And Cara's room is too empty. My new room, the beige room, the spare room, is just right for now. I still can't believe I lived—was trapped—in this room not knowing it was a room in my house; or that it is in fact a room that I furnished. Did I suggest the dreaded potpourri? That terribly dated armchair? I'd ask Paul if there wasn't already so much else to ask him.

He tells me he's getting Cara's things from where they're stored. Says it was too painful for him to keep them in the house. A courier is going to bring them round in a bit. I'm ready, dressed for the occasion. A full skirt, in purple, because Paul says that's the colour she liked best by the end. And I'm wearing a yellow sleeve-less shirt decorated with pink cupcakes. I look present-able. As if I'm meeting Cara herself rather than…

I still can't bear it.

Perhaps if I had another child, it would be better. A 'spare' for times like this. One of my clients told me once that was why her belly was protruding for a second time.

Perhaps if Belle had lived.

But there's always just been Cara. Really. She always seemed to be enough, once I had her. She seemed— seems—to be everything.

I stare at the ground. My feet, I notice, are not what the outfit requires. Colourless. I have no shoes on, and my toenails are au naturel. If Cara was fifteen again, alive again, we could have had a girly afternoon painting each other's toenails. Because that's what some mothers and daughters do, right, in the teenage years? Cara wouldn't have been the moody type to storm off to her room, or hide inside earphones at family gatherings. I know that. But even if she was, I would take that. I would take a thousand days of silence over this lifetime of it.

Close my eyes. Try to stop imagining small hands painting my toenails. Aquamarine, purple, pink. I'd let her choose. Open my eyes again. Paul is there, lurking by the open door, fiddling with his phone.

'Any update?' I ask.

He nods. 'The courier's on his way.'

'Good.' I nod too.

'Cup of coffee?' he asks me.

I shake my head. I don't know why. Coffee would be good. Pick me up. Restore me.

'I'll put the kettle on anyway,' he says.

He knows me well, then, Paul. I watch him as he leaves the doorway and heads off towards the kitchen. I should follow him. He's being good to me. Protecting me, cushioning me. Somehow normalising what is happening to me. Many husbands would throw their hands up in horror, take me off to some institute and leave me there. Visit diligently, of course, talk at great speed about nothing, after I answer silently the question of how I am. Then delightedly resume their daily lives when free of seeing my captivity.

Not that I'm bitter, Craig.

I plant my feet more firmly on the floor. Maybe there are some slippers somewhere I can use to cover these toenails that are now haunting me. I'd put on socks, but that would be so wrong with a skirt that I'd know why I was wearing them and I'd see my naked toenails straight through them. Grief giving me X-ray vision.

When I get to the kitchen, Paul isn't making coffee. He's talking on his phone, his back to me.

'Just stay across the road,' he's saying. He sounds angry. Then he must sense my presence because he turns round. And hangs up the phone.

'Everything OK?' I ask him.

'Fine.' He nods. 'The courier is just being a nuisance. Says he's going to drive off. I'd better go out and meet him. Why don't you back to your room and I'll bring the coffee and Cara's things through?'

I nod and I turn in the direction of my new room. But I'll be missing something if I go. The journey of Cara's things back to us. It's like an after-life voyage. I want to see the means of transit. Paul can't shelter me from everything. So, when Paul goes to the door, I'm hidden behind a pillar that separates the kitchen from the hall. I expect to have a clear view of the doorway.

What I don't expect is to see Craig there when Paul opens the door.

And nor, I think, does Paul. Because he immediately hisses, 'I told you to stay across the road!' and steps outside, putting his hand round to pull the door shut behind him.

But before he can do so, he sees me.

Paul freezes. His face goes pale and his mouth gapes.

Craig, the ex-husband who I hate. Who Paul knows I hate. He's the 'courier'? Why does he have Cara's things? I know he is Cara's father but why would Paul give them to him? Why be so generous to Craig, so callous to us? Craig hasn't seen Cara since she was one. When he left, because it was all too difficult. For him. Not enough to have me committed all the years before. Had to leave me alone with our baby too, just when I was beginning to rebuild myself (baby steps).

I step forward. Craig can see me too now. We stare at each other. I expect to hate him. But I don't. I just see a man who has memories. Physically, in his hands, with boxes of Cara's possessions. But in his mind, too. He will have memories of Cara. Ones that have escaped me and that Paul wasn't around for.

'Come in,' I say.

Paul finds his voice. 'Craig can't stay, sweetie, he's very busy, on his way somewhere else. He's just dropping stuff off.' I see Paul glare at Craig.

Craig brushes past Paul and comes into the house. He holds his hands open to me. 'Susan,' he says. And he hugs me. And I let him. Because even though, so far as I remember, this man has shown no interest in his daughter for the last—oh what must it be, now we're back on real time?—seven years, she was of both of us. Somewhere within Craig is a piece of Cara.

And Belle too, of course. But Belle never existed as a person for Craig. Not really. Otherwise how could he have dealt with it all so inhumanely, in a way that I will now never forgive him for?

Yet we still have Cara, in this moment, Craig and I.

Paul clears his throat. He wants to end the hug. Claim me back. Annoying. Selfish. Let me just have this.

But the moment has passed. Whatever Cara-ness was flowing from Craig to me is lost. We move apart.

'You've got Cara's things?' I ask.

He nods. 'Paul was generous enough to give them to me.' Is that a smirk in Paul's direction?

'I don't understand,' I say. 'You hadn't seen Cara since you walked out on us, you bastard. Complete, complete bastard.' My voice rises, wobbles. I take a breath. Focus. This is about Cara. 'Why did Paul give you her stuff?'

There's a glance between Paul and Craig. Paul hasn't regained much of his colour from the shock of seeing me where I wasn't supposed to be a few moments earlier.

I turn back to Craig. There's a lazy smile crossing his face.

'Do you want to tell her or shall I?' Craig asks Paul.

'There's nothing to tell,' Paul says. 'Craig just turned up here asking for Cara's things. His claim seemed better than mine. And you were—well, you know how you were. I wasn't thinking clearly.' He's gone straight from pale to red.

'She deserves an explanation, Paul,' says Craig.

Paul is clenching and unclenching his jaw.

What's going on here? More than just a natural rivalry between two husbands?

Whatever it is, I can't be bothered with it just now. I'll decide what I need to know. All I care about is Cara. Park this testosterone fest.

'Get Cara's things,' I instruct Craig. 'Then come in and sit down.'

With a shrug and a nod of deference, Craig lopes out of the door.

'I don't think this is a good idea, Suze,' Paul whispers to me while Craig is—maybe—out of earshot. I ignore him and settle down on the sofa, fanning out my skirt.

Craig returns with a stack of box-files and carrier bags.

Cara's world!

He puts them down on the coffee table and sits down next to me.

'Thanks, Craig. I've got this now,' says Paul. He is hovering behind the sofa.

Craig and I turn round.

'The "this" you're talking about is mine and Susan's daughter, Paul,' Craig admonishes him. 'I'd say you should let us get on with this.'

'I think you forfeited the right to have anything to do with Cara a long time ago,' Paul somehow manages to say, out of that tight jaw. He has a point. But Craig doesn't seem to think so because he's raising his eyebrows. He raises his chin slightly, looks defiantly at Paul.

'By comparison, Paul, I'd say—'

'Oh for goodness sake,' I cut in. 'Paul, we need to go through this stuff and I'd like Craig to be here. And, Craig, not seeing your daughter for the last seven years—abandoning her, and me—doesn't count as great parenting. Let's get on, shall we?'

Craig raises his hands and makes a 'backing off' gesture. But his eyes are intense. 'You heard what the lady said, Paul. Let's just get on.'

Paul glares at him and doesn't say anything.

Craig opens up the first box. I think I see sequins. I get a little thrill. Sequins. I remember sequins.

'Look, these are from her designs, that skirt she made!'

Blank look from Craig. And a blank look from Paul.

'She made clothes, didn't she?'

Paul wipes a hand across his face. 'She did crafts, I guess you could maybe call that design…' He trails off.

Design. Crafts. I don't know which is real. But these sequins are real. Cara used to collect them, either way. Kept trying to make me sprinkle them on cakes, even though they're not edible.

I pull out a small toy sheep from one of the boxes. 'Remember this?' I ask Craig.

He wrinkles his brow. No he doesn't.

'We bought it for Belle,' I remind him. 'But we gave it to Cara.'

If hearing the name shocks him, he doesn't show it. 'Of course,' he says. That's it. He cares as much now about Belle as he did then. Bastard.

He hands me the next item from the box. It's a recorder, one of those brown things. Ugly. 'Where's her flute?' I ask.

There are tears in Paul's eyes.

Oh. I get it. Cara, the virtuoso recorder player. Hadn't yet graduated to a flute. Fine. Another element of 'Cara' I have to bury. It's OK. I can take it. I have this recorder. Perhaps it's not so ugly.

'She had that with her when I saw her,' Craig says.

I hear a sharp intake of breath from Paul.

I don't know why.

But then it dawns on me.

'I'm sorry, I don't understand. When did you see Cara?'

Because so far as I know, the last time he saw Cara, she was one year old.

SIXTY

Suze

CRAIG PLACES THE lid over the box again and turns to me. Slowly. Casually.

'Craig,' Paul says. His voice is low, tense.

'Craig?' I ask. Like so much else, I just don't understand.

'I've been a better father than you think, Susan.'

'Craig,' Paul says again. 'We had a deal.' His voice is so low and quiet, perhaps he thinks I can't hear him talking about deals concerning my daughter.

'I think Susan should know,' Craig says. His tone is casual, light. 'I was seeing Cara once a week.'

I stare at him. 'What? Rubbish!'

He's messing with me now. Right? He must be. There's no way I would have forgotten that. Or let him see Cara without supervision. You can't just turn up after years of absence and expect unfettered access to a mother's daughter.

'Rubbish, Craig. I might be piecing things together, but I know that's not true.'

Craig turns to Paul. 'Paul, you going to verify that for our Susan? Can't have her thinking I'm a liar now.'

Paul doesn't say anything at first, just pushes out his

lower jaw and gnaws on his lip like he's trying to resist the urge to spit at Craig. Then untightening his jaw just enough so he can speak, says, 'It's true.'

'What?' I'm standing now. Craig was seeing Cara? With Paul's knowledge? 'Why didn't you tell me? How did this happen?'

Craig smirks. 'Paul does like his little secrets, doesn't he?'

Paul turns to me. 'I'm sorry. It was just twice, a fortnight before she died. He appealed to my better nature. I knew you'd be upset, but…he found me at the client I was working at, because like a smug idiot I'd posted it on LinkedIn. And he was so persistent, and he made such a good case, about not keeping Cara from her father. Threatened to come and find you if I didn't let him. I'm sorry. I know it was wrong and I'm sorry.'

I can't believe it. How could Paul break my trust like that? OK, so this is a guy who can imprison his own wife. But that was for good motives, wasn't it? What about this? This was a betrayal. This was Paul looking at Craig and me and Cara and deciding to make himself moral arbiter. Taking a view on who was right and who was wrong—and found me wanting. After everything he knew about Craig. And how hard I'd tried to keep him out of our lives, out of Cara's life, after he left— moving house, cutting all communication, hoping he would never decide to come looking.

I shake my head. I can't process this now. I just want to see Cara's things. I reach out towards the box with the sequins. I have it in my hands when Craig speaks again. He leans forward conspiratorially.

'Do you know what Paul likes as much as a good secret, Susan? He likes a good drink.'

'Shut up, Belvoir!' Paul shouts. 'Shut up or I swear I'll kill you!'

'Sometimes he likes a good drink, or maybe two, before driving. Before driving your daughter.'

Craig's face vanishes as Paul moves in with a punch. I drop the box-file and sequins fall to the floor, scattering the carpet with reds and greens and blues.

And inside me there is an explosion. An explosion of hate. Because I remember now. I remember the way Paul tasted when I kissed him after I arrived at the hospital. I remember he'd been drinking when he drove Cara to her death.

SIXTY-ONE

Paul

'I WASN'T OVER the limit!' I shout before Suze can say anything else. I need to get in there quick. I can't have this happening all over again. 'I wasn't over the limit. The police breathalysed me. I'd had one drink. You know this!'

She's shaking her head. Not the rational shaking you do when you disagree with someone. Shaking it enough to make her brain ricochet. Shaking it to free herself of my existence, of any existence.

'You were drinking. You were driving my Cara and you were drinking,' she tells me.

Craig is climbing up from the floor. I consider punching him again but it's too late. And I think he'd win.

'Suze, listen—if that drinking had affected my driving in any way, I'd be in prison now, wouldn't I?'

Craig is rubbing his jaw. I'd expect him to be ready to punch me back, the old security guard in him ready for a fight. But no. Words are his weapon this time. He's opening his mouth to speak.

'Like before, you mean?' he says.

I don't know if Suze has heard. But I need to act as if she has.

'Balls, Craig! You know that's rubbish! I never went to prison. I got a caution. That was all.'

'For drink-driving,' Craig says. 'You got a caution for drink-driving and then you did it again and our daughter died.'

Suze has stopped shaking and stands completely still. She is staring at me. 'What?' she whispers.

'It's time you knew the truth, Susan,' says Craig. 'You'd never imagine the lengths Paul went to so you wouldn't know.' He spreads his hands out, indicating Cara's things. 'Gave me all this, for a start. And I bet he didn't let you see this particular newspaper article.'

Craig hands Suze an old newspaper, the same vintage I've been looking at with her. I can see he's highlighted a sentence. I don't need to read it. I know what it says: 'The police breathalysed the girl's father and, although he had been drinking, he wasn't over the limit.'

'Kind of set me thinking, you know?' Craig says. Laconically.

I want to kill Craig. I want to find the gun, reunite it with the bullets, wherever Suze has put them, and I want to kill him. How dare he turn up here with his 'truth'? I wasn't drunk when I drove Cara. I wasn't. I sometimes wish I had been, those other times. The first time was the worst. When I had to explain to Cara where we were going. That horrible conversation in the car, my hand on her knee, explaining to her that she wasn't to me what she thought she was (by blood, anyway—I still loved her just as much). It wasn't the drink that distracted me on the last visit. I'm sure it wasn't. I've lain awake night after night thinking about whether it was because I'd had a glass of wine. A large glass of wine. Remembering what I saw, how I felt, before I hit that wall. Were my reactions slowed? Was my vision wavering from the straight line at the centre of the road? No. No. If my mind wandered—if—it was the thought of how I was betraying Suze by taking Cara to Craig. Questioning whether I was doing the right thing. Knowing that I wasn't by Suze. But that I might be by Cara. Plainly, I wasn't. If it was the right thing, she would still be alive.

And I wasn't even supposed to be seeing Craig that day.

It was Suze who made me. Indirectly.

Suze is moving her hands up and down her face, pulling in her cheeks so that I can see the red tissue under her eyes.

'So, Paul—let me get this right,' Suze demands, her voice cracking. 'You have a drunk-driving record you didn't tell me about? Then you drink while driving Cara, which kills her—'

'I wasn't over the limit!' I tell her again.

'Which kills her,' she continues, 'and then you give away all my mementos of her to my shit of an ex-husband, who you've been letting Cara see, so that he won't tell me your disgusting little secret, thus robbing me of my daughter two—no, wait, three—times?'

'If I might just add,' Craig says, putting up one hand. 'He was driving her to see me that day.'

Then Suze flies at me. Nails, hands, teeth—in my face, my hair, my groin. And I'm bent double beneath this flurry of hate. She hits me and hits me and hits me, and I don't defend myself because I deserve it, do

I (even though I wasn't, I wasn't over the limit)? All I can do is curl up on the floor as she kicks and sobs and hits and shouts over and over again, 'I hate you, I hate you, I hate you!'

I can't take this. I can't be the martyr. I have to defend myself.

'You knew, Suze! You knew I'd been drinking, and you sent me to get her!'

She flinches and pauses in her assault. Is that a memory returning?

'What?' she asks me.

'You knew. You phoned me, and you asked me to collect Cara because you'd had a last-minute booking at the studio. A hen party, their other plans had fallen through, you said. Great for business, you said. And I told you, I'm at a lunch with a potential client, he's just buying me another drink. Another drink. And you said it would be fine. You knew.'

She is almost spitting at me. She shouts down at me from her elevated height. 'Don't you dare blame me! You were the one who was driving! You were the one behind the wheel. And I thought you were just collecting her, not taking her off on some other journey to Craig!'

'But you lied to me, Suze! You told me you had clients. You didn't. You didn't. You confessed it, in the hospital, don't you remember? You made up the clients. You just wanted some me-time. A soak in the tub. Your hair was still wet at the ends when you arrived, from where you'd been reclining in the soapsuds. You let me go and kill your daughter because you wanted a bath!'

Suze is staring at me, stunned. Even though I'm lying
on the floor and I'm convinced she's broken all my ribs
with her kicking, and that my internal organs will burst,
I'm somehow in charge again. We're back in the hospital
again, realising how much we hate each other. The moment before the moral truth reaches me that yes, she's
right, I'm more to blame. I'm the one who drove when
I'd had a drink. The one who took the opportunity to
take Cara that little bit further to see Craig to get him
off my back. Drove a little bit faster to get there and
back in the time we had. But I wasn't over the limit.
Suze was. She was over the limit of what I should have
been asked to do.

Suze is attacking me again. Does she hate me more
because now I've made her hate herself too? There are
hands in between us, pulling us apart. Craig. Maybe
he didn't want to witness a murder. Suze killing me, of
course. Because I forgave her. I had to. At the time. I
understood why she needed the time. Her fragility, ever
present. The spectre of that weak mental health. That
she's played upon? Maybe. But look at what's happened.
It's true. She clearly does have 'mental health issues'.
And I've had to look after her. Because I can see all of
her and still love her.

But it doesn't mean that she is absolved of the guilt
of that decision she made. I cannot take all the blame.
Can't be made to, by her.

'Susan, Susan, shh.' Craig is trying to comfort her.
What's his game now? Does he want her back? Or just
to expunge years of guilt? I try to stand up, but I'm too
bruised, inside and out. He keeps talking. 'I'm sorry. I

should have asked you to see Cara. Made it up to you, slow-time. But I'd missed our little girl. Wanted to see how she turned out. How you'd turned out. Susan, if you'll believe me, I'm sorry I walked out, it was all too much, it was selfish, I couldn't—'

Suze is shaking her head and pursing her mouth. She looks like she's about to explode. Craig sees it too. 'Anyway, look, so when I moved back to the area, after the business went bad, I tracked Paul down at a client's office. Did some digging. Saw her a couple of times. Didn't say much to me, but she would have done in time, understood that she was truly my little girl. But Paul, he robbed me of that. So I wanted those things. I still want them. We can share them. If he hadn't given them to me, I'd have instructed my solicitor to try to get the police decision not to charge Paul reversed. But I wanted her things more. Getting Paul locked up won't bring her back, but seeing her things, it—'

I shake my head from my heap on the floor. 'Rubbish, Suze. He wanted money. He blackmailed me with some notion that he could get my decision to "drink-drive" reviewed, challenge the police decision not to arrest me, use his "contacts" to trump up some charge. Or just that he would tell them what he suspected about you being here against your poor confused will, and they'd take you back to that institution again. He would use your liberty, your mental health, as a pawn to get our money. All the money that we have, that we built up, that's what he wanted. And I bet… I bet if she hadn't died, he would have blackmailed me so that he didn't tell you I'd let them see each other. It's only ever been about the money. Now he's had a payment, I guess he's just being a shit.'

I can see Suze begin to wriggle free from Craig.

'No,' she says. The head shaking has started again, and she has her hands raised now too. 'No, no, no, no. We're not doing this. This little spat. You don't get anything. Neither of you. You get nothing.' She grabs at Cara's belongings. 'These are mine. They're mine.'

'Susan—' Craig tries to control her, but Suze pushes him back with a force that sends him flying into the coffee table. He stays were he is; I guess he doesn't want to end up like me. Or he doesn't value Cara that much after all.

And Suze falls to the floor. She starts picking up the sequins one by one, then, when they cling to the carpet, she makes these big sweeping gestures, trying but failing to scoop them up into her fingers. She stays like that, grabbing at the sequins, crying, until she has picked up the few that she can. She pours them gently into her shirt pocket, then grabs up the other box-files and bags, and drags them down the corridor. I hear the sound of a slamming door.

Craig turns to me. Looks down at me on the floor where I still lie curled.

He's going to say something. Something nasty. One of his smug, callous, offerings. Special Craig one-up-manship. A new reminder of how pathetic I am. Of his notional brilliance as a father and a husband. Had he been boring enough to stick around. I tense, ready.

But no. Instead he kicks me in the ribs on his way out of the front door. Not enough to break them. Just enough to hurt.

SIXTY-TWO

Suze

I HAVE IT all now. In front of me, behind me. All the knowledge that I need. To assimilate, understand, digest. The key was Paul's breath. That has unlocked it all for me. The hate. The sheer blinding hate anger rage despair grief terror I felt at the hospital. How I arrived after the Visit, the ring on the front door no mother wants to receive. The police told me what had happened. An accident, they said. Your daughter in a critical condition. Your husband uninjured but being treated for shock. Sinking to the floor.

I'd been expecting a delivery. Cupcake cases. The ones Cara likes. Liked. I'd opened the door smiling with fresh relaxation, straight from the tub.

Not that.

And so. Police. Doorbell. Like the other day. Except that time they were never there. A flashback so real it felt real, and, if not real, then like a hallucination. Oh hello again my illness; how I've missed you.

But I mustn't wallow. Because my mind is taking me back. Arriving, distraught but hopeful, at the hospital. Seeing Paul wrapped in a silver sheet. Too distracted to kiss him at first. Being shown to Cara's bedside. Little, eight-year-old Cara. Still covered in blood and glass—my child! My child, like this! And the tubes, and the monitors and—Oh! It's too much. It's still too much. Sitting behind that curtain with her, holding her hand, life invisible through a veil of tears.

Her hand is so fragile, so tender. If I squeeze it, will she squeeze back? Please let her squeeze back.

A mother shouldn't have to do this twice.

Then Paul appearing beside me. Putting his arm round my shoulders. Kissing me. Then me knowing. Knowing he'd been drinking. Understanding, what he'd meant about his client lunch. Not questioning, then, because he was 'in shock' and because Cara was alive. She was alive for seven days. I was awake for seven days. In that one room, in that one chair, staring at her. Keeping one finger on her wrist so I could just keep feeling the pulse. Talking to her and begging her to hear me, to respond. Praying that her eyelids would flutter. Offering all kinds of sacrifices and deals to a God I usually only meet at weddings and—funerals. That I would give up my business. That I would take her to and from school every day. In a sedan chair rather than a car, if I had to. That if she had any residual brain damage—please, God, no, take my brain instead—I would sit with her day in day out to recover what I could, that I would get her into the best special educational needs school in the world, re-re-mortgage the house to pay for it, start a charity in her name. Anything, anything, everything. I doubt I ate as fluid was dripped into her by tubes.

And then. And then.

The end.

I can't—I don't think I can go back to that. It's not really a memory. It's more bursts of images, colours, emotions and horror and noise and silence. Holding her hand one final time as she drifted into a permanent sleep. The sheet pulled up to cover her face, a veil for death's bride. And turning to Paul. Seeing him for the first time ever. As a drunk who killed my daughter. How was this possible? My two most loved people dead to me. It cannot be possible, said my brain. For those next few days—it cannot be possible. I won't let it be possible.

And of course I remember the guilt. Now Paul has told me. That awful terrible guilt. That if I had been there collecting her, if I hadn't told a white lie, if I had asked him what I suspected—'Have you had much to drink?'—but conveniently decided not to question his judgement, just so I could have an indulgent soak in the tub, then she wouldn't be dead. If I'd remembered that 'me-time' is something that really, if you thought about it, you'd never really want because it means 'me without child' time. Which is something you should never ever ever want because it might happen. It did happen.

Then, here. My poor ill brain's solution. An alternate reality. Total disassociation. Cara here but not here. Paul responsible but not responsible; unrecognisable to me other than a figure of hate who has separated me from my daughter (and from himself). A ball of hate surrounding his face, obscuring him, so I couldn't really see him at all. Turning his features from the most familiar and loved man to a hideous stranger, while my Paul, my safe good Paul lived elsewhere in my brain, his features intact, and could come and rescue me. Rescue me from himself, and the apparent kidnap, but really the whole situation. The death, the drink, the hate. That kidnap reality had hope—my other reality didn't. All the while Paul trying to drug me out of it as I desperately sought to rescue unreal Cara into a false reality. For both of us to escape the evil we were in, a blessing compared to the true evil of her death and absolute separation. And then, of course, the flashbacks, slight recollections, once the medicine for psychosis began to kick in. The questioning of why the Captor, still anonymous to me, seemed familiar. A déjà vu creeping in with every hot drink he drugged. My mind allowing me to think separately of Paul, my rescuer, and the Captor, my curious nemesis, without linking the two.

How boring for this mental creativity to be a simple clinical case. Am I 'better' now, then? Is it all over? Now that I have finally, actually, lost her. Not like I imagined that I lost her when she was an imaginary teenager then brought her back to me through treats and temptation—actually lost her. Now that I know that, do I get to be just an ordinary mother whose child has died? Oh, privilege, oh luxury, oh lucky me. Can I unmedicate myself back to a place when my daughter was alive? Any of them—Belle, Cara, Belle-Cara? Worth a try, surely?

Or can I rationally deal with this reality that has been forced upon me? Can I think that, as Paul says, it was just one drink? If the police had thought he was at fault, it would be him who was locked up now, as he says, right? Can I ignore the other, alternate truth, that everything might have been different if he hadn't had that drink? And even if I can ignore that, can I ignore that Paul was driving somewhere he should never have been headed? That my Cara was being taken to the father who had forsaken her? Do I rationally and empathetically analyse that, do I understand in an objective way that Paul was doing what he thought was best for Cara, and also best for me by not telling me? Do I forgive?

Am I still 'ill' if I refuse to do so, if my insides scream that it was all Paul's fault, that I should spend the rest of my life making him suffer for my loss? For Cara's loss? Or if I will blame myself, and blame him for having to make me blame myself, for ever? Like I questioned for years whether I should blame myself for Belle's death. All those questions. Did I eat the wrong thing? Do the wrong thing? Somehow commit little Belle to her neverness? Did I not cook some blue cheese well enough, rinse out the soil from spinach thoroughly enough, quiz and re-quiz waitresses about what was in the meals intensely enough? That's why it's so important, you see, to always watch what you eat.

As for Craig, he's an irrelevance. I have hated him ever since he left me, fragile still, even years after the stay in that institution—sorry, mental health unit—with only my new little daughter, barely a toddler, to cling to. How weak for a man to leave someone for their weakness. His words, not mine. I would not say weak; I would say poor mental health. A lack of 'resilience'. But for him, daytime crying, night-time insomnia, the guilt, the fear of relapse, the reliance on my medication, they were all weaknesses. Boring. Unliveable with. Not the

sort of 'sickness and health' he'd meant when he said
his wedding vows. A wheelchair he could have coped
with. Not a refusal by an able-bodied person to get out
of bed. Not their night-time crying. Their daytime crying. Their all-time sadness. And always his threat that if
I didn't 'snap out of it', he would call the mental health
team again. That they would take Cara way from me.
That he would take Cara away from me. Like Belle, and
my vision of Belle, had been taken away from me all
those years before. Taken from him too, but he didn't
seem to care. The surface of his testosterone didn't even
seem to be scratched. Perhaps he's even used it as a 'sad
story' over the years to get women into bed. His 'sensitive side'. Paul's right. Craig's a shit.

Well, he made good his threat about taking Cara
away, didn't he? All these years later. Even though back
then he didn't care enough about either of us to stay, or
even to kidnap Cara. Only Paul cared enough to kidnap. Too bad Cara was already dead.

So yes, I have all that. I have love and hate and guilt
stretched out behind and before me. How to blot out
Craig. How to deal with Paul. How to deal with myself.

But perhaps all that is just noise. Because what I
also have now is all of Cara. Bones fleshed out by the
books, drawings, games, ribbons, loom bands, sequins,
magic kit, recorder and all the other components of her
eight-year-old world. Here a well-thumbed copy of The
Witches; there a pencil drawing of a cat. Here a set of
Frozen Top Trumps; there a rainbow of plastics and
embroidery threads and macramé and beads. And all
her clothes—tops and skirts and trousers and pants and

pyjamas. All Cara's. All familiar. I lay out an outfit on the floor: a pink T-shirt with a smiling white unicorn; pale-blue jeans with little purple bows embroidered on the pockets; a white cardigan with buttons shaped like cats' faces (oh, I remember how she loved that, treasuring the buttons in her little hands). At the top of the outfit I place a hairband—one of those black ones with the name written in colourful paint across the top, beloved of teachers so they can remember kids' names. I didn't like it. I thought that if she was having a dim day, a stranger could approach her and pretend he knew her by reading 'Cara' from the top of her head. But it turns out strangers weren't what we needed to be afraid of.

A friendship bracelet at wrist height and then the outfit is complete. I sit back on my heels and look at it. A wave of nausea fills me. The outfit isn't comforting. It's heart-breaking. It mocks me. It is all empty. Empty of Cara, empty of life. I scrunch the clothes up and throw them across the room, then immediately run to pick them up again. I'm sorry, Cara. I love you. I didn't want to hurt you. Let me just hug you, your clothes, one moment longer.

Is this normal? Is it normal grief? Am I sick? I don't know. How do I judge? Is the fact of my asking this enough to show 'normality'? What would I tell myself to do, rationally? Leave the room? Visit her grave? Talk to people?

But what would I say to them? 'Do you have my daughter?' 'Can you bring her back?' 'Do you remember that cute way she stuck her tongue through the gap in her milk teeth when she smiled?' 'Wasn't that a lovely day she and I spent in the kitchen the day before she died?' 'Why didn't I collect her from school myself?' 'Why did I remarry?' 'How do I fill this emptiness?' 'Help me, help me, please.' They are hardly conversations to have over cupcakes.

Lie on the floor and breathe. Just breathe. A moment of stillness. A moment of love. Because she was lovely, my Cara. How delighted I am that she even existed. How blessed. My beautiful daughter. Daughters. Try to take that feeling out into the world. The world? Really? Am I ready? Stand up, climb to the window, look out at what I can see of the world.

There she is, the little girl. Skipping away. Skip, skip, skip. Pretty pigtails flying.

I stare, drinking her in. Now I know she is roughly the same age as Cara was, she has more relevance. So much more relevance.

Yes, perhaps I am ready for the world again. Or at least, what I choose the world to be. Because it must be on my terms, this new world. Just like my little interim world was. Paul owes it me to let me face the world as I choose, after all that has happened. Because it won't be the same world I left, without Cara in it. And now it has this revised version of Paul. I must decide what to do about Paul.

Perhaps I should travel? Is that what people do? Try to escape their grief by going halfway round the world? Or do they stay, sipping tea in quiet rooms? Hiding under duvets? That's what I'd rather. But that's weak. Craig said that. So is going out strong? Do I need to be strong for Cara? Will travel ease the pain? I imagine sitting opposite Paul in the living room. Drinking tea. Making small talk. Hating him. Longing for my little girl. That doesn't seem very positive. You have to do one positive thing every day. That's what they told me, back then. To stop the depression setting in. And having the medicine doesn't count as a positive thing. I must do something else. Something positive. What, then, shall that be? I give a last look at the girl outside the window.

And I have an idea. An idea about how to make a positive new world. One little skipping step at a time.

SIXTY-THREE

Paul

'I'M GOING OUT,' a voice from behind me announces.

I jump a little. I've been alone for four days. In limbo. No, hell. The hell of not knowing whether Suze will forgive me. For the drinking. For the driving. For the captivity. For reminding her to hate herself. Whether I've lost her. Whether we'll ever get back what I was trying to save. Suze has kept herself in the captivity suite, her 'new' room and Cara's room. Sometimes I think I hear her potter around at night, going to the kitchen. She must be eating, mustn't she? And sleeping a bit?

Taking her medication?

I turn round. Suze does indeed look like she's set on going out. She has on a coat, shoes, make-up even. It's on the tip of my tongue to tell her she scrubs up well, but that would underplay the significance of the moment. Plus it's not totally true. She is beautiful to me, of course. But even through my prism of love and with my IT-geek dress sense, I know—because I've heard her say it enough times—that navy shoes don't go with black tights. And that there's a limit to what concealer can hide. Slight bags and wrinkles from general wear and tear, not the deep purple and blackness brought by trauma and illness. By me.

So instead, I smile at her. 'Shall I come with you?' I ask.

She shakes her head. 'I could do with a bit of time by myself. If that's OK.'

Oh. More 'me-time'. I nod, although I'm not sure she's really seeking my agreement. And I'm not sure I really agree. Perhaps I should insist on going with her? Or just follow at a safe distance behind her?

No. If I want normality—which I do, I really, really do—I need to trust her. Trust that she's well. That she can go out of the house, not do anything stupid and come back in one piece. Without the police. Because I'm aware, what I've done, holding her here, may not be strictly legal. Quite apart from what she might think about Cara's death.

'Where will you go?' I ask her.

'Oh, just to the village and back,' she says.

Some things don't change, then. She's still insisting on calling Crouch End a village. It's a suburb, I want to tell her. A leafy London suburb. Not a village. But then, her world has been turned upside down enough recently without my contradicting her outlook on geographic locations too.

'OK,' I say. 'Just make sure you take your phone with you.'

She gives me an odd look. Then I realise. Her phone. I still have it, don't I? Locked away upstairs. You don't let kidnappees have mobile phones in their cells/recovery suites so they can phone the police. Nor do you let your ill wife have a phone that lets her endlessly stare at social media apps in case they will magically bring back your daughter. Or at least show some sign that she was alive. Even if I hadn't kept Suze in confinement, I would have confiscated her smartphone. They aren't healthy for people like her, all those internet windows perpetually open in our brains. Refresh, refresh, exhaust. And phones are part of my business. So I know what I'm talking about.

'Actually, I'm not sure where it is, and I think it's out of charge anyway,' I tell her. 'I'll have a look while you're out.' I'm not sure I'll find it.

Suze shrugs. 'Don't worry. I'll be OK.'

'And you're sure you don't want me to come?'

She gives me a faint smile. 'Sure. Thank you.'

Suze ducks round me. I realise I have been standing between her and the door. I must have shifted unintentionally.

As she undoes the latch, she turns round and gives me a kiss. The very faintest brush on the lips. No tongues. But still. A kiss is a kiss. It's a definite start. She must have been thinking about me in the four days. Doing some real deep thinking. When she went in, she had just attacked me, tooth and nail. But she's had time to reflect now. To come to terms with things, and to understand why I did what I did. That I love her. That I loved—love—Cara too.

And then, as I'm still savouring her touch, she is out of the door. I stand watching her until she rounds a corner and is gone.

I consider standing with the door open until she returns. So that I can see as she rounds that corner. So that I know she's all right.

But no. It's trust again, isn't it?

Or maybe I should go and visit Cara's grave. I haven't been for a few days, not since I released Suze. I needed Suze to know I was there for her all the time—couldn't have the daily excursions through the trees to the grave any more. I could go and get some more roses—only the most beautiful flower for Cara. The petals of the ones I left last time must be brown and falling now. I owe her more than that, don't I? Even though I already did everything. I read to her, I sang to her, I tested her on spelling. I went to school concerts—even if I was a bit late and had to stand at the back—listened to her playing the recorder, clapped louder than almost anybody there. I took the moral high ground and decided she should see her real father. I took myself out of the pub after just one drink. I did up the seat belt as tight as can be.

I just didn't manage to stop the car spinning into a wall.

Even Cara's pitiful cry as she must have seen it looming towards her couldn't stop us. Help me! And then—wham. A horrible echo of that first collision with Suze and Cara's shopping trolley. Cara's world stopping for real.

And so then came watching Suze sit by that bedside for those seven long days. Seeing her at first hugging the unresponsive Cara, stroking her hair. Whispering into it that all would be fine, that she'd protect her. Then Suze realising all the hugging and stroking and whispering in the world wasn't enough to protect Cara. That we had lost her. And then, of course, unrealising that again. Going into her own make-believe world.

But it's not my fault, about Cara. It's not my fault. It isn't, it isn't, it isn't. I'm not the child-murderer Suze accused me of being when she saw my self-inflicted blood in the bathroom. The constant lump in my throat is sorrow, not guilt. I have done nothing wrong. I was not over the limit. I was safe. Life isn't safe. But I am.

I will continue to tell myself that every day. One day I might even believe it.

We have to move on. Suze is my primary responsibility now. It's Suze who needs me. Suze, with all her weaknesses. Suze, who needs me here when I return. Cara isn't coming back.

So I come inside and close the door. I sit myself down on the sofa. Even put my feet up for a moment. Then I put them down again. It just feels wrong, over-indulgent, to relax quite that much. Even though I can. Because she's well again now. She'll come back. I'll be waiting for her. And we can move on. Or back. Be like we were before.

SIXTY-FOUR

Suze

FANCY ASKING IF I wanted him with me.

Fancy keeping your wife in captivity then be her accompanying jailor as she walks outside the prison gates.

Fancy not understanding what I have to do.

Although, to be fair, I wouldn't mind someone walking to the road-ward side of me on the pavement right now. Acting as some kind of noise and car filter. The world seems louder than I left it, as if everyone's activity levels have increased to make up for my own dwindling. For all the noise, though, there's a kind of fog. I feel like I'm wading through particularly thick icing. Like my feet have to make double the effort they used to just to propel me along. And that I might suddenly get stuck, like a reluctant bride atop a cake.

When I get to the centre of the village, they're all still there, the shops and the cafés. They shouldn't be. They should have burnt down. They should have been replaced by funeral parlours. How can they still be flaunting their wares for the child-centric existence? Cafés with signs declaring 'soft play area inside'; children's bookshops advertising readings; restaurants boasting kids' menus, high chairs stacked by the entrance. And then you look to the other side of the road to them, and you see yet more children's shops—clothes, toys, arts and crafts cafés. The mummy economy, all desperately trying to convince you that motherhood is about entertainment, cultural development and prettifying your offspring. About succeeding in having some coffee while they do something else. Covert me-time disguised as good parenting.

But it isn't. Parenting's about keeping them alive. The bottom line fundamental is that your children must live. I want to scream this at the mothers with their pushchairs, half watching little kids on scooters—no helmets, not even any stopping at pavement edges—while they themselves drink another latte and pat themselves on the back for not being helicopter parents. I want to claw back all the play dates and parties and coffee mornings. The shopping for pretty outfits while Cara begged to go home because she was tired. The allowing her to spend just two more minutes or two more pounds in the toy shop. The saying if she was very good she could walk back from her friend's house without me, if she phoned before she left and didn't dilly-dally on the way home. All this, giving her a sense that life is just play, that she can exist independently of me, that fun frivolity and froth triumph overall. It isn't about that. Life is about living. The state of being alive. Being able to breathe.

But, most of all, I want to scream at all these mothers: what is your husband doing? Your partner? Your parents? Your au pair? Can you trust them? Are there rules you have written down? Had tattooed onto their skin, etched into their brains? Do this, don't do this? Because there is no point, even if you are good and grip your child like you can never let them go, when you are out and have sole responsibility for them, if whoever you share your childcare duties with couldn't care less. Thinks they are immune. Thinks it is acceptable to let the children play near cliff edges. Thinks it's OK to keep medicine where children can see it. That it's OK to leave them unattended in a car just for a few minutes. OK to drive drunk. Or, yeah, after 'not being over the limit'. Of course.

The black dots appear in front of my eyes again and I prop myself up on a window ledge. Come on, Suze. Positive, yes? This is a positive trip. A move forward. Part of the plan.

The dots start to fade and are then gone. I look up to see what lies behind the windowsill I've been leaning on.

Of course.

A toy and clothing store.

The front window so pretty. Bunting and fake grass. A miniature deckchair. Dragon and unicorn buckets and spades, wooden pull-along whales, sunhats bearing Union Jacks. Little green dresses with blue bicycles printed on. Blue trousers with green bikes.

Froth. It should make me angry. I should turn away. But it is beautiful. A celebration of childish play in the great British outdoors.

And necessary, of course, for what must happen next.

My feet carry me into the shop.

Once inside, my hand shoots out before I can think.

I'm suddenly holding a little handbag in the shape of a kitten's face. Then my brain forms the reason: She'll like this. Even though she's not here with me, I know. I know what my little girl wants and needs. I know she'd want to fill it with that pretty beaded necklace. And the purse with a peacock on it. And that little crystal mobile phone charm.

Oh. And look at that. Perfect. The skipping rope with Punch and Judy as the handles.

I pay for my purchases and step back over the threshold. The brown paper bags give me a euphoric glee. Everything is OK! And such a sunny day! My step is easier. My stride lighter. My eyes able to take in the families around me without a frown. Another shop, then another. A coffee. A cake. One more shop before I go home.

As I walk back, the effect starts to wane. Maybe the caffeine is wearing off. The froth round my lips licked away. I remember what I am returning to. On the other hand—I remember what I am returning to. This will take determination. And guts. But it will be worth it. Let's just hope I can make Paul play along.

SIXTY-FIVE

Paul

SHE LOOKS LIKE a different person, Suze does, when the she appears at the door again. Or rather, not a different person. Herself. Before.

There's an energy to her. A glow in the cheeks. A light in the eyes.

'Hello, darling!' she almost sings to me, kissing me before we've even got inside.

My Suze. She's really back.

'Make me a cup of tea and I'll tell you all about it,' she says. 'My trip into the big wide world.' Her voice has a light tone, as though she's intentionally mocking herself.

Red buses with forgotten destinations, cafés with little gardens outside, cutesy purveyors of beautiful cakes, all spring from her tongue, and from her hands, which she waves as she talks. There's an energy and drive about her that I can't remember her ever having before. The world is in her. I just let her talk. She doesn't need a response and I don't need to give her any; I'm content just to absorb this new super-Suze. My judgement was right—it was fine to let her go out. To see the world of which she's been deprived for so long, to indulge her senses. But it wouldn't have been fine before. No. She needed her period of treatment, here, with me, first. Otherwise it wouldn't have worked. She would have returned still in mourning and despising me. To look at her now, you wouldn't think she'd ever had a daughter, or ever had reason to hate me. Not that she did have reason to hate me, of course. Or I her. Not really. Life deals what it deals. I'd happily let her take a thousand baths on a lie if it made her glow this much.

Then, just as I'm beginning to worry if she's perhaps too manic, the smile fades. She looks down her lashes into the mug of tea, and I think I see a tear.

'What is it?' I ask.

She tilts her head to one side, embarrassed almost. 'I was a bit silly while I was out,' she starts.

My heart beats a little faster. Silly? What does silly mean? Silly is what happens when people don't take medicine. When they act on hallucinations or irrational fears. Or they talk to the police about what the police cannot understand.

'What did you do?' I ask, on full alert.

'I bought a few little trinkets. The sort a little girl might like. The sort I might have bought if Cara was still with us.'

Is that all? I try not to show my relief. Poor darling Suze. But nothing could be more natural. I will still have those 'I saw this and thought of you' moments in shops for Cara for years to come.

I smile at her. 'Show me,' I say gently.

She gives me a smile of thanks and rises from the sofa to get her bags.

Very carefully she places four or five tissue-wrapped items in front of me.

'There,' she says. 'You can see how silly I've been.'

I'm reminded of a cat presenting a succession of dead birds in front of its master, asking for praise. Except Suze would be a cat who knows she's done wrong. But wants to be patted on the head regardless.

I open up the packages. Yes, they are absolutely what a little girl would love. A cute bag, a pretty purse, a necklace, a skipping rope and some kind of key ring thing with a tiny animal attached.

I look up at Suze with tears in my eyes. She does a tearful little shrug. I put my hands over hers.

'It's OK,' I say, because it is. This is natural grief, manageable grief, grief that we can share together.

'What shall we do with them?' she asks.

I shrug. 'Don't know. Put them on the mantelpiece?'

She looks at me and bites her lip. 'I'm not sure. That might—get to me. More than it should.'

Of course. Now I'm the one being silly.

'I don't want to just lock them away,' she says. 'It seems wasteful. Unless we have another!'

Suze laughs like she's making a joke but she looks up at me and lets the words hang for a moment. She must see the shock in my eyes—she's almost forty-five, for goodness sake, and with everything we've just been through… That she went through before…

But she carries on at speed before I even have time to respond her pause. 'Or if we could maybe give them to someone, one of her classmates maybe, or…' She trails off, then her eyes brighten like she's having an idea. 'Hey, I know!'

'What?' I ask. Whatever it is, I'm sure I can indulge her. If it's biologically possible. She's suffered so much.

'That little girl, you know the one who's always skipping out back.'

Yes, I know the one, I tell her. 'The one who Cara used to play with? Lizzie, or something?'

'Yes, that's it. Lizzie. Well, what do you think?'

It's a nice thought. And I'm sure the little girl would like them. But we can't just go round giving her presents, can we? Won't her parents think it's a bit odd?

'We'd better go round to her parents' house, Suze. Give them the things. Explain ourselves. They might think it's a bit funny otherwise.'

Her eyes well up. She shakes her head. 'Forget it, then. I don't feel like explaining myself.'

Damn. I've upset her again. I just want things to be normal. And it's such a small thing—means so much to Suze, and I can always explain to Lizzie's parents afterwards, on the sly.

'Tell you what,' I say. 'Let me have a look out there now, see if she's having a skip. If she is, I'll get her to come in.'

Suze sits up taller. 'Really? You don't think I'm being daft?'

I shake my head. Yes, I think she's being silly, but what does it matter? We're a couple. Our own world. We can do silly things.

I cross over to the door and open up, hoping that little Lizzie will be outside.

She isn't.

I tell Suze and her shoulders slump slightly.

'Never mind,' she says brightly. 'I tell you what. Let's make some cakes. I'd love that. I haven't made cupcakes in so long. I was thinking that on the walk home.'

'Whatever you want,' I tell her, leaning forward and kissing her. Personally, I'd have thought cosying up on the sofa, reconnecting, would be more appropriate. But perhaps we can do that later. With frosting.

'Great. Let me just put my bags upstairs then we'll get started.'

Soon, Suze is back. She strokes the surfaces of the kitchen aka her studio, cherishing them, then gives them a good wipe down (I admit the food waste from those trays has built up a bit). Before I know it, she has her pretty baby-blue apron on, the eggs are broken in a bowl, and the flour and sugar are getting a good sifting. I love watching her work. She is so quick, so deft. With what seems like no effort at all, the cakes go in to bake.

'Good seeing you with one in the oven again,' I joke.

She blushes.

Oh.

Was she serious, before? I take a deep breath.

'Suze, if you want to—'

'Shh,' she says, and puts her index finger against her mouth. 'Don't let's worry about that now.'

Then she kisses me. A proper kiss. Full, deep, tongues and everything. It feels like everything we've been, everything we've lost, everything we're going to be, is in that kiss. I love her. She loves me. Our future lies ahead of us.

'I was thinking we could have a little fun while the cupcakes cook,' she whispers to me. Her hands are on my crotch, her tongue in my ear.

If it wasn't for that kiss, I'd say it was too much, too soon. But I share her urgency. It's been months now. I know how badly she wants me, because I want her just as much. There's something about the deadline of having the cakes cooking that turns me on. The sense that she can't wait, I can't wait—it must be now and it must be fast. And I'm hardly going to turn down afternoon sex. So we don't even make it to the bedroom; the kitchen surface will have to do.

SIXTY-SIX

Suze

DING!

The oven timer goes.

We're done, too.

It's all over too soon. Me and Paul, in our kitchen table push and pull. But, in another way, just soon enough. I don't want my carefully prepared treats to go off. That won't do at all.

Paul is smiling down at me. His eyes say afterglow, caresses, pillow talk. My eyes close slightly for a moment; perhaps best he doesn't see what's in mine. But only for a moment, then I open them again. Show him I'm not hiding anything. Show him I want to drink him in now, while we're so intimately close. Like I'm trying to commit it to memory. The little puckered pores of his neck. The way his arms imprison me on the worktop. The prominent collar-bone covered in tiny beads of sweat from the exertion of being with me. Lock it all away, upstairs, in the brain.

Remember what it was like when Cara was alive? Constantly alert for a creak on the staircase or the opening of our door. Never a chance to abandon myself fully to my senses. Thinking of what to say to Cara if she saw us.

Now, we have all the time in the world.

Apart from the cakes. I cannot burn the cakes. That would undermine everything. Stick to the plan. That was part of the point of being with him, just now. Get him to buy into the plan. Or at least, what he thinks the plan is.

Paul strokes my face, and looks poised to kiss me full on the lips again.

'No time for that,' I say, kissing him on the nose. Gently, I push him off me. He lies prone, watching me, as I move to the oven and turn off the cakes.

'Now you can come back here,' he growls to me, putting out a hand and making to grab me to him.

'Tut tut,' I say to him, darting out of his way. So much easier now, that his brain and movements are made heavy by lust. 'You know full well I need to take the cakes out and let them cool. Come on, get your clothes fastened. You'll pollute the cakes.'

He makes a sulky face, but you can see from his smile that he's not in a sulk at all. He believes he owns the world. As we readjust out clothes and I tend to the cakes, he declares his love for me.

He's so pleased I'm better.

So in love with me still.

So looking forward to taking me on a mini-break, or a world tour if I need it, to fully restore and regroup. To talking seriously about having more children, if I really want to—there's IVF, adoption, if I want to go down that route.

He'll support me, he says—of course he will.

This is all very well. But I have more immediate plans. Starting right there, outside the window.

SIXTY-SEVEN

Paul

I'M JUST BEGINNING to wonder out loud how much IVF costs when Suze cuts me off.

'Oh, Paul!' she says. 'Look, there she is, walking past the house. Lizzie. Be a darling and get her in, won't you?'

Now? Really? Are we post-coitally inviting little girls into our house? After possibly the most intense, emotional lovemaking I've ever experienced? I think that's why the orgasm was so intense, because I'm more in love with Suze than I've ever been. We've seen the whole of each now, emotionally, and we've shared so much. Everything is on another level. We're so blessed. Cursed, of course. Cara, Cara, poor darling Cara. But so blessed too. Because we still have each other. Because of what I did. And because Suze is so strong, and so wonderful.

'Come on, Paul, stop staring at me, and pop out or we'll miss her again.'

'Suze, come on, after that, do you really want to?' I entreat her. 'And we were talking about our future, our plans.'

'This is the plan now, look lively!' Her voice is light, jokey.

I think she sees I'm still unconvinced, because she sidles over to me, hips swinging. I can see her naked, totally naked, even though she's fully clothed.

'Come on, Paul,' she says, her voice low, flirtatious. Full of love. 'We might as well—it's done then, and we can enjoy our evening together.'

The suggestion isn't lost on me. I kiss her again, my darling, darling wife. Then I tuck my shirt in and check my flies. Perhaps it's not such a bad thing the conversation is averted. I'd be happy with the act of trying for more children (possibly I just have—I should have paused to think about condoms but it seemed such a tawdry concern at such a big moment of being with Suze again after so long, and it's not likely to result in a child), to go along with adding our name to long IVF waiting lists, or starting on the adoption process (we'd never pass the screening for that—come on!) if she can't conceive naturally. But, actually, I'd rather not have any kids. If I'm honest. I don't mean about Cara. Of course I want Cara back. I would give anything for that. Anything apart from Suze. But a new baby—no. Because from what friends told me, back in my thirties, babies have a tendency to cry and shit more than you'd think from one so small. And sleep a whole lot less. And adopted problem teenagers are probably much the same. Plus what if something goes wrong again? Like it did for Suze with Belle. Now that I have Suze back, why would I want to jeopardise that?

So after planting a kiss on the lips of my beautiful, beautiful restored—and did I mention beautiful?—wife I go outside to talk to Lizzie. It's a magical glowing afternoon—the sun is gently kissing the trees and little rays of light flirt with the golden leaves. Why have I wasted these years working in IT? I'll live much more of an outside life with Suze now. Pavement cafés, field, fjords, whatever—just exploring and rejoicing our saved world together. Take her away from here, from dark inside thoughts. From loss.

By the time I reach Lizzie, I must have a big goofy grin on my face, so I try to tone it down a little. I think she remembers me from playing with Cara, but you never know, do you, with children, so I remind her who I am. Even then, she's reluctant to come into our house, so I talk to her of cupcakes. She gives me her hand.

As I lead her up the path I'm oddly reminded of the wicked witch in the fairy tale, leading children to her fabled gingerbread house. I don't know why. I can't remember what happens to the children, but it's nothing good. I shrug off the feeling and we step inside.

SIXTY-EIGHT

Paul

WHEN WE GET inside, it's not how I left it. Suze has her apron on again and she's sitting on the sofa. There's a smile fixed on her face. A little tissue-papered package is on her knee. I don't know what she's done with the others.

Suze pats the sofa next to her.

'Lizzie, isn't it?' asks Suze.

The little girl nods.

'I've seen you skipping. You're very good,' Suze tells her.

I smile. Suze is lovely with children. Some women naturally are, even when the children aren't their own.

Lizzie does a shy little smile and turns her face to one side, hiding it in her hair. Cute. Maybe we should try IVF after all, if we haven't just made our own new child the old-fashioned way.

'I think you knew my little girl, Cara, didn't you?' says Suze.

Lizzie nods.

'Something very sad happened to her,' Suze continues.

Lizzie nods again. 'She died,' says Lizzie, very matter-of-fact.

I flick a glance at Suze to see how she'll react. The

smile is still on her face. If that veneer helps her then so be it.

'She did,' Suze agrees. 'She died. And we're very, very sad.'

Lizzie nods sagely.

'And sometimes when we're sad, we do silly things, Lizzie. When I was out shopping—you like shopping, don't you?'

Again Lizzie nods.

Suze nods too, establishing some joint understanding. 'I knew you would. I thought when I was in the village earlier, I bet that little girl loves all these shops.'

Lizzie does a shy little giggle. She doesn't know, like I do, that the little girl Suze was thinking of was Cara.

'Now, guess what I bought back for a lucky little girl.' Suze hands Lizzie one of the tissue wrapped packages.

Lizzie opens it eagerly. It's the charm thing. The crystal creature on it is a little sheep, I see now. Obviously enthralled, Lizzie stares at it in her hands, turning it over and over.

'Isn't it lovely, Lizzie? I'm sorry Cara can't have it, but you're a very lucky little girl.'

She nods. 'Yes, I am. Thank you very much Mrs Cara's mum.'

Suze ruffles Lizzie's hair, like she used to with Cara. Lizzie giggles. I wonder what's happened to the other presents. Did Suze want to keep them for herself?

'Now, Lizzie, if you can believe it, you're an even luckier little girl, because I've got more little presents just like that in Cara's room for you. You'd like to see them, wouldn't you?'

Lizzie nods. What are the presents doing in Cara's room? Maybe Suze couldn't bear to give them away without seeing them in situ first.

Suze takes Lizzie's hand and leads her to Cara's room. I trundle along behind, feeling a bit redundant. I remember I used to feel this way when I first came to stay with Suze and Cara. The mother–daughter relationship already established.

In Cara's room, the other tissue-papered items are laid out on Cara's old bed. Nestling on the pillow is the soft sheep toy Suze and Craig bought for Belle, and was passed on to Cara. If Lizzie wonders why the room is bare of other toys she doesn't say anything; perhaps she's distracted by the hope of more crystal animals.

Suze bends down to speak to Lizzie.

'And once you've opened those, the cupcakes will just about be ready to eat. Would you like one?'

'Yes, please!' chirps Lizzie.

'Open up those little surprises quickly then!' says Suze.

Suze stands up to her full height again and gives me a 'thank you for indulging me' smile. I wink at her.

'There's a little surprise for you in the bedroom too,' Suze whispers to me.

'I like the sound of that,' I say, hoping Lizzie is too distracted by the kitten handbag to notice me flirting with my wife. And, even if she does notice, who cares— I don't care who hears my joy that the whole of our marriage will be resumed.

'I didn't mean that, silly—perhaps later! But for now, go on, toddle along there and see what you find. You know, in the room you kept me in.'

A bit disappointing that she hasn't put the surprise in our bedroom; that would be more alluring. But there's no malice in her reference to the room I held her in. So, with another kiss, I do as she says and wander off along the corridor. In the centre of the bed, there is a tissue-packaged item. Before I start to unwrap it, I want to savour this moment. This moment that shows Suze's kindness towards me. I want to savour the warmth of feeling love, reconciliation and gladness. It surrounds me like the hug that I want to give Suze later. Not a sex hug, just a hug. A hug that means: we know each other now, totally, and we will cherish that.

Peace. Happiness. Love.

Of course we will miss Cara. We will mourn Cara. Every day I will feel guilt, whether I ought to or not. But so will Suze. We will feel everything together.

I move to unwrap the present. I hear Cara's bedroom door shut. They must have finished looking at Lizzie/Cara's presents. They'll be coming through here next, then, or maybe going to the kitchen for cupcakes. Better open up my present so I can seem as grateful as I am.

The soft tissue paper almost unwraps itself beneath my fingers. The layers fall away, opening up to reveal a beautiful grey silk tie. I unfold it and stroke it. It's almost exactly the same as the tie I wore for our wedding. Tears form in my eyes. It's so delicate, but woven together so strong. Like us. I know what it means. It means we can truly begin again.

I see something flutter to the floor. Must be a receipt. I shouldn't look. I should crumple it up and consign it to the bin.

But I want to know. I want to delight in how much Suze has lavished on me. Despite everything. Because of everything. I bend down and pick it up.

It's not a receipt at all. It's a note. From Suze.

I smile as I see her handwriting.

But then I read the words.

'I will never forgive you.'

I freeze.

Something grips my heart. It must do, because I'm sure it's stopped beating.

And then those same words spoken, behind me.

'I will never forgive you.'

I turn round to see Suze standing in the doorway.

With the gun.

Then, before I can react, she closes the door.

And locks it from the outside.

Her footsteps retreat.

'Suze? Suze!'

Nothing.

I'm alone.

Surely…

No.

She can't have done!

A taste of my own medicine?

No. No! We're starting afresh, it's fine, she loves me, the world is ours.

But I see the words of the note again in my hand. Stark, black against white. The message is clear.

Then it hits me.

The girl. What about the girl?

SIXTY-NINE

Suze

AND SO, THERE we have it. The plan I conceived now brought to life.

My happy little girl, playing in her room.

She won't play outside again. Can't have that. I expect she'll want to. But she'll learn. And if she doesn't—well, she's got the new skipping rope in there with her. Like Paul has his tie. If he gets desperate.

Because I knew, when I saw her playing outside her window after I learnt what I learnt about Cara, that this other little girl was made for me. That she was brought by fate. I didn't quite understand how, at first. I needed my thinking time. I needed to test my brain, my emotions, to make sure they were working correctly. Hence the walk to the shops. And, of course, I suspected I wouldn't be going out and about again for quite some time. Because I can't leave them here, now, can I? Not my new family. Plus I needed all the gifts, didn't I? The draw. To supplement the cupcakes.

And I'm true to my word. There will be cupcakes. For my new little daughter. My little Lizzie. Frosted with my own fair hands. Not for Paul. He can starve, for all I care. Or put his new tie to good use. Because there's not much hope of escaping from that room otherwise. I know. I've been there. And I had someone to escort me to and from the bathroom. And bring me food. Sorry, Paul. But those are luxuries you don't deserve.

Never mind him though. He is not my prime concern now. He had to trust me. That is all. If I'm pregnant again, after that last liaison, so be it. If I have to see his face close to mine when I shut my eyes, even to blink, on the occasions I don't see Cara or Belle, then so be it. If my spine continues to shiver at the thought of his touch, so be it. That changes nothing. We are done.

All I must think about is you, my new daughter. We'll be so happy together. I'm longing to tell you how much I love you already. Maybe I will tell you. Maybe I'll write to you. And I can ask you to put on that lovely little outfit I laid out for ghost Cara. Complete with cat buttons on the cardigan. There's no hurry, though. I know where you are. I'll always know where you are.

Safe, here, with me.

I'm thinking already of the fun things we can do together, even from the confines of the house. All the things my practice daughter couldn't do with me in the end. The teenage shopping trips. The boy chats. The champagne afternoon tea in town. The shopping, we can do online. The boy chats we can do using Tinder—which way will you swipe? And the champagne afternoon tea can of course be on a tray, right inside your own room. We might have to start soon. Accelerate the programme. I don't want to miss all that again.

Oh hush, little baby, please don't cry. Mummy will sing you a lullaby. You're safe, darling. Safe, here with me. I whisper that to you through the door, the locked door. Shhh, darling. Shhh. These are happy times. Crying subsides. Just the odd sob. Or perhaps that's my own?

Your parents will worry, of course. Or rather, your former parents. They may even think they miss you as much as I miss my Cara. My Belle. But they don't deserve you. Because they're not careful enough. They haven't learnt the lessons that I have learnt. How to be a good mother. One, keep your baby wrapped up in cotton wool. Two, never let them leave your sight. Three, no one else can be trusted. Four, with my new knowledge, I can get it right this time. Otherwise, what was the point of Cara dy—going? If I can't learn from my mistakes. Remedy Paul's mistakes.

And if the outside comes in to find me—well, they won't find me. Or the other two. Because in the worst-case scenario, I have the gun. And I have the bullets. They're reunited. The gun, too easy to find, in the bottom of our wardrobe. The little bullets were waiting for it in the base of the kitchen blender, the one I don't use any more. And all of us will be reunited in heaven, or in the sodden earth, if need be. No one is taking my little girl away from me. Not this time.

And so just like that, I'm a mother again. I don't know for how long. But I'll savour it while it lasts.

* * * * *

Get 2 Free Books,
Plus 2 Free Gifts –

**just for
trying the
Reader
Service!**

Get 2 Free Books,

Plus 2 Free Gifts—

just for trying the Reader Service!

Get 2 Free Books,
Plus 2 Free Gifts—
just for trying the Reader Service!

HARLEQUIN
ROMANTIC suspense

Get 2 Free Books,
Plus 2 Free Gifts—
just for trying the Reader Service!

♦ HARLEQUIN
HISTORICAL

Get 2 Free Books,
Plus 2 Free Gifts—
just for trying the Reader Service!

Get 2 Free Books,
Plus 2 Free Gifts—
just for trying the Reader Service!